I0823657

PRAISE FOR
A Season on the Drink

"The joy of this wonderful book is the hunt. We search for ourselves in each of the characters. Adapt, examine, identify, discard. Like a great painting, *A Season on the Drink* is immersive in the best sense. The great baseball book is literate. Elusive. I've always liked Pat; now I admire his artistry.

—Mike Veeck, former MLB executive
and current Minor League team owner

"*A Season on the Drink* is a story of challenge, hope, and coming together as a team to do something extraordinary that can transform—even for a moment. It's a story of redemption, dignity, and purpose."

—Dave Winfield, National Baseball Hall of Fame

"First pitch and you're in. *A Season on the Drink* is an original cocktail of true characters, orderly chaos, broken dreams, and a shaky team of outcasts desperate for redemption. Its free-swinging narrative neatly weaves through a lineup of complicated lives that intersect through personal pain and shared inspiration. It's a winner!"

—Dave Whitaker, author of *Cabrini-Green in Words and Pictures* and *Live from FitzGerald's: Songs and Stories of an American Music Club*

"Finding your place in the world isn't always a fastball down the middle. *A Season on the Drink* captures the hopes and struggles we all face—on the field and off. Full of heart, humor, and hard truths, this one connects. I call 'em like I see 'em: It's a hit."

—Tim Tschida, Legendary MLB Umpire

"*A Season on the Drink* is a powerful and compassionate portrait of the men living at the St. Anthony Residence—fittingly named for the patron saint of lost things. While Harris offers an honest account of all they have lost—stability, relationships, health, and purpose—he also reveals what remains: moments of connection, resilience, and the hope of being seen. At its heart, this is a story about our need to belong, even in the most overlooked and forgotten places."

—Pat Plonski, Executive Director, Books for Africa

"The best baseball stories are deeply rooted in a love for the game while also casting an unflinching eye at the world beyond the foul poles. Count *A Season on the Drink* among those stories. Pat Harris masterfully blends wry humor with an honest, moving portrayal of addiction to create a memorable cast of characters who keep readers rooting for them even after the last pitch is thrown."

—Jack Heffron, author of *The Local Boys: Hometown Players of the Cincinnati Reds*

A SEASON ON THE DRINK

A NOVEL

BY PAT HARRIS

Adventure PUBLICATIONS

A Season on the Drink: A Novel
Based on a true story

Cover design: Travis Bryant
Text design: Hilary Harkness
Editors: Brett Ortler, Emily Beaumont, Holly Cross
Author photo: Michael Murray
Front cover: ballplayers: Shutterstock AI/shutterstock.com;
bottle cap: xpixel/shutterstock.com; bottle: Maryiana M/shutterstock.com
Back flap: social icons: webhazrat/shutterstock.com
Front case: foil ballplayer stamp: mugiberkah/shutterstock.com

Library of Congress Cataloging-in-Publication Data
Names: Harris, Pat, 1966– author
Title: A season on the drink : a novel / by Pat Harris.
Description: Cambridge, MN : Adventure Publications, 2025.
Identifiers: LCCN 2025021105 (print) | LCCN 2025021106 (ebook)
ISBN 9781647555825 hardback | ISBN 9781647555832 ebook
Subjects: LCSH: Softball teams—Fiction | Alcoholism—Fiction
Self-realization—Fiction | Friendship—Fiction | LCGFT: Novels
Classification: LCC PS3608.A783265 S43 2025 (print)
LCC PS3608.A783265 (ebook) | DDC 813/.6—dc23/eng/20250530
LC record available at https://lccn.loc.gov/2025021105
LC ebook record available at https://lccn.loc.gov/2025021106

Adventure Publications

Published by Adventure Publications
An imprint of AdventureKEEN
310 Garfield Street South
Cambridge, Minnesota 55008
(800) 678-7006
adventurepublications.net

Printed in the United States of America

To Mom and Dad.
You taught us to honor every story
and to speak up for those who cannot.
I share this one for you.

"I will be able to help, but first I must find myself.
I am happy, for negativity always breeds discontent."

—MARTY PETERSON, 1984

This novel is based on a true story.
Some names have been changed,
but the people are real,
the Saint Anthony is real,
and what happened in 1986
on the diamond in Saint Paul was real.

The Saint Anthony Residence Softball Team Starting Lineup

1B	Marty P.
2B	Harry O.
SS	Jim B.
3B	Jerry N.
LF	Freddie
CF	Wesley
RF	Ray
C	Jerry
P	Terry T.
Utility	Johnny Luck
Missing	Eric
Lost	Donald
Player/Manager	Marty P.
Player/GM	Terry T.
Real GM	The Queen
Player's Rep	Jim B.
Investors	Mr. Long and Mr. Ryan
Charitable Mobster	The Padre
Owner	The Patron Saint of Lost Souls

PART ONE

THE PATRON SAINT

DIAMOND PRELUDE

FIELD OF DRINKS

Late summer, 1986 (final game of the season)

The Saint Anthony Residence Softball Club was at bat, bottom of the seventh inning.

Marty knew the count was 2-2. Freddie was on second physically and Jerry N. was loitering near first and leaning toward second, but not because he wanted to steal a base. Even though that summer day in Minnesota never went above 70°, everyone was sweating.

The young fast-pitch hurler had seen *The Breakfast Club* at the Highland Theater no less than five times. It was 99¢ for the movie and $2 for the popcorn-soda combo. He was an Emilio guy. He would later see *Top Gun* and immediately change into a Maverick guy.

"That's right, Ice, I am dangerous!"

He took a full college windup and fired the ball past Marty's head. Marty didn't take notice of the brushback.

Jerry N. was green on first base, listing, and looked sick to his stomach. On second, Freddie was looking up at the sky, his eyes following the clouds like a typewriter carriage.

The Saint Anthony Residence for chronic alcoholics and the drywall company were tied. It was the final game of the season.

It was also the last inning, and the ice was melting in the visiting coolers. The weathered Saint Anthony squad didn't have coolers. They had paper bags, which were hidden out of habit.

Except for a diminutive and lonely player in right field, the team from the drywall company was burly and gigantic.

The drywall pitcher was a typical ringer, aka an intern in the sales department. He jumped the line on the summer intern list when he walked in for his interview at 6 feet, 4 inches, with arms like howitzers. His summer job immediately became softball.

The right fielder was the obligatory brother-in-law who was required to satisfy his sister by acting man-friendly to her hubby's sporty coworkers. He only drank to excess on softball night, with the beer escorting him through jokes of prowess and primordial chest-bumping.

The intensity of this season finale escalated quickly. The drywallers challenged a play at the plate in the second inning. It was just a game at a city park, but somehow it mattered to them as though jobs and manhood were on the line. The owner, and son of the company founder, had never even been to a game.

In 1986, there were no official challenges in any league. No replay systems to consult. No redress for diamond grievances. In rec league, someone had to give. In a second-inning dispute, it was the Saint Anthony Residence, the home for chronic alcoholics.

The drywall team knew they were facing up a team of chronic alcoholics. It was an open secret among rec-leaguers and a brewing rivalry, literally.

The inebriates were wiry and disheveled, yet annoyingly good at softball. They angered the oddly chiseled squad of mostly half-Windsored office workers. The actual drywallers were at worksites.

Marty stood square in the sandy box, the chipped wooden bat hanging on his shoulder like a yoke. He knew exactly how his counterpart felt on the mound—the loneliest place on the diamond. The pitcher nervously paced, wanting nothing more than to impress his purportedly future colleagues. He didn't want to be Bender, the burned-out Judd Nelson bully in *The Breakfast Club*. He was Emilio, the cool wrestler in detention.

He unleashed the ball as fast as he could. It was right down the pipe. "Time!"

Marty jumped out of the box and looked around to see who called time. It quickly became obvious.

Jerry N. had passed out on first base.

Marty rushed to help Jerry N. off the ground. Terry darted over for the assist. Terry was the sophisticate at the Saint Anthony, the fast-talking former real-estate magnate from the North Shore who handed out embossed business cards as though the next deal was right around the corner. The phone numbers were disconnected. He had a joke for most occasions, largely for a shrinking audience of the familiar and intoxicated, but he could still hold a boardroom and a card game, if necessary, and at the same time.

The drywall team looked on in amazement.

Jerry N. did not smell of whiskey or vodka. His breath was not medicinal.

Terry and Marty knew it right away: Lysol.

Jerry N. had opted for a crafted cocktail that only Saint Anthony mixologists could conjure.

First, he found the can. That was the hardest part. He removed the spray cap, blasted the remnants into a cup of flat

Coca-Cola, and downed the concoction. The rumble on his faculties commenced shortly thereafter.

He was not belligerent by any stretch. By the time Marty and Terry placed him on the bench, he was stoic. He didn't know what was happening, but his environment was stable enough to settle and perhaps assess an upward trajectory.

It wasn't the first time for Jerry N. Terry and Marty were perfectly accustomed to the managerial challenge.

The first baseman of the drywall team approached Marty and Terry. He was the self-appointed captain. He was a towering figure tricked out in full softball regalia—headband, wristbands, eye paint, and the unmistakable whiff of entitlement. Marty immediately noticed that his fingernails were manicured.

"What's the plan, boys? Looks to me like this young man is now ejected, and by my last count, you only have eight players. I would say forfeit."

Terry and Marty were dumbfounded. After an entire season of mishaps, Jerry N.'s slip was a minor transgression. Passing out was passé. Players had even thrown up at home plate—sometimes on it. It was a different kind of rain delay, but still not a rainout.

"Uh, I don't think so." As Terry moved toward the captain, the fast-talking salesman thought of his last fight. It was in high school in Duluth, and he was pummeled in front of God and everybody by the captain of the chess team. He permanently transitioned from brawler to negotiator.

"OK, it's the bottom of the final inning, we're at bat, and we're playing rec ball. How about you call him out and we go from there?"

"OK, I'll go with that, but let's just get it over with."

Jerry N. was paying attention from afar and offered insight, "Bullcrap!"

Terry was at his finest when there were crumbs on the negotiating table. He put the captain on the ropes and closed the deal. Terry didn't want to forfeit. He wanted to vanquish.

It was clear to Marty what was happening. The drywall team could not lose to this conflicted band of bedraggled alcoholics. It would not go well at the watercooler or the next staff meeting.

It would also not go well with Marty. His life was fair and square. He accepted the consequences of his actions, which almost always meant his own loss. Not this time.

Jerry N. yelled out again from the bench, "Bullcrap!"

A few Saint Anthony players left the bench and were sharing a single cigarette around a garbage can. A few others went into the bushes.

Freddie was still idling on second base. He didn't think to get involved in the commotion on the mound. He could hear the conversation escalating only a few feet away, but it was intentionally out of his mind. He stood square on base with a permanent smile. He was sober.

The second baseman turned to Freddie, seemingly bored with the proceedings. "You tracking this?"

"What?"

"I know. I feel the same way." The second baseman was burly like his teammates—shorter but also with arms like sewer pipes. He was wearing a thick gold chain, and his dark hair was parted to the side. He had seen *Top Gun* in the first-run theater. "These guys get a little competitive sometimes. I just come for the beer. Where you from, dude?"

"Saint Paul."

"I'm from Edina. "Way out in the 'burbs."

"Never been there."

"Well, maybe some of your guys can come check it out one of these days. I'll buy."

Bottom of the seventh inning, game tied, now one out, two strikes, man on second.

Marty stepped back into the box. If he turned sideways, only the rims of his duct-taped glasses would be in view of the small crowd assembled.

He focused on the ball. His life was dismantled by a torrent of alcohol in unimaginable volumes, but this one moment on the diamond was all his and he knew it. Marty had been there before. Many times.

He wasn't drunk. He wasn't nervous. He was in the game.

At the plate, nothing had changed with Marty since high school. Strategic alterations were useless. Watch the ball.

His eyes focused above the rim of his scuffed glasses.

The intern-pitcher was embarrassed by his captain's intensity, but he still wanted to win. He had grown curious about the opposing team, and he felt bad for the stranger who passed out on first base.

The pitcher stared at Marty and pulled his arm back in a slingshot, hoping his next clutch would be in the cooler.

The captain screamed out, "Finish him!"

Marty ducked as the ball sailed over his head and rattled into the dusty backstop.

Terry pounced from behind the backstop, making a hard stop at the third base line. He knew the rules of engagement and what alpha-male preening looks like on a ballfield.

"What the heck was *that,* sonny boy?"

The pitcher looked sheepishly at Terry. His face was contrite, his eyes wide and his mouth stretched downward.

The captain yelled to Terry from first, "Just softball, dude, you know, ball-and-bat stuff. Need a lesson?"

The Saint Anthony team refocused on the brouhaha. Saint Anthony residents would protect each other in a fight, but usually the fights were fueled by a lunge at the communal rubbing alcohol, with loyalties, fists, and reason flailing in a myriad of unexpected directions.

The team watched in unison as Terry negotiated the incident. They were accustomed to blame and its requisite excuses, and they knew that this boy had made a mistake.

Terry didn't respond to the captain. Without alcohol, his strategy was clear.

Terry nodded to the young hurler. He was never sure if the brother-nod led to brotherhood, but he used it often, hoping that a short drop of the head would lead to battlefield loyalties. It never led to war, which was a start.

In an instant, the pitcher returned the nod, his lips pursing with understanding. They were brothers.

The ringer really wanted to tell his captain to calm down or, better yet, to shut the hell up, but his position as young sidekick and rising company star was at risk.

Marty remained calm in the box.

The next pitch sped toward the strike zone. Marty took a short step into the ball, making full contact with the old wooden bat. He immediately knew its trajectory. The ball sailed deep down the right field line and landed with an audible thud just to the right of the barely visible boundary. The miracle wasn't in Marty's ability to pull a ball that far with his frail body, it was that a chalked line existed on a municipal field. Foul.

Marty was thankful for the anonymous city worker who snaked the foul line from first base to the fence. Without the line, his hit would have caused World War III between Terry and the captain.

Marty stepped back in the box. The pitcher smiled and gave him a brother-nod. Marty's head moved too slowly for the brother-nod, but their eyes locked and it sufficed. They were brothers.

He bent his knees and held his bat loose and low like Rod Carew in '77. He stared straight at the intern-pitcher. They knew where they were, on a municipal field in a rec league. But they both wanted to win.

The pitcher didn't know that sharing beers after the game would be a bad idea. With memories on the Saint Anthony squad already muddled, warm hands plunging into an icy cooler could only lead to the ugly opposite of revelry and brotherhood.

The pitcher hunched forward with the ball in his glove, but just as his windup exited the gate, a synchronous gasp of hacking cigarette lungs hailed from the Saint Anthony bench. One charred set of lungs could hardly make a whimper, but eight of them could be heard across Raymond Field and into the gardener's house across the street.

"Look out!"

The right-handed Marty stood still in the box as his teammates roared in unison. Marty thought they were either trying to rile the pitcher, or they were entirely focused on something other than the game, which was not unusual. At last week's game, throwing dice was more important than scoring runs. Even Jim and Harry chose dice over softball.

Marty focused on the pitcher through the one lens on his thick glasses that wasn't covered in dust or fingerprints. He only needed an opening.

He didn't hear the screams. He was locked in, like he was back at bat for Wilson High School. Cauzy was on first base, Schribes was leading off second, and Jimmy wanted the squeeze from home. The game was all that mattered, then and now.

The roar returned, "Look out!"

The pitcher snapped out of his windup. Everyone except the captain was now yelling. With the windup paused, Marty heard the noise and peered over his shoulder toward the bench, and then again to third base. Everything Marty did was in slow motion, even drinking. As his head slowly turned, his eyes widened to the impending collision.

Freddie missed the foul call entirely. As soon as Marty's bat connected with the ball, Freddie flew off second and kept chugging. By the time the ball rolled on the other side of the foul line, it was too late. A row of dump trucks would not have stopped him. He rounded third wide enough to throw a grin toward the Saint Anthony bench and then lowered his head and body for the home stretch, pumping his arms like a vintage locomotive. He was either heading home or somewhere way past it.

Marty had suddenly become a softball matador. As Freddie lumbered toward home in front of a stunned, yet entertained, audience, Marty moved his hips away from the plate while his body stayed bolted in the box.

It wasn't enough. Freddie was picking up even more steam, barreling downhill toward the plate. Not only did he miss the foul call, he believed he was going to beat the tag.

Marty backed out of the box when the train hit. Freddie dove headfirst into home, sliding across the plate with his head and taking Marty to the ground with his right arm and leg as a mushroom cloud of ballfield dirt exploded in front of the backstop.

When the dust settled, there were two men lying on the ground, one face up and one face down.

The dust cloud lingered with the same slow motion as Marty.

The Saint Anthony bench was silent. Even Jerry N. was at the edge of his seat, this time for reasons other than being drunk.

The drywall squad didn't know what to make of it. They kept looking back and forth at the dust and then at each other.

When the air cleared, Freddie was on his stomach all the way past home and up against the backstop, and Marty was lying flat on his back next to the plate.

Freddie turned to Marty with a smile. Marty leaned up on one elbow, his body miraculously intact and his almost indestructible glasses still in place. He turned to Freddie and made the call.

"Safe!" It wasn't close.

The cheering Saint Anthony squad unloaded off the bench and ran to Freddie, mobbing him in a game-seven dogpile. Marty stood up, brushed off his pressed jeans, and turned to Terry, who was standing next to the pile with a stub cigar in his mouth.

"Thinking we should tell him?"

"Not yet. Maybe not ever." Terry and Marty both saw the point. Baseball or softball—the game was made to make the world feel better. Even in failure, it offered victory. Teams made brothers, and brothers made teams. For the Saint Anthony team, and for Freddie, the game carried them.

Terry had a plan. "You realize that it doesn't matter if we don't tell him." Marty smiled.

Terry approached the mound with a plan. The Saint Anthony players were still mobbing Freddie in front of the backstop.

"How about we just call it an out and go from there?" Terry said, for the second time in the same inning.

Terry knew the rules. It was a foul ball, and Freddie should return to second, winded and soiled. But it was about the game, not the score, and Terry and Marty would take the out over negating Freddie's heroics.

Terry had won over the young pitcher. The company side-kick didn't need to be a forgotten, chronic alcoholic to know what was happening. There were no *Moneyball* moments at Raymond Field, and for the youthful hurler, there were no grudges. Years from now, he could be the captain, but today, it was about playing neighborhood ball with nothing to prove. Victory is forgotten after the first Budweiser. The joy remains, even through the hangover.

"Works for me, dude."

The captain moved toward the conference on the mound, and he was irate at the circus.

Terry talked his way out of many fights, usually enjoying post-argument drinks and brotherhood with his would-be combatants. There was no bar on the mound. This time, Terry was on his own.

The captain was ready to convert a recreational soft-ball game into a brawl. Forget the snazzy corporate softball uniforms and Saint Anthony's tattered Goodwill outfits. This was class warfare, and the self-proclaimed gatekeeper took no prisoners, shocked onlookers included. Weeks later, city council members would hold forums, maybe even convene a task force. Inevitably, Saint Anthony would be blamed, and in a matter of months, the community would fear "those people."

Terry was incredulous. The successful so-called executive seemed to be moving on a team of chronic alcoholics. It should have been the other way around. Instead, the alcoholics were sharing cigarettes while the corporates were lunging toward an ignominious playground rumble.

"Take it easy, Jack, he's out. It might also be in your interests to take a break," Terry said quietly, lobbing a veiled threat from a team of chronic alcoholics with nothing to lose.

With Freddie secretly called out at home by his own teammate, the captain lost his skin in the game. It was also obvious that he would get clobbered by a mob of disheveled locals in an embarrassing David-and-Goliath melee.

The captain retreated against the threat, volleying his best and final leverage in a contest between the haves and have-nots, "I swear to God I don't know where you people came from . . ."

But Terry cut him off, "Where we came from? You're correct. Yes, we're from the Saint Anthony Residence. Yes, we're poor, we're drunk, and we're hiding in the shadows to scare your kids. Unfortunately for you, these crusty old drunks," Terry pointed to Marty, his voice breaking, "this crusty old drunk, is going to kick your butt."

Marty didn't say a word. He didn't need to. He looked at Terry, and then the captain. He walked slowly to the batter's box, turned around slowly, and waited for the pitch, his cigarette dangling from his yellow fingers as he clutched the cracked bat.

No one noticed that Jerry N. had passed out, again.

CHAPTER ONE

EXODUS

April 1984, Saint Paul, Minnesota. 6 a.m.

Marty Peterson thought of his mother every day. When he was drinking, he thought about her kindness. When he was sober, he thought about her drinking.

Always, he remembered her words: “Pray to Saint Anthony and you will find it.”

It was motherly advice that Marty never forgot. How could he possibly forget after hearing it *ad nauseam?* The Peterson house in the historic Frogtown neighborhood of Saint Paul was reliant on a saint to locate lost items. A wayward set of keys, a book, or a toy, Saint Anthony was the patron saint of lost articles. Peterson family logic dictated that any offer of assistance, even from an apparition or a fable, was worth a try. Marty prayed to multiple religions anyway, thinking that one of them had to be right.

“Pray to Saint Anthony and you will find it.”

Marty Peterson knew that he had lost many things. He was pushing 50 years old, and he wondered if the patron saint would ever help him. With his heavenly summons thus far, the only thing Saint Anthony found for Marty was a sock monkey under his bed.

He sat on the cement bench in the detox center and wrote in his spiral notebook.

MARTY INTERLUDES

"Bound"

By Marty Peterson, 1984

Bound in chains and shackled feet
waking from a nightmare dream
drying, watered room
cemented damp
and clinging floor
locked door
echoes of your voice
no more

Spring was starting to melt the dirty snow, and downtown Saint Paul was bustling with the season's first crew of newly arrived homeless. Word on the street had it that the annual pilgrimage had traveled from Chicago. No longer rail-riders, the unsubstantiated theory was that these fine men and women were given bus tickets to Minnesota by eager Cook County social workers anxious to deconcentrate poverty and gentrify the brownstones on the South Side. Alternative origins included Denver and San Francisco. It was more likely that Minnesota folks disappear in the winter and return in the spring. Snowbirds jump all social boundaries when temperature and wind chill combine to make staying unfathomable.

Marty's whole world was in a two-block radius. He had closed the Depot Bar last night for what he thought was a last hurrah. He always thought it was a last hurrah. After he passed out in the tiny parking lot behind the bar, the last hurrah turned into a night in detox, which was conveniently around the corner. His demise was equally convenient.

The door buzzed open. Marty walked the two blocks from detox in bright sunlight and hunched over on the bench in front of the Ramsey County Department of Human Services.

Just across downtown, Harry Opus was getting ready for work.

Harry wasn't in the saving business. He had little time to think about travelers from the Windy City. As day manager for the Saint Anthony Residence for chronic alcoholics, Harry needed to make sure Jack didn't steal from Wesley, Jerry turned down the music, and Charlie didn't sneak in a fifth of Karkov. He needed to provide three meals a day, an evening snack, and a vomitless bathroom floor, which was a word that Harry used with regularity: *vomitless.*

At 19 grand a year, this was not a bad gig for Harry. In fact, it was the best gig he could get. In truth, he was an hourly worker at $9.14, but since he worked exactly 40 hours per week, he declared himself salaried.

Standing at 5 feet nothing, Harry was nonetheless a giant in the homeless AA crowd. Twenty years on the sauce, a marriage, a couple of kids, and enough jobs to adjust the federal unemployment rate, Harry had been ridden hard. He was 43 years old, but he looked 70, and his inability to smile was well documented. But it was also well understood to the select few who truly knew him. He had been to the depths and returned. With a half-gray beard, jet-black hair, and a scar from eye to chin whose origin was unknown even to Harry, he was a cross between Lou Reed and a Depression-era hobo. When he wasn't suspended in a cloud of cigarette smoke, he smelled of Club Man deodorant and spoke with a softness in his voice that only years of apologies could explain.

After slinking out of bed, Harry's ritual over the past five or so years of sobriety was to pray. He was a Catholic in upbringing and a self-made Christian in sobriety, and he prayed as a way of thanking somebody, anybody, for one more day.

"Hail, Mary, full of grace, the Lord is with thee. Blessed art thou amongst women and blessed is the fruit of thy womb, Jesus. Holy Mary, Mother of God, pray for us now, and at the hour of our death. Pray for the life I have, pray for those who have not, and God grant me the wisdom to know the difference. Amen."

It was Harry's amended Hail Mary Serenity prayer. He'd written it down.

As he lifted his tired body from its penitent state, he lit a Marlboro Red, sipped coffee from his 99¢ refillable cup, and muttered to himself, "OK, Harry. No more prayers or you'll miss the bus."

At 7 a.m., Marty was first in line at the county. He took a number anyway. The room slowly filled. It seemed like detox to Marty, but without the concrete accoutrements.

"I'm here to see Chemical Dependency Services."

"Step through the door on the right when it buzzes." Marty was aware that his life was being defined by buzzing doors.

Harry put on his trademark brown corduroys and plaid shirt and stepped out for another day, each one a beginning.

He thought, *Another day. A gift, but I'd rather go back to bed.*

The large bus driver announced Harry's entrance in an operatic tone. "A coin from Harry, and a good morning to you." Harry used bus tokens.

"Mornin', Teddy, not a great one, but a mornin'," Harry returned, looking toward a cluster of homeless men around a trash can in front of his downtown apartment building. "It might be a better morning if those guys would get a job."

Harry's apartment was walking distance from the county offices. It was a shorter walk to the Saint Paul Downtown Alano Society.

He wasn't sure if the bus driver's name was Teddy. It sounded good, reminiscent of a time when folks knew their bus drivers. It was an old-school scene that Harry wanted, but without the five guys sharing a bottle of Canadian Club in front of his home.

Harry took his seat in the back of the No. 16 bus and began his journey to the Saint Anthony. He purposefully lived as far away as he could without jumping bus fares. He had the job before the apartment.

On the bus ride, life in Saint Paul appeared traditionally boring yet conventionally on the rise: historic neighborhoods in a gentrifying slow cooker spotted with period-designed commercial nodes neatly wedged in by cosmopolitan developers. "The Biggest Small Town in the Midwest" is how Saint Paul wanted to be known, with requisite kindness and a smattering of new cobblestone. Not Minneapolis, as they covertly desired. In fact, Saint Paul is correctly deemed by urban planners to be "urban small-town chic." Nice people and quiet streets with late-model vehicles dotting the acceptably crumbling curbsides.

Harry's bus inched its way past the serenity. After heading out of downtown, the diesel icebreaker plowed through University Avenue, zipping past Hmong grocery stores, chicken wing shacks, and Smoker's Haven.

Marty took a seat on the side of the county worker's desk. The county worker was middle-aged and looked like a well-dressed banker.

"I see that you are a referral from the Union Gospel Mission."

"Yes. Bob Earl was the one who called."

"Treatment six or so times, detox 30 or 40 here. Looks like you had a job at the post office? The one across the street?"

"Yes." Marty was calm, and not uncertain about his future.

"Well, it looks like the Saint Anthony Residence has a room, if that works for you. You're tapped out, but I would be willing to fight for another round up at Pine Shores if you think it might click." The county worker liked Marty, even though he had only known him for about 20 minutes.

"I'm sure you've heard of the Saint Anthony. No rules on drinking, but you get a bed and three squares. They have a 12-step thing going, which you could try. You should, actually."

Marty ran his hand through his dense hair. His eyes were wide open, and he looked confused through his thick glasses. He looked like Stan Laurel, if Stan had lost Ollie. He had heard about the Saint Anthony.

"I'll go there."

Inside Teddy's bus, the global tour continued as the community joined Harry—a mom with kids, an older Russian couple, and a few habitual truants, or so Harry thought. They nodded to Harry as they took seats. A few of them slept, and a few of them played their Walkmans loud enough to violate the no-music rule. Harry felt connected to his fellow riders, but he didn't smile. He wondered who the leader would be if they were trapped.

University Avenue soon opened into Minnesota's industrial boulevard. Prefab buildings with off-street parking had replaced TV repair shops and diners. Tall cobra lights eased out the above-standard lanterns that brought old-world charm to a neighborhood on the brink.

Harry had names for everyone. Weird Larry awoke to get off at Dell's Cafe, and Grandma Gaudy stopped talking to herself and trudged her collapsible shopping cart over to the Rainbow Foods superstore.

Harry stared blankly out the window. When the lighting was right, Harry saw his reflection. He recalled that he had once held a job on University Avenue, but that was all he could remember. He remembered Christiansen's Pub on the avenue and that the job and the bar were intertwined. Harry lost many jobs, and usually a watering hole was involved.

He would sit by himself and drink Windsor sodas until his face slowly descended toward the wooden bar rail. Alcohol did not please Harry. He just needed it. His time at each job soon lessened, and the booze began to control everything. Harry definitely remembered Christiansen's.

The bus went from empty to full and now back to empty. Even Skinny Pauly got off, just in time to catch the bus going the other way.

Forty-seven minutes into Harry's journey, Teddy announced, "Hampden Avenue!"

Ten seconds later, Harry stretched his short arm to reach the stop cord. His wrist had a jailhouse tattoo, but Harry had never been to jail.

"See ya tomorrow," he muttered to Teddy.

"Have a nice day," Teddy returned without looking at Harry.

Every day, Harry wished that Teddy had a stereotypical quip. Even a "We're sucking diesel" or a "Back at ya" would have sufficed.

As the bus filled the air with exhaust, Harry stopped for a moment and wondered what it would be like if he had stayed on the bus. Maybe he could have become friends with the driver. They would share Twinkies in the break room of the bus garage. Maybe Teddy would let him take the bus for a spin around the parking lot.

With the bus out of view, Harry shook his head for a moment and checked his watch.

Fifteen minutes to 8, right on time.

Two buses later, Marty Peterson got off at the same stop.

Walking around the corner off University Avenue, it would be easy for Marty to get lost in the industrial zone. Industrial zoning allows for a pleasant and businesslike experience for all who enter. That is, of course, if one believes that "pleasant" is a series of square buildings that have little use unless the visitor is an employee, salesperson, or thief.

On his way to the Saint Anthony, Marty traveled deep into a lattice of ghostlike roads and occasional sidewalks. There were no schools, corner stores, or even scrubby edgeland woods in sight. It was a place to do business, which for any robust community is a good thing.

Marty's destination was obscurity by design—a term not found in journals of architecture but a guiding principle of the homeless shelter planners of the 1980s.

The Saint Anthony Residence was nestled deep in the prefab neighborhood. Semis and dump trucks rumbled past the turn to Saint Anthony, their drivers none the wiser about what transpired around the corner. It was bliss for an institution like Saint Anthony and a founding intention. Not-In-My-Backyards—the ubiquitous NIMBYs, city council members, and activists—could hardly object. Who could be bothered by the homeless if no one knew they were there? The *feng shui* homeless planners were thinking straight.

The only people who noticed they had neighbors were weary-eyed second shifters, 10-key operators, the occasional salesperson, and, of course, area thieves.

It was also one of the cleanest industrial neighborhoods in town, all due to intoxicated men. Around mid-month, after traditional forms of financial assistance were depleted on mood-altering liquids, dozens of sullen residents flanked the industrial neighborhood. Recycling for money was the objective. One would be hard-pressed to find a can or cardboard box anywhere.

As he walked through the neighborhood, Marty was isolated but content. He should have expected anticipation, fear, or excitement. Marty experienced none of these. He was relaxed. He had lost his family and his job, and the government had only moments ago provided a room for him at a home for chronic alcoholics. In some respects, it could be the end. In others, it could be a beginning. At this point, Marty was just walking. He had a small backpack with a toiletry kit, a change of clothes, and a baseball. They also gave him two bus tokens, which Marty didn't understand. He was only going one way.

Walking toward the Saint Anthony Residence, Marty noticed the suburban twists and confusing street corners. This was another positive for the City Hall folks. It was next to impossible to find just about anything here, let alone a weaving platoon of the forgotten. Marty walked past the White Castle corporate offices, tucked in between nondescript industrial buildings, and deceptive because of its prominent castle-adorned sign and lack of 24-hour access to steamed sliders. He stopped to look at the sign and wondered how many Saint Anthony residents knocked on the door.

A Special Conditional Use Permit allowed for Saint Anthony operations outside the standard city codes. The Saint Anthony was special in many ways. Its condition was to be covert.

The building was alone, and the people were alone. For the City Council, it was an easy vote yes.

It was all deliberately confusing, but Marty knew exactly where he was going.

Harry was still walking. As he passed the industrial neighborhood, he dreamed of working at one of the businesses. He would have a cube, a Rolodex, maybe a Rolex, and maybe even a computer. At Thanksgiving, he would get a free turkey. At Christmas, his boss would stop by his cube wearing half-tinted glasses and give Harry a bonus for being the best salesman of all time. He would have a fine car and tell hilarious lawyer jokes. Happy hours would be rowdy.

People would like him. When he got home from work, his

family would greet him at the door like a hero and his wife would hand him a tall glass of lemonade.

Harry was turning off Hampden Avenue onto Wycliff Street and into the parking lot when his daily fantasy was rudely interrupted.

"Greetings, Mr. Harry, greetings on this fine morning." The man erupted in a world-record burp.

Harry's face turned sour. "Jesus, Jack, isn't it a little early for you to be at it?"

"Early? I never went home."

"Good God, man, you smell like a brewery, and we're in the middle of the month. Do you have any money left?"

"I got some from the new guy on a bet. He thought I was lying about my tongue."

"You showed him?"

"That's right, good Harry." Jack proudly unfurled his unusually long tongue and shoved it halfway up his nose.

"Enough already!" Harry stepped up his pace.

"Catch you later, Harry. And lighten up, would ya?"

Harry's olfactory senses were hardened, but profound. He was certain that any money Jack had made was only enough for a 99¢ bottle of rubbing alcohol. He smelled medicinal.

It annoyed Harry when he ran into clients before work, even right in front of the building.

In the 1980s, they were clients. Years later, the first-ever employee manual would replace "clients" with "guests."

The early morning was Harry's, all the way up to the front door, and he didn't want anyone spoiling it—clients, guests, or anyone else. He grumbled to himself, "Everybody else in this world gets paid overtime, but not Harry. No, he has to sit and talk to Jack like a Good Samaritan. That millionaire down the street at the widget shop writes a big check once in his life and gets a standing ovation and a plaque. He'll be at the club by 1 o'clock. I care all day. I want a plaque and a handshake from the mayor."

Despite years of extended helping hands, Harry was an unabashed conservative, mostly of the "dollar for a day's work" variety. He believed he picked himself up by his bootstraps and had a license to be irritated.

At the end of Wycliff, amid the eclectic morass of entrepreneurs and industrialists, the Saint Anthony Residence loomed like an abandoned roadside motel. Years of vegetation hung over the L-shaped building and into the street, almost by design. The parking lot was winter-beaten asphalt with flora creeping through the cracks. A lone basketball hoop leaned on the right side of the lot.

Harry didn't know the origin of the hoop and never asked about it. It was obvious it had been there since the building had hotel customers. The net was torn, the rim was bent, and the gray metal backboard, surprisingly, was without rust. A number of Saint Anthony residents would take drunken turns throwing round objects through the hoop, none of which were basketballs. Games lasted only a few points, but they were entertaining in a circus-like way.

Bodies bouncing around, players passing out in the middle of the court, bench-clearing brawls with spinning roundhouses that never made connections, and even the occasional vomit trick—a surefire drive to the basket without interference. Bill Russell used to throw up before Celtics games, but never during a game. He might have considered it if he knew its efficacy. While flagrant, it would not be unsportsmanlike.

Harry wondered who in their right mind would put up a basketball hoop at a hotel. He often thought it was a diversionary mechanism—like weights in prison.

In the parking lot, cars were not the issue. With most residents on the state's "do not drive" list and none with any real income, the lot was used mostly for staff and, occasionally, a first responder.

Nothing else in the parking lot provided any indication of what lay within. Church groups and high school service classes were nowhere to be found. While homeless shelters could count on upbeat campus crusaders to lend an annual hand at planting flowers and playing nervous gin rummy with the homeless, the Saint Anthony was dark and quiet, with an appearance of abandonment. Lights dimmed through the faded windows and crisscrossing broken, uneven blinds.

From the parking lot, there should have been a sign at the old hotel with hourly rates and an old soda machine with Orange Crush handwritten over the Diet Rite. The beds in the rooms should vibrate.

But the Saint Anthony Residence was not a hotel. It was not a motel, either.

It was a home.

Fifty-five beds, with a fifty-sixth and a fifty-seventh bed depending on the aging structure and regulatory mood swings. Each bed was a home. From the outside, it looked empty and abandoned. Inside, every bed was full.

In the parking lot, Harry took a thousand steps back in time. It was a brief moment every day when Harry remembered the days in God-knows-what-city when he ended up in the parking lot of another roadside motel, kicked out of the party and 17 bucks short of $17.95 for clean sheets and all the *Barnaby Jones* he could watch. The only thing missing was the pool, where he would bathe before being forcibly thrust on his way by a skinny hotel manager with a dangling cigarette in his mouth and scrambled eggs on his shirt.

In the blink of an eye, Harry could remember a life lost.

Today, he stood in front of the Saint Anthony and remembered his last job. It was at the potato factory only a half mile from the Saint Anthony. Frozen French fries by the millions jammed into small brown bags and shipped to restaurants across the Midwest. Harry remembered signing the paperwork to be a Teamster and then walking to the line, thinking about retiring with a pension. He stood in front of the giant sifter picking out brown French fries and throwing them into the pig feed bucket.

After about an hour, he was in front of a Windsor soda. After another hour, his face was on the bar.

The metal double door looked like it came from a schoolhouse, and it clanged at recess. Kids and chronic alcoholics can both be unruly. At the Saint Anthony, the smallest amount of traffic in the entryway was cause for extreme caution.

Harry slowly opened up the uneven rusty barrier. It was never locked.

There was an unmistakable elixir of foot odor, some usual body odor, a heavy bathroom fragrance, and an excessive seepage of cigarette smoke from all corners.

While it appeared to be a standard roadside hotel in an industrial zone, the building was a two-story structure with a sunken first floor.

Harry descended a handicapped-accessible linoleum walkway to reach the first floor.

Today, the walkway was free of slippery obstacles.

Harry's office did not have a door, so the unofficial invitation was always public.

Morning had broken at the Saint Anthony.

- -

Marty stopped at the corner of Hampden and Wycliff to have a cigarette. He had five left in the pack and only two matches. He could take only one break from smoking before he would need to borrow a match or another smoke.

- -

It never took more than a few moments for the slinking in the hallways to begin. Right around the time that Harry procured a cup of coffee and sat down in his metal chair, Professor John stood in the doorway. He was breathing halitosis fire from the hallway to Harry's nose hairs. "Harry, someone threw up in the second bathroom."

"Was it you?" Harry's standard response would make the employee manual. Blame the guy who told you.

"No," the Professor cautiously responded, as though it was the first time he could answer negatively.

Professor John was one of many legends at the Saint Anthony. A chronic alcoholic like everyone else, he held two badges of dishonor that were neither confirmed nor denied. He had a PhD of some kind, and he had the state record for number of times in treatment, a staggering 180 visits.

Harry knew that the old man's name was John. After names, backgrounds at the Saint Anthony grew hazy due to boozy embellishments or saucy forgetfulness. Paper records were passed from agency to agency in a game of telephone. The only constant was a name and a Social Security number. Other records required sleuthing.

Harry had a feeling that the Professor's number of treatment stints was accurate, as he heard it from a county worker in a tweed jacket. In order to enter the Saint Anthony, an individual must have demonstrated a propensity for at least two things—expending large sums of taxpayer money on treatment and failing all structured attempts to release the grip of alcohol addiction. Most residents passed with extraordinary skill. Harry ordered the cleanup like a submarine captain. "Tell someone to get a mop on it, doc." He knew there was no one to tell.

The Professor cracked a yellow smile and shuffled backwards to the utility closet. He didn't open the door.

Harry offered the Professor the courtesy of a professional moniker even though he was unsure of his doctoral status.

Nicknames were ubiquitous at the Saint Anthony: Docs, Dutches, and Stoshes were everywhere.

The Professor's treatment record, on the other hand, was not ubiquitous. It intrigued Harry. Everyone at Saint Anthony had been through treatment at least four or five times, and many had more. Harry never liked math and rarely calculated the average of anything except the number of cigarettes versus time, but he surmised that the average amount of completed treatment visits was somewhere around seven per resident. Walking in the door and walking out a few hours later didn't count.

Harry had done five turns in various centers, the last of which was successful. Others had done far more. Completing 25 turns accounted for almost a year and a half, which was a decent run at prison, or for some, a run at marriage. It was also akin to a stint in the Peace Corps. If the Professor's average stay was one week, two weeks less than the typical full term, then his minimum stint would have been about three and a half years.

Detox was a different story. Almost everyone at the Saint Anthony had a distinguished record of overnight stays in the detoxification center. Detox is scientific terminology for "drunk tank." For those unruly and inebriated enough to arouse the attention of law enforcement, a free pass to the tank was awarded. If they were just unruly, they would go to jail.

Nestled behind an alley in downtown Saint Paul, detox was almost a speakeasy in that none of the powers-that-be wanted anyone to know what was behind its old red doors. City planners wanted guests out of sight, and perhaps out of mind.

The Fortune 500 Ecolab, just two blocks away, had little idea what was behind those alley doors. The CEO of the industrial cleaning products company spoke often and eloquently about commitment to eradicating poverty, and he backed it up with millions of dollars from his company and his own pocket. He was an actual pillar of the community. Around the corner, his products washed away the outcomes of lives gone awry.

The Professor returned to Harry's office. "I asked around about cleaning up the mess. No takers."

Harry half-smiled. "Appreciate it."

The Professor visited detox 300 times—300 times dragged from the gutter, 300 times eating a PBJ, and 300 times walking through red doors into an alley, squinting in the light.

The Professor continued to stand in Harry's office to offer commentary on the day's happenings. He had nothing else to do, except drink.

"Saw Larry passed out last night in the kitchen."

"Yup." Harry made a point not to engage the Professor. If he did, the ensuing conversation would last through lunchtime. Harry just let him stand and look professorial.

"My dissertation had more substance than that," he would regularly comment to the TV in Harry's office.

Harry never saw the Professor's dissertation, but he believed it existed. Some residents he wanted to believe, and some he did not. Harry believed the Professor.

Harry was far more skeptical of the myriad business backgrounds at the Saint Anthony.

He was even more skeptical about military history.

Did everyone at the Saint Anthony serve in Vietnam? It was unfortunately possible. With a closet full of denim shirts emblazoned with American flags, Harry was a patriot.

He never served in the military, but he respected veterans and wanted so much to have the same stories and the same feelings, even if some stemmed from horrifying memories of violence in a foreign land. He wanted a valiant purpose, but it was too risky.

Lying in the gutter 20 years ago, not thinking about America and hating everyone around him, Harry brought himself to treatment under the premise that America had more to offer. It was the same premise he brought to his previous visit. Emerging from treatment on his fifth run, he became a patriot. The county gave him a chance, which meant that America gave him a chance.

Harry did not know how to respond to claims of military service. It was important to respect those who served. He respected the contentions and never wanted to argue. One day, Harry would do the research on every resident's background. Hopefully, he would not discover that America had forgotten so many.

Marty lit another smoke with the butt of the previous one. Unless he was drinking, he was never tardy. He could rationalize truth out of anything, and in this case, he was correct in that there was no expectation for the time of his arrival. He was not going to prison. He had never been to actual prison. He was in jail once when detox was full, but never prison. Today, he had time for a few smokes.

- -

The Professor's intoxication never seemed to dissipate, as though it was permanent. He eventually tired of the one-sided conversation with Harry and stumbled to the Saint Anthony library, a lonely shelf of books in the kitchen.

"Headin' out now, Harry."

"Catch you later."

If Harry saw him tomorrow, the Professor's ongoing state of inebriation would erase the day's one-sided conversation and allow him to begin anew. The Professor's daily ingestion of alcohol was the norm at the Saint Anthony. In-house intelligentsia, or just the quiet and lonely, almost everyone bellied up to some sort of bar.

Saint Anthony was not a treatment center, halfway house, or sober house. It was a wet house. Visitors to Harry's office were drunk, drinking to get drunk, or looking to get drunk.

All were welcome at the Saint Anthony. Pray to Saint Anthony and you will find it.

- -

Marty pinched the end of his cigarette, put it in his pocket, and walked into the parking lot.

CHAPTER TWO

BOTTLE SERVICE

Harry made the same request at least seven times: "Bottle, please."

A furrowed brow and the revelation of an aperitif would ensue each time. Residents were allowed to own alcohol but never possess it on the premises. Despite some attempts to smuggle bottles in, residents followed the rules as though it was a brotherhood to protect.

Bottle check at the Saint Anthony was no different than coat check at a fine restaurant. Instead of a number and a coat, it was a slip of paper with a name and brand. Sneaking bottles into the residence was a serious offense at the Saint Anthony. The opportunity for disruption was immense. Drinking to the edge of fatality, fighting, and overall mayhem was almost guaranteed. It was General Order Number One for Harry, and he believed it was tantamount to the survival of the program.

Walter handed Harry a large plastic bottle of whiskey. "Harry, my check didn't come last week. Can you spare a few bucks?" Handing the bottle was an afterthought.

"Not today, Walter. You know the score." Harry took the bottle from Walter and put it in a box with 10 other bottles, all plastic. Harry knew that Walter's check from the county had arrived, and he knew that Walter spent the money. Walter, as nondescript as they came, had been at the Saint Anthony for about five years. No funny stories, no doctorate, and no preposterous story about the glory days. A quiet, middle-aged, average-dressed male—he just drank a lot.

"I really need a few bucks, Harry."

"Even if I could, and I can't, why do you need it?" Harry wondered why Walter needed money when his checked bottle was a third full.

"I just need it."

The conversation never lasted more than a few minutes, but it happened every month.

Walter also forgot about his bottle every month. The lost and found was the drain.

The reality of rock bottom was that everyone was out of money. It also meant loss. They had it, they lost it, and they were looking for it. Pray to Saint Anthony and, this time, you won't find it. The patron saint of lost articles is wise.

Marty Peterson stood in Harry's doorway. Harry thought it was a bottle check. "I'm Marty Peterson. The county sent me for a room."

"News to me, Mr. Marty. I thought we were full."

"I just came from downtown. They told me to come here."

Harry was frustrated. He was typically informed of new residents at least a day in advance. He hoped it was not a sign of demise, either of his brain or his job. He made up the part about being full.

"Have a seat. I need to figure this shit out." The expletive was whispered.

In 1984, the average cost of chemical dependency treatment was $10,000 for a 30-day stay. The cost of detox was almost $150 per day, which made cement floors and PBJs almost as pricey as the nearby Saint Paul Hotel. At the four-star Saint Paul, guests could substitute peanut butter for smoked ham in the room-service omelet. No one over did.

For the Saint Anthony, defense was more important than offense. The stock speech for Catholic Charities leaders focused on money instead of dignity.

"The average resident has been to treatment seven times and detox 25 times. At an average cost of $10,000 for treatment and almost $200 per day for detox, one person on the streets costs over $80,000."

Audiences of elected officials and business leaders would harrumph over Styrofoam cups of strong coffee. "Saint Anthony costs less than $50 a day. What are the choices? People on downtown streets, cold and hungry at almost a hundred grand, or at the Saint Anthony with three meals and a roof?"

Another popular opinion was to get the homeless out of sight. Drunks on the streets were bad for business.

The Chamber of Commerce liked the Saint Anthony.

In a different speech for advocates, the Saint Anthony was a matter of dignity. "Society may give up on curing the disease of alcoholism, but the afflicted are still our fellow citizens. Dignity calls for the basics of life—food, shelter, and maybe something for the soul."

The patron saint of lost articles would not allow a community to lose its own.

Even for the arguers of dignity, it was impossible to avoid the spreadsheet fact that the Saint Anthony saved money and removed people from the streets. Dignity was a bonus. It was left and right wing.

Financially, the Saint Anthony was organized with laudable efficiency. The federal government gave the county a fixed amount of dollars per resident. Official qualifications included lack of stable housing, a diminished hope of near-term self-sufficiency, and a unique and lengthy history of chronic alcoholism.

While government could pass these dollars directly to individuals to fend for themselves, county and nonprofit leaders created a unique plan in the Saint Anthony. The county would accept the money from dear old Uncle Sam, they would take the daily cost of a Saint Anthony resident off the top via a contract with Catholic Charities, and they would give the rest to the resident.

For Catholic Charities, this amounted to barely enough to operate the facility. They had to rely on donors for the frills.

For the residents, this meant three squares and an actual bed. Management even threw in a late-night snack.

It also meant that each month they would receive a check for $47—no strings attached.

Checks at Saint Anthony arrived like any government check—on or about the first of the month. This made for an unusually regular calendar at the residence.

It was April 14, 1984, and Marty was still sitting there in Harry's office.

Tax Day was tomorrow, which meant little to anyone but Harry, the cook, and the occasional custodian. For everyone else at the Saint Anthony, it was the middle of the month, and the money was gone.

Howard peered into the office. He looked at Marty. "Harry, do you have bus fare?"

"If you mean, do I have money, then you know the answer."

"C'mon, Harry," Howard gurgled. He was still looking at Marty. Howard's breath wrapped around the room like a serpent.

"You know the rules. If you want to actually get on a bus, then I have tokens. If you're looking for money, then you know the score." Harry never looked up at him.

"Then can I have some tokens?"

"Two tokens—one there and one back," Harry offered. The fact that many residents rode the bus to the end of the line and back without getting off was an acceptable flaw in the Saint Anthony transportation plan.

Harry didn't know too much about Howard. Rumor had it that at one time in Howard's soaked life, he worked at a bank. Preposterous stories developed of him being a bank president and even a millionaire. Howard was good with numbers, but not much else.

Howard bargained, "How about three?"

"How about you just take one and not come back?"

"Funny, Harry," Howard's face cringed as he grabbed two tokens. Then he turned to Marty, "How about you, stranger, do you have any tokens?"

Marty looked at him and said, "Actually, I have one." He reached into his pocket and gave Howard the token.

Howard would sell the tokens and net himself almost a dollar. That would get him started. Maybe he was a bank president.

"What was your name again, Mr. Whatever?" Harry said to Marty. "Marty Peterson. The county sent me."

MARTY INTERLUDES

An insanely cold day in 1990

The case manager put his tattered coat on the rack and sat in the dank office at the Union Gospel Mission. He took the short bus ride from downtown, and he knew that he would be cold for the next hour.

The case manager waited for his next appointment. It was a referral from the adjacent Christ Center, the mission's religious-based treatment center that catered to homeless men. The case manager did not have a clue what transpired behind its doors. It only mattered that his appointment was sober.

"You must be Marty Peterson. You're here for the jobs program?"

"Yes. Can I smoke in here?"

"I guess so. Do you want coffee? I'm getting some, so it's no problem."

"Sure."

The case manager walked past Marty and procured two cups of excessively dark coffee from the overused Mr. Coffee in the staff room. It looked like it hadn't been cleaned since its purchase.

The case manager was taken aback by the gentleman's frailty and apparent age; Marty was recommended by the staff but wasn't old enough to get Social Security benefits. He might not tell stories in corporate boardrooms about how he came from the streets to the corner office, but he could use a job. The case manager would soon realize the same for all his clients.

Intakes took two hours of coffee, cigarettes, and box-checking. If the applicant was open and truthful, he could delve into their lives. After the names and usual multiples of jobs and addresses, the conversation would tunnel deep.

"Where was your last treatment?"

"Pine Shores, I think. I was there for two weeks."

"But I thought you were at the Christ Center?"

"I thought you meant one of the regular treatment places. Yes, I came over to the Christ Center from the Saint Anthony."

"How long have you been sober?"

"I don't know."

By the time he completed Marty's intake, the case manager knew about his years of alcoholism and the path on which it took him. He also knew most of Marty's spotted work history, his military service, and a little about his family. The case manager struggled to make conversation with his new, seemingly elder client. He wondered if he should order him a psychological evaluation and perhaps a sheltered work environment.

"Thanks so much for coming out today. I know it's freezing out there. I look forward to working with you. I think you'll find that we have some unique resources to get folks moving in life."

"It was only across the parking lot."

Marty smiled and shuffled out the door. The case manager leaned against the office door and watched him slowly walk into the lobby and out the door into the frigid air. Marty didn't talk to anyone in the crowded lobby.

The case manager went back to the office and looked over the manila file. Nothing stood out—no drug use, no prison, no rail-riding, no embellishments. Marty seemed unusually local to the case manager.

It would be weeks before they talked about baseball.

"Are you guys giving out bus cards in this program? If so, I'm in."

The man in the doorway did not have an appointment, but for the case manager it was either another intake or a bone-chilling wait for a bus that was always late. The case manager was optimistic that even two hours closer to springtime would be warmer.

"Yes, we are. Have a seat."

PART TWO

PEOPLE ALWAYS ASK US WHO WE ARE, SO WE TELL THEM

CHAPTER THREE

MARTY IN THE HOUSE

Early spring, 1986

Exactly two years after he walked into the Saint Anthony Residence, Marty Peterson was Harry's favorite.

Billy Martin or a grizzled 1800s prospector—Marty could have been either.

The hard-drinking, hard-playing, World Series title-winning Yankee had no relation to Marty Peterson. But Marty was frazzled, he had a history of prodigious imbibing, and he loved baseball, excessively. He looked the part, and he acted it, but he was decidedly less intense than the great Mr. Martin. Marty didn't know how to carouse.

As for a prospector, Marty just looked like one. Not the Yosemite Sam one with the wild-eyed growl or the thirst for gold. It was just the look. His weathered face, sunken eyes, crooked fingers with smoke stains on every digit, and listing frame added up to an ideal prospector, with and without his 1980s-style quarter-inch rectangular, gray-framed glasses.

His face was sallow and forlorn. His secondhand clothes were far from the homeless stereotype—he wore a cheap blue windbreaker, a plaid shirt, and seemingly prehistoric blue jeans that looked pressed on his frail, skeleton-like body.

He walked with a slow, shuffling motion. His K-Mart shoes were standard homeless issue—bright white and, at size 12, out of place for his smallish frame. They looked like Reeboks, without the logo for everyone to see.

There was also something about homeless socks. Marty was supposed to be disheveled, drunk, odorous, and ornery. His socks set a properly opposite tone—crisp, white, and pulled tightly over his varicose veins. Maybe it was just Minnesota nice, but in shelters everyone seemed to have white shoes and crisp socks. Marty had to start somewhere. Smelly feet and duct-taped kitchen shoes would fail to impress on the résumé, if he had one.

Atop his listing and shuffling frame was an enviable swath of bright-white hair that went from Green Beret short to artsy long in a cycle that closely followed the rounds of the volunteer barber. Marty was 55 years old, and he lacked a bald spot. The white mane had been present for decades. It inexplicably appeared one day, enshrouded in chemical stimulants and likely genetic predisposition. He was just a white-haired guy. Like so many in Minnesota, he was German-Norwegian.

Marty cared less about the color of his hair, a designer label on his jeans, or whether Jimmy Connors wore his shoes. His body was grizzled, but the rest of him was neat as a pin.

His appearance fit in nicely at the Saint Anthony.

Experts could conjure a range of theories as to why the average Saint Anthony resident was fastidious about appearance. The chemical dependency counselor would indicate that there was an underlying co-dependency to one level of accomplishment, and the psychologist would assert a predilection for obsessive-compulsiveness.

They would pass over the most likely and most simple theory: Time.

Marty and his colleagues walked the halls of Saint Anthony with groomed figures and clean clothes for a simple reason. They had time. Time in the morning, time in the afternoon, and time in the evening was all they had, along with a washing machine, a dryer, and a monthly visit to the secondhand store with a voucher.

Marty also took the time to enjoy a clean shave every day. The act itself did not feel particularly good over his weathered skin, but when the last splash of warm water hit his face at the penultimate moment, it was worth a thousand nicks. Millions of men—some with millions of dollars—enjoyed the same moments. It did not make Marty feel equal. He just liked shaving, and each day's razor-sharp travel across his face revealed the weathered lines of a grizzled man.

Years ago, Marty toiled in the depths of the post office as a federal employee, entrusted with sorting America's mail. He was likely the only former federal employee at Saint Anthony. He was also the only federal employee with enough visits to detox to warrant the rare federal termination. Resident careers at the Saint Anthony were spoken of in the present tense, even though, without exception, they were all in the past.

"What do you do?"

"I'm in construction." Destruction skewed reality.

Before the sun peeked through the prefab concrete and made its way past the chipped paint and overfilled gutters, Marty would complete a round of the facilities, first the shared men's room and then the shared shower. "Shared" is a loose term, as the bathrooms only fit one person and there was a sometimes-working lock on the door. Marty would arrive long before Harry cleaned out the first mess.

The bathrooms were clean but oddly odorous. Long ago, Harry tasked a professional cleaning team to attempt permanent odor removal. Normally suited for dead animals and crime scene eradication, the cleaning team failed. Marty knew the stink could never get better than at 6 a.m.

He quickly executed the three S's of male life: shit, shower, and shave. Like everyone else, Marty's enjoyment of the three followed a perfect bell curve against age: burden when young, solace at middle age, and painful when old.

After, Marty fired up a low-dollar filtered cigarette that helped compose him. His brand was Parliament. It would be Marty's first cigarette before coffee.

Smoking was the norm at the Saint Anthony. Old-school theories of alcoholism would indicate a correlative addiction to nicotine. Alcoholics need cigarettes as a complement to their more serious addictions.

A resident might ask at any moment of the day, "Do you have a smoke?"

Another theory was social. Notwithstanding its horror-film effect on his teeth, Marty liked being in the club.

"Sure." The gift was an invitation to brotherhood. The giver would then join the taker for an enjoyable 7-minute confluence.

After drawing down the cigarette to its filter for one version of tar, Marty would shuffle to the cafeteria for a hot cup of the other. He never understood why the hallway smelled like feet and the bathrooms a mix of lavender and something horrible. It was 7 a.m. when Marty entered the dining room. Breakfast would be served in 30 minutes, but the large, industrial coffee urn had been turned on since late-night snack. By sunrise, the urn was a bubbling tar pit—the Saint Anthony preferred roast. The kitchen crew of one was just arriving, so if a resident chose to wait for the fresh stuff, relatively speaking, it would be available at 7:30 a.m.

Marty never waited. Staring at the coffee urn, Marty paused and looked at both taps. He knew they dispensed the same coffee, but it was a decision.

Dave was the only kitchen staffer at the unaptly coined Café de Saint Anthony. He smiled at Marty every weekday morning, and sometimes on the weekends.

"Morning, Mr. P."

"Morning, Dave. Did you get that Michelin star yet?" Marty asked.

"It's still in committee. I'll let you know." Dave knew that his job was to satiate the masses.

Dave was a success story. Addiction and mental health rode him from the West Coast to an SRO apartment in Minneapolis. Treatment and support found him a job as a dishwasher at a Catholic Charities drop-in center. Stability brought him to the Saint Anthony. Dave was likable but not talkative.

Marty was unsure if Dave was either the right name or the right alias. Almost everyone at Saint Anthony had an alias, some for their role as community provocateur, a few because they wanted to hide from noble efforts, and many because they wanted a taste of the intrigue that can only come with an alias. Marty did not have an alias.

Marty did things slowly, and everything around him complied. Even the coffee flowed like actual street tar.

"Big plans for the day?" Dave hesitantly asked, knowing that striking up conversations with residents could lead to the dreaded recurring conversation.

"Just headed downtown."

"Downtown is nice."

"Yep."

His daily kitchen conversation complete, Marty would make

his way out of the cafeteria and down foot-odor alley. He made a point to see Harry.

Every day, Marty would sit with Harry. Their time together would last a minimum of 7 minutes for a smoke. Sometimes they would talk. Sometimes the sessions lasted all day. Others occasionally joined the party.

"Had to bounce Monroe today for throwing up too much," Harry mumbled. He had powdered sugar on his beard.

Marty slowly looked up, "Monroe?"

"The chubby guy from Duluth."

"I know Monroe," Terry Thomas chimed in over a stub cigar as he stood in the doorway.

Terry alternated between cigarettes and cigars, depending on his mood. His lips had a brown ring around them.

The soft-spoken conversations of Saint Anthony residents had neither a specific point nor any air of judgment, condescension, or other qualities that would suggest the appearance of flawed character.

Marty never said a negative word. His brow never furrowed, his rotten teeth never bared in rage, and his yellow fingers never whitened in a clench, except around a baseball bat.

Marty was comfortable at the residence. Like a veteran home from military service, which Marty actually was over 30 years before, he was just happy to be there, even though the only combat Marty ever saw was long after his service and in the face of a bottle, not a gun.

Harry wanted to explain it in a psychological way, but it was too simple for analytics, and he didn't know how to do it anyway. Marty was just a nice guy, and he was Harry's favorite. It helped that he never fell on his face in the bathroom.

CHAPTER FOUR

FROGTOWN BASEBALL BAR

Marty did not have storied tales of reaching the pinnacle, then miserably crashing to the inglorious depths of failure. He was just woeful. Long before he was predictable in Harry's office, he was predictable in life.

Marty was born on June 22, 1937, on the North End of Saint Paul, where union halls hosted wedding receptions and the American Legion and VFW clubs had veterans lined up three-deep at the bar. The neighboring Whirlpool plant and Hamm's Brewery were the rocks of the community, almost making the neighborhood an old steel town—ethnic churches, bustling corner bars, and meatloaf.

The Petersons did not linger in the North End.

Family and hard work. This was Frogtown in central Saint Paul. Solidly blue collar, the families were large and the churches numerous and powerful.

As amateur historians had it, Archbishop John Ireland was so struck with the incessant cacophony of frogs from the former marshland that he dubbed the neighborhood *Froschberg,* or "Frog City." It was unclear if it was a term of endearment.

Frogtown was surrounded by a community of overlapping neighborhoods with arguable boundaries, and one of those was Rondo. In the 1950s, over two-thirds of Saint Paul's Black population lived in the Rondo neighborhood. In 1956, planners purposefully chose to saw Rondo in half by building Interstate 94 right through it. Over 600 Black families lost their homes and businesses. It was an unfortunate time in America.

The neighborhood had resilience, but now it meant business.

Frogtown's taverns were less raucous beer halls than they were community centers. Dads would argue about management and the mayor over locally brewed Schmidt beer. Intransigence was cursing the union or voting Republican. Abject failure was not making it home for dinner.

Marty fit nicely into the neighborhood. He grew up in a modest stucco home on a tree-lined street. Curmudgeons had nothing on Marty and his friends. Kids outnumbered everyone.

He attended public school. He occasionally wondered why he went to church every Sunday, but he only went to Catholic school for two years when they lived with Grandma. Did they change religions? It didn't matter to him. He excelled in school, but like most kids in the 1950s, all he really wanted to do was play sports and drive cars. None of his friends had cars.

In most Saint Paul neighborhoods, it was all about hockey. Minnesota itself was a hockey state. On the East Side, Rice Street, and the North End, where scrappers are born of 8-to-5 trade jobs and sloppy joes in church basements, hockey was redemption.

Everyone played hockey in Saint Paul. Each team had a hard-nosed coach with half-tinted glasses, a terry-cloth shirt, and polyester trousers, and each coach was a community icon.

Teams were Olympian in nature, and legends were born on ice that never melted. At the bar, stories of hockey glory were not only tolerated, but they attracted ears of all kinds, including the cauliflowers.

Across town from Marty, Herb Brooks was laying the foundation of sports immortality.

In Frogtown and Rondo, it was baseball.

From future legend Dave Winfield to unknown scrappers like Marty, America's pastime ruled the streets, literally. Baseball brought enclaves together to become communities. Tension in the neighborhood became friendship on the diamond.

Marty played hockey because he was supposed to play hockey, but he was never good at it, and he never liked it. Marty was a baseball player.

Years later, he drank at a baseball bar.

The Nickel Joint was a classic corner tavern. Tucked in the shadow of stately Saint Agnes Church, drinkers and storytellers flocked to its long bar. The only beer was Schmidt, and the scotch and sodas were poured strong into small glasses. Sunday mornings were busy.

Marty knew about the Nickel Joint in a different way. In the 1940s, the Saint Paul Saints served as an affiliate of the Brooklyn Dodgers. Every team had a home bar, and for the local Saints, it was the Nickel Joint. During their brief runs with the Saints, Roy Campanella, Leo Durocher, Lefty Gomez, and Duke Snider all lined up at its wooden dais. They became legends of a neighborhood first, then legends of baseball.

For his short time in Saint Paul, Roy Campanella lived at the Rideaux Boardinghouse, not far from Marty and his pals in Frogtown. The segregated hotels in normally progressive downtown Saint Paul wouldn't let the legend stay overnight. The downtown hotels remained, but Roy's home eventually became a freeway.

Marty liked Roy the best. All the kids liked Roy the best. As a young fan, Marty squeezed his eyes through holes in the fence to watch Roy play at Lexington Park. After the games, Ron, Jim, Terry, and Marty would run to the park and imitate their heroes. They would fight over who got to play Roy.

Marty eventually drank from the same glasses at the Nickel Joint, and he knew it. His life traveled from carefree times playing baseball on the diamond to talking about baseball at a bar. After the first drinks, the bar would be carefree. After the last drinks, the baseball was gone. Then it would start over.

MARTY INTERLUDES

Friday, May 6, 1955, Saint Paul, Minnesota

Peterson stepped into the box for Saint Paul Wilson High School in the top of the third. Schreiber stole second after a bloop single, Senske walked. Causton was on deck. With the game tied 0-0, the meat of the order was coming up.

It never crossed Marty's mind that any of the opposing Saint Paul Johnson Governors would ascend to baseball immortality. The Governors were good, but not that good. It was even harder for Marty to predict that one of the Governors would lead Team USA to gold in the most important Olympic hockey game in history.

Marty didn't know Herb Brooks. He just wanted to get on base.

It was midseason in the City Conference, and the team from the tiny Saint Paul public high school looked like it could make a run for it.

It seemed not to matter that Marty's mother was drinking every day. Marty had his boys, and, together, they had baseball. When the snow was gone, Marty didn't need to be at home. He didn't eat much anyway, but if he was hungry, there was always a warm plate somewhere else. His mother was usually passed out by the time he needed his bed, and by that point, he could dream that mom fell asleep from the hard work of being the world's greatest mom. Years later, Marty sold a dozen or so World's Greatest Mom T-shirts at the Union Gospel Mission Thrift Store. Some were tattered, and some were unscathed. He only briefly thought of his own mom when he sold the shirts for 50¢ apiece.

Marty took the first pitch. Called strike one. It was outside. Marty never complained. Herb Brooks was covering first base.

Herb was the anchor of Johnson's soon-to-be-legendary Minnesota AA Champion hockey team. The Governors hockey team was the pride of Saint Paul. Twenty-five years later, Coach Brooks and the Miracle on Ice team were the pride of the democratized world, a squad of anonymous, likable scrappers who faced up to global intimidation and toppled the giant.

Herb Brooks was also a baseball player; right then, he just wanted to get Marty out. He would have been good with a strikeout, but he wanted to be in the play.

Ball one, outside. Ball two, outside.

Herb Brooks elevated everyone around him. Even those he berated were better off for having known him. After the Wilson team, Marty elevated everyone around him because he was going the opposite direction. It just seemed like they were elevated.

In his historic path from the North End of Saint Paul to Lake Placid, New York, Herb Brooks may have had a few lite beers to celebrate a thousand victories.

Marty just had the beers.

The Johnson pitcher was locked in a full count with Marty. Not much in the way of stuff, but he was a hurler.

Fastball. Foul tip.

Schreiber yelled to Marty, "Let's make it happen, Petey!" Causton was quieter, "You got this, Peterson."

It was not the first time Marty played against future Olympic gold. Two years earlier, on Monday, May 18, 1953, an up-and-coming Wilson team squared off against Jack McCartan and Saint Paul Marshall. McCartan would go on to lead the Minnesota Golden Gopher baseball squad to the NCAA title, but he would also make history by winning hockey gold for the United States in the 1960 Olympics. He was named "All World" goaltender for the US squad. It was a miracle on ice before the Miracle on Ice.

Marty Peterson and the Wilson boys outlasted Jack McCartan and Marshall 7-4. Two weeks later, Saint Paul Marshall closed permanently.

The pitcher was in a groove. It was just the third inning, so his arm was strong. There wasn't an overabundance of heat in the City Conference, but today, the Johnson pitcher was bringing it. It was Frogtown versus the North End. Marty's summer would be defined by this game.

Marty didn't think about neighborhood wars or tavern pride. He just liked playing ball. Ten years later, Marty would sit at the Nickel Joint and overhear stories of Frogtown thumping the North End. He would also sit at Vogel's on the North End and hear the opposite. He just cared about the beer.

Fastball.

Marty was focused. The pressure of staying undefeated and making it to the state championship failed to overcome his love for this moment. No one could tell him anything.

He stepped into the pitch. His swing was in perfect concert with the unusually sinking fastball, connecting in a single, slow motion. The bat and ball stayed together and then released into a curve down the left-field line.

Schreiber and Senske could see it. They took off before Marty even dropped the bat. By the time Senske made it home, Marty was standing on second base, his pants still clean.

Wilson 2, Johnson 0.

It was only two runs, but the game was lopsided. The Governors picked up two runs for themselves, but Wilson crossed the plate another eight times to earn summer bragging rights.

Four players on that field would wear the same college uniform the following year at the University of Minnesota, including Herb Brooks and Marty Peterson.

Herb would eventually take off his Gopher baseball uniform for a checkered sport coat and one of the most iconic gold medals in history.

Marty took off his uniform for a shirt he found at Goodwill.

CHAPTER FIVE

GOING FOR THE CYCLE
FIRST WEEK AND MIDDLE OF THE MONTH

At the Saint Anthony, middle-of-the-month blues were created by first-week highs.

Payday was the beginning. As soon as checks arrived, most residents were quickly standing in front of a check-cashing counter. The term "underbanked" was not in the dictionary in 1986. After the fee, residents would stuff $45 and change into their pockets, just enough to test their stamina.

Marty usually hung around in Harry's office for the first half of payday.

Most of the other residents would enjoy the fruits of their non-labor. Marty would greet them on their way out. Chronic alcoholics with money and a plan offered few words.

"Catch you later, Marty." Phil slapped the doorframe as he whisked down the hall.

"Roger that, Phil, save one for me." He was invited, but Marty would never join the crews, and he was OK that they quickly forgot about him. They were focused on one day of tavern normalcy.

Not far from the Saint Anthony, three bars stood out on University Avenue: The Ace Box Bar, Johnny's, and The Cromwell. Ace Box was home to a long and comforting wooden bar rail, Johnny's was home to "World Famous Sandwiches," and The Cromwell was home to its own check-cashing window, for a fee, of course. Depending on the employee, Saint Anthony residents were welcome. It was a short list.

All of them were within walking distance. Most other establishments had come to recognize Saint Anthony residents and their problematic intoxication. Some had been pressured by community leaders to refuse service on the grounds that residents were in recovery. The bottom line was that most bars did not want Saint Anthony residents disturbing the regulars, even though the regulars could similarly drink to intoxication. Someone had to be worse, and that ignominious honor fell to the Saint Anthony residents.

For the three bars, it was only a few days anyway, since they didn't sell rubbing alcohol.

The Ace Box was a classic tavern. By day, regulars encased the long bar for cold ales and conversation, and by night, college students populated its darkness. A handful of regulars would stick around for the evening festivities and eventually become folksy locals.

At the Ace Box, Saint Anthony residents were monitored. The owner was a good Irishman. Like the Saint Anthony, he had both a moral and business intention. Morally, he would not serve Saint Anthony residents over their limit, whatever that was. Business-wise, he didn't want residents to make his gathering place unwelcome to the community. There was nothing folksy about a sweaty, odorous inebriate. He arrived at a balance to make a little money and retain his obligatory role as a publican.

Carl's red nose shone through Harry's doorway, "Hello there, Mr. Marty. Say, Harry, am I stupid to ask for a few bucks?" Harry could only see the nose, but he assumed Carl was smiling, even though he was almost out of money.

Harry responded in his best Ed McMahon, "You are correct, sir." Harry heard a guffaw, the squeak of tennis shoes, and the front door opening and closing.

Marty liked Carl. He was smiling all the time, he wore tattered suit coats, and he had a red nose. He appeared to enjoy his life position. He had lived at Saint Anthony for years, and no one knew anything about his background. Everyone liked Carl. He never fought, he only vomited when he had the flu, and his body odor was graciously slathered with Hai Karate cologne.

Harry was thankful that Carl didn't know he could drink the cologne.

Carl's first-week bar choice was Johnny's. Johnny's had been on the avenue for years, but it never earned "local gem" status and had no desire to do so. The regulars were happy, which was all that mattered. The sign said, "World Famous Sandwiches," but sandwiches were not on the menu. Carl took a seat at the bar and enjoyed the cheapest ale in town—$1 per glass in the morning and the afternoon. No Saint Anthony resident was sure if it was the same price in the evenings because no one went there after 6. Carl was not even sure it was open at night. He was passed out by 5. On the first of the month, he was passed out by 2.

Johnny's staff enjoyed the company of Saint Anthony residents and served them accordingly. No matter one's place in a recovery program, a cold beer would appear in front of even the lowliest patron. And another, another, and another.

For everyone else at the Saint Anthony, the story was mostly the same on the first day of the month and for the entire first week.

In the beginning, the taverns were raucous. And on the seventh day, they didn't rest.

They passed out.

After the first week of the month, it was time to pool funds, hit the liquor store, and share bottles.

This was the period that Harry disliked the most. It meant that residents were drinking in the neighborhood. Harry cared about the health of the residents, but getting crosswise with neighbors could sink everything. Luckily, the neighbors were a long walk away even for a buzzed resident.

"Say, Harry old boy, I heard there were extra bus tokens at HQ," Robert said, peering his closely shaven face through the doorway.

"You heard wrong."

"Just keeping the man down, is that it?" he responded with a wisp of a smile.

"That's right, sir."

"How about you, Peterson? Spare change for a housemate?"

"All out today, Bobby," Marty quietly responded. He still had a sawbuck in his pocket. Robert was a veteran, and he wore his service on his sleeve daily.

"Fourteen days in the wake-up till payday, I guess," Robert muttered. He was off by a week.

Harry coined the second week of the month "the bottle period." It was mostly a continuation of the first week, although residents could consume more from a large plastic bottle than they could at a crowded bar. Odor was pronounced, and accidents were ubiquitous. The building was full of activity that needed to be managed toward calm and sanity.

Harry worked harder in the second week, and Marty remained a responsible observer. As the middle of the month waned, the creative period slowly wafted into the building.

This is when innovation took over from convention and legitimate danger covered the residence with a creepy twilight fog and a noxious smell of cleaning fluids, mouthwash, and rubbing alcohol.

At the hump of the second and third weeks, it started with the obvious and readily available. At just over 50 proof, a bottle of Listerine contains roughly the same amount of alcohol as a fifth of E&J Brandy. Listerine was available in any drugstore, and it was about one-third the price of the E&J. It was also easy to find for free.

Listerine or other mouthwashes were also present in the standard care package donations for the homeless. Harry never blamed anyone for the mouthwash donations, nor would he have expected them to understand the intricacies of caring for the chronic inebriate. The mere location of the Saint Anthony lent itself to abandonment.

Harry would promptly empty any donations one-by-one down the drain. Unfortunately, residents could easily make their way to another service agency to pick up care packages. The "Listerine Ripple" would flow.

After the obvious, supply and demand necessitated alternatives. These strategies traversed a desperate path. Rubbing alcohol, Lysol, or any combination of alcohol-based cleaning agents would be on tap for a potentially deadly elixir.

CHAPTER SIX

GOING FOR THE CYCLE
THE CREATIVE PERIOD

The alchemist labored over an elixir, waiting for that special moment when a batch of swirling, uncommon elements would transform into untold riches or a universal cure for the ills of the world.

Saint Anthony residents didn't wear lab coats, they weren't medieval, and they were unaware that among the nutritional components of barley *(hordeum vulgare)* are β-glucans and polyphenols. Most of them knew that barley in liquid form can be *vulgare,* but they didn't care.

Alchemists would mix chemicals that underwent "inexplicable and mysterious transmuting," and some even drank the resulting concoctions.

Saint Anthony residents were community alchemists. They mixed common household items for speculative happiness. Cocktail hour began with rubbing alcohol and Gatorade or a can of Lysol with Kool-Aid.

It sometimes took a few months of acclimation for the desperate, but eventually, most residents were taught the ways of alchemy. Not everyone took to it, but almost everyone tried it.

The creative period was explosive, almost literally.

The scenario was troubling. By the third week, basic economic theory is proven. Residents were out of money. Supply was low and demand was high, and innovation took command in the quest for survival.

Residents were scientists of the downward spiral. They sold bus tokens or took cans to the recycling center and then promptly headed to Walgreens. On lucky days, there would be stray Lysol cans in the neighborhood. Small groups would gather in hidden locales to share. Usually, it was rubbing alcohol. The hard stuff was cut with Kool-Aid, and the bottle would be passed until empty.

The results of alchemy during the creative period were swift and often tragic. Residents were quickly overtaken. The circles of alchemy in the neighborhood would immediately result in a mass exodus to bed or the floor. Participants would be completely out of their bodies as they followed the wall to their rooms. The third week was the most dangerous.

It was a deeply troubling time at the Saint Anthony.

It was not unusual for Harry to rely on professionals for the serious cases. Cause of death: extreme alchemy.

It happened enough to numb Harry.

Harry and the residents would line the hallway as the paramedics wheeled the stretcher up the ramp. The soft female voice of the dispatcher on the paramedic's radio traveled slowly down the hall as an eerie reminder of how close residents were to the end.

He would look sullen and serious, but Harry tried to block out the sight by thinking of Roy DeSoto and Johnny Gage from

Emergency. He assumed the paramedics were about to dig into a delicious bowl of Chet's chili before he called them to wheel out the chronic alcoholic. The diversion never worked, and all he could do as the ambulance doors closed was cover his mouth and sigh.

It was too frequent. It could have been a year prior, but the vision of a covered stretcher always seemed like yesterday.

The last one was a month ago.

Billy had lived at the Saint Anthony for just over five years. Harry knew him as personable and non-intrusive. He drank every day, and it was obvious to Harry by his empty Gatorade bottle that Billy was an alchemist. He would leave in the morning and return calm but despondent. He would say hello to Marty in the morning and fail to recognize him in the evening. He had family in town, even in the suburbs, but Billy stayed his course.

His mind and body slowly deteriorated. His face aged rapidly, and his eyes began to lose focus. He was literally lost in a reused plastic bottle of Gatorade.

Harry knew the path of deterioration, and he saw it in Billy.

Eventually, Billy departed the residence under a sheet. In a rare moment, there was an actual funeral. Harry attended the sparsely attended service, wearing a clip-on tie and light-blue polyester slacks. He shook hands with Billy's mom. His father chose not to attend.

Harry checked doors during the creative period. He knew the thought leaders, but the newbies were harder to find, so Harry knocked on all of them.

Marty never joined the alchemists. He was a chronic alcoholic, but he didn't seek the blackout. For 35 years, he just drank beer. By the time he arrived at the Saint Anthony, even the beer had grown old.

The creative period lasted only a week, often shorter and never longer. It was simple and destructive.

So went the Saint Anthony Residence—not-so-nefarious characters crisscrossing through demons to stay upright and out of sight. It was a home and a theory. Perhaps by realizing bottom, they could see the top. It was a canvas of struggle and horizon. The Saint Anthony Residence was a last stop—a formal determination of the end while living.

Marty Peterson was a lost soul. He had been gripped in an undertow of alcoholism and by a social theory that enough was enough. He was home.

CHAPTER SEVEN

ALL HAIL THE QUEEN

Spring, 1986

"Ladies and gentlemen, the Queen of Housing has entered the building," Jerry Tork sang through the fog of Marlboro Reds, knowing that the only woman in the building was now the Queen herself.

The Queen barreled through the metal doors and down the ramp. Allison was the Director of Housing for Catholic Charities and a boss who took the title of Director to mean "get it done or get out of my way." She was the nexus of the Saint Anthony, commanding all around her to make it happen or suffer an undetermined fate.

One would assume that a board member or CEO had assigned her the moniker.

"I am the Queen of Housing." Only this queen could choose her royal title and only this queen would hear "Yes, my lady" from her loyal subjects. It didn't matter that it was the 1980s.

Physically, the Queen commanded a presence by her imposing size and her piercing-yet-heartening stare. No one knew her age, and it seemed never to change. She was a glorious performer—funny, irreverent, and always with a purpose for the poor. She commanded stages in the halls of government, corporate boardrooms, and in every kitchen and community room where the last rungs of society dwelled. CEOs retreated quickly to their checkbooks at her comments, and the homeless rallied to her as a grandmother. The Queen was full of all the good things.

It took her a while to get there.

The Queen said it. "Life is an adventure in forgiveness."

Allison was technically not from Minnesota, but she was an original person.

She was born in Los Angeles, California, date purposefully unknown, where her parents worked in defense factories to make ends meet. Times were good, briefly, and the young Allison was a long way away from disdain for weaponry.

The largest native group in Minnesota today is the Anishinaabe. Other monikers have been assigned by outsiders, but the name Anishinaabe remains true to history. It means "original people."

Hundreds of years ago, the Anishinaabe lived peacefully off the land. Slowly, their land was taken away, and along with it, many souls. When the white man arrived to collect the goods, he also brought alcohol.

Allison's mother was born on the White Earth Reservation and raised at the White Earth Mission School in northern Minnesota. Despite the warmth of neighbors and the sun, Los Angeles was a job, not a home. When the work dried up, it was time to return home.

The alcohol wasn't original, but it was there waiting for them all the same.

The White Earth community was resilient and proud, but discrimination, poverty, and alcoholism came poking through the Norway pines at every switch in the trail. Allison's family was strong, but she was a young queen. She saw the mirage of independence in the forest and ran for it.

The trail markers didn't take her to the big city to throw her hat in the air like Mary Tyler Moore. She wasn't ready to make it, after all. She stayed up north, where independence was a bed at Grandma's and the white man's gift.

The trail was not long, but it was rocky and looped. She was 16 years old.

The return to grace usually has an inexplicable moment. Somehow, either for a monthly check or because a tiny ray of light slipped through the pines, Allison visited a county social worker. Assessments can go either way. Right or wrong, her alcoholism was deemed a mental health issue, and she was thrust into a state-run, residential program in southwestern Minnesota. Seeing nowhere else to go, she went along for the ride. It was a bent ray of light.

Many turns of the trail later, including a stint in chemical dependency treatment, Allison was living back up north in Duluth. This time, she didn't follow all the trail markers. She was sober.

Along the way, she had a son. It was how things happen. He was a wake-up call and a treasure, so the young Allison took him seriously. The trail took her round and round, but she had found her way.

She was now a trail guide, first for her son, then young queens, finally for anyone who was lost.

The Queen had emerged, and she knew where she had been. "A year ago, I was drunk and hiding and now I'm riding around with these two old broads going for cupcakes and cappuccinos." She said it every week, and the two old broads could have been anyone.

She wasn't simple, but she kept things simple. The Queen wanted to get to the point, and she did it with her life. She never went into specifics about the path she'd traveled, instead sprinkling out just enough street cred to make a difference.

The Queen visited the Saint Anthony Residence every week. It was her other baby. Employees drew paychecks at her behest, and the operation and bottom line were within her purview.

"That's right, boys, the Queen has arrived," the Queen would play along, knowing she could eschew certain workplace rules and let them all have it.

When the Queen rolled into the building, she strode down the hallway as though she were the actual Queen, with men following behind her in a phalanx of fear.

Most of the Queen's visits, while appearing to be surprise quality-control reviews, were largely rekindling efforts for the Queen herself. The Queen decided that serving the lowest of the low was not only the mission of Catholic Charities, but it was the driving force of her life. There were questions about the rightness or wrongness of the Saint Anthony, but the lowest of the low were still God's children, and they should not be forgotten.

When a city council member thought otherwise several years before, the Queen steamrolled him.

"I'm not sure you understand what we are trying to accomplish here," the Queen quietly pleaded in the council member's office. The council member was attempting somehow to invalidate the Saint Anthony's permit over a single incident of public urination.

"What's it going to be—you standing down or me telling lefties that you put people on the street and righties that the homeless problem downtown is your fault? I have my speech written and ready for delivery. You can't win."

The council member stood down.

"OK, I get it. Seriously, I get it." Fear and endearment permeated the stately office.

"I thought you would see it my way."

It wasn't the first time the Queen and the council member came to political blows. It also wasn't the first time they had lunch after a kerfuffle.

"How about the Saint Paul Grill for hash browns?"

"As long as you're buying," the Queen responded, never losing a battle.

The Queen commanded that the Saint Anthony Residence join the Catholic Charities program list, and it was the Queen who protected it, maintained its position in the hierarchy, and used it as fuel for the fire of service.

Rumor had it that Boston had its own Saint Anthony. The Queen was certain that the Cradle of Liberty purloined her idea.

Today, the Queen spent her morning at the main office trudging through the administrative duties of a boss—budgeting, performance reviews, and an ongoing morass that she did not enjoy. At the end of the day, she stared blankly at her computer.

The touchpoint drove the Queen. "Out of sight, out of mind" terrified her. The longer she stayed away from the front lines, the farther removed she would become from her mission of change. She would lose the urge to hug the homeless man in the wheelchair and instead worry about his impact on her budget. She needed to look into his eyes.

She stood up from her desk, took a deep sigh, and lumbered to her large, always Detroit-made vehicle for the journey across the river from Minneapolis to Saint Paul.

Turning into the industrial neighborhood made her feel better. The broken curbs and industrial activities were harbor lights for what drifted in the mist.

She stood in the doorway to Harry's office. Harry was not expecting the visit and visibly shocked, and Marty was in the chair, legs folded and smoking a Parliament.

"Greetings, Mr. Opus. I thought I would stop for a quick walk-around, assuming you have the time."

"Of course. Didn't know you were coming, but yes, yes, we're always available here at the Saint Anthony."

"I should hope so." She turned to Marty and smiled. "Greetings to you as well, Mr. Marty."

"Greetings, Queen."

Marty gave the Queen pause. The Queen liked Marty. He was downtrodden, but she saw something else. She felt that he knew where he was. Every time the Queen saw Marty, she wanted to know more. She wanted to sit with him in the cafeteria and just listen.

The feeling was mutual. Marty only had the endearment part for the Queen, not the fear. Outside of her humorous power banter, Marty knew that she was there to look out for him. The feeling made a difference.

"You know, Mr. Marty, why don't you and I grab lunch one of these days somewhere besides this greasy spoon?"

"I'd like that, Queen." They would never have lunch, but they talked about it enough to make it real. Coffee in the cafeteria eventually sufficed.

Today, the Queen had a different mission. She turned to Harry. "Let's move. I can't spend all day here."

Barreling down the yellow hallway through the din of smoke, the Queen wore a game face.

“Get that ceiling tile fixed. It’s gonna fall on someone and we’re gonna get sued,” she said, pointing to a dangling piece of asbestos. She cared less about being sued than she did about providing an equal playing field for the community’s forgotten.

“You got it,” Harry responded, even though it was Jerry’s responsibility.

“The problem with you people is that you need to look around once in a while. If you cleaned the joint up, fixed the holes, they might consider it a home and they might for the first time in their god-forsaken lives realize that someone cares about them,” she bellowed in what seemed to be a predetermined oratory. “And if they belong, they might finally understand where they’ve been and try to move the other direction, for god’s sake.”

It was a speech she gave that morning in a downtown boardroom filled with three-piece suits. It was the reason that Saint Anthony came to be, and a central tenet for those who believed that the solution to poverty was not just programs and helping hands, but respect. It was Christ-like.

“Something stinks like crap in that bathroom,” she cringed as she walked by a main-floor bathroom. Harry couldn’t smell a thing.

Turning the first corner of the horseshoe past the kitchen on her way to the laundry room, which was fertile ground for complaints, the Queen peered into the kitchen. It was 3 o’clock in the afternoon.

“What’s going on in there?”

“Nothing. Just guys having coffee,” Harry returned.

The Queen snapped, “Nothing, huh? What is that supposed to mean?”

"It means nothing. They tend to gather before supper." Harry was cautious.

"What time is dinner?" the Queen fired back, knowing that dinner was nearly two hours away.

"5 o'clock."

"5 o'clock?!" The Queen was visibly upset. "Maybe you should close the kitchen until dinnertime, so they actually go out and do something." It was the Queen's occasional bootstrap argument.

"Then you'd have people in the neighborhood looking for trouble. The kitchen keeps them under control. Just saying," Harry continued, hoping that his experience earned him the opportunity to speak his mind.

The Queen was infuriated by the prison line of thinking. It was a philosophy of penning residents so they would remain out of sight. If she wanted to run a zoo, she would have done so. The Queen furrowed her brow and continued into the laundry room, where she discovered mouse droppings, an overflowing lint trap, and an empty plastic bottle of Karkov vodka. At $4 a jug, it was top-shelf.

On her way out, Marty was still in Harry's office. With Harry dripping in sweat behind her, she stopped in the office and gently put her hand on Marty's shoulder.

"Good to see you, my friend. Keep that Harry in line or I'll replace him with you by the end of the week." She was out the door before Marty could even turn his head.

Later that evening, the Queen and Jim Brunson were at home watching the Twins game.

It was unclear if they were married, or if they even shared a room, but they were together.

Jim Brunson was tall, skinny, and weathered. He had long, stringy brown hair that hung out the side of a ubiquitous baseball cap. He was the Marlboro Man who smoked too many Marlboros and lived too much, so he switched to Camel straights. He had a terrible ulcer, or so he thought, and he rarely spoke. His gaunt, sallow, and listing physique made him appear to be a Saint Anthony resident, but the only liquid he drank was the blackest coffee and dated samples of Ensure dropped off at the shelters.

Jim was a prodigious imbiber of yesteryear, and his return to grace was also a rocky path. He didn't have enough time or breath to tell the whole story, but he knew that he could make a difference with as much as he could share. Like the Queen, when Jim's path straightened, he also became a trail guide. He joined like minds to found Eden House, a recovery home in Minneapolis for ex-convicts and returning soldiers from Vietnam. Heroin and LSD were the drugs of choice. Eden House eventually became one of the largest and most respected providers of re-entry support services in the Midwest.

Jim looked like Bigfoot, and he lurked in the background to become legend.

Jim and the Queen briefly converged at Eden House. Jim was saving historically tired souls, and the Queen was running chemical dependency groups for women. Their paths eventually joined at Catholic Charities, and the Queen was in charge, just the way Jim liked it.

They were a couple.

Jim had one of those management roles that arrived without convention. There wasn't a promotion or job to fill. Jim just did it, and no one questioned him. He held maintenance court every day over thousands of square feet—cavernous, musty, and largely weathered facilities serving thousands of America's poor.

He had a right to be quiet. His mind was filled with a never-ending to-do list. He should have used index cards, but his fingers were too sore and shaky to write. Broken windows, dirty floors, and wobbling washing machines converted his mind into an old metal filing cabinet with executive-level efficiency.

Jim and the Queen stared at the glowing TV.

"We should make sure that those windows at Mary Hall get in the budget," Jim said.

The red ember on his cigarette was the only other light in the room.

"And Puckett stretches out another double on a short liner to left. That's how it's done, folks," Bob Kurtz, the Minnesota Twins announcer, relayed to the two fans in the smoky room. Bob Kurtz had a Charlie Brown name. No one called him "Bob," and no one called him "Mr. Kurtz." It was Bob Kurtz.

The room was silent. The Queen talked all day. She hollered demands. She grumbled and roared. Home was for her heart, and she needed a moment.

Jim repeated his statement over a mid-sentence Camel draw, "Did you get that?"

"Yeah, I got it. Puckett got a double and you want me to spend money on windows."

"Good."

The fruits of Puckett's hustle would be short-lived.

". . . and the Twins leave one on with no runs as we head into the bottom of the 7th. Brewers 4, Twins 1. We'll be right back," Bob Kurtz announced.

"Why does he sound so chipper when we're getting clobbered?" the Queen exhorted. "You would think we were at the top of the division."

The Queen continued to slink into her chair, not in a depressive mood, but in a manner befitting of a leader who spent her days wrestling with budgets, board members, politicians, and the city's most difficult clientele. The woman had a right to be quiet and sit in the dark.

Like most nights, Jim nodded off while his cigarette burned in the oversize ceramic ashtray. The Camel slipped into the tray and petered out without incident. Jim knew his cigarettes well. They would never betray him.

The Queen enjoyed her moment, even though the Twins continued their painful descent.

The Queen sort of cared, and she sort of didn't.

CHAPTER EIGHT

JOLLY TERRY

It was the end of the month, and Terry Thomas stood square in Harry's doorway, "Harry, did you hear about the talking dog?"

"I didn't." Harry rolled his eyes and lit a smoke. He heard it a thousand times. He even read it once or twice.

Harry knew Terry, and he knew the 7-minute rule on an end-to-end Marlboro Red.

The joke would be over by then.

Terry was a longstanding Saint Anthony resident. He was a provocateur, easily mistaken for "Caretaker" from *The Longest Yard.* He even looked like Caretaker. But Terry wanted to be Fast Eddie Felson. He sat through the *Color of Money* three times in a row, watching it twice and sleeping off a 12-pack for the third. He was kicked out before the fourth.

Terry was humorous, conniving, and sad. His story to tell was reaching the pinnacle of success, then watching it miserably crash beneath him. He was too proud to fake it.

"A man walks into a café with his dog, and the two of them take a seat at the counter. The man turns to the cook and says, 'My dog can talk.' " Terry was smiling as he talked and sweating at the same time.

"Uh-huh," Harry mumbled, taking a long draw of the cigarette.

"The cook said, 'That dog can't talk.' The man said, 'If my dog can talk, will you give me a free meal?' " Terry's heart was racing like he was onstage.

Terry grew up near the top of Minnesota and eventually made his way down to Duluth to dabble in a range of ventures, all of which were designed to bring him wealth and privilege. He was a shrewd businessman who could talk his way in and out of everything. In America, a chosen line of business for the fast-talking and ambitious is real estate, and Terry excelled at it.

In scant time, Terry made his mark buying and selling homes. He married another fast-talker, and they eventually produced a small brood of fast-talkers. He soon built his real estate effort into a company. No one at the residence knew why he called it Dryco. It had nothing to do with sobriety.

Harry knew it all to be true. Terry still carried his business cards, and he had a stack of embossed stationery. He also had yard signs in a storage container with an unpaid bill and a cot.

"So the cook says, 'Yeah, if your dog can talk, I'll give you a free meal. Heck, I'll give you both a free meal.' So . . . the man says, 'Alright,' turns to his dog, and says 'What's on top of a house?' The dog says, 'Roof-roof!' The man turns back to the cook and says 'See?' "

Terry paused with a grin on his face, the sweat now traveling through his shirt from his armpits to his chest. The temperature did not matter. Sweat was common in the creative period.

"Is that it?" Harry grumbled, drawing past the halfway point of his smoke.

"No, no, no," Terry giggled. "The cook looked at the man and said, 'Are you nuts? Don't try and razzle-dazzle me, pal!'

The man said, 'Wait, wait, let me try another, and he turns to the dog and says, 'Who's the greatest baseball player of all time?' "

In Duluth, Terry quickly became a recognized man of substance. He was also a man of other substances, like drinking excessively and enjoying every minute of it. Like any tale of alcoholic woe, Terry's drinking escalated to the point of strain. His home life suffered, his business suffered, and he started telling the same jokes repeatedly at local functions. He was long off his pinnacle, and for those who know the shores of Lake Superior, he was heading downriver like a smelt into a bucket.

Despite his round-the-clock imbibing, Terry's downfall was a combination of his drinking and the simple fact that he picked the wrong business. Real estate was cyclical, and he hit a down cycle. That's when the drinking took command. Unlike stories of economic recovery, this one never found an up cycle. Terry lost his wife, his business, and almost his life. Several runs in treatment and he was in the smelt bucket.

Terry escalated his voice toward the punch line, "The dog turned to the man and howled, 'Ruth-ruth-ruth!' "

"Bus tokens, Harry?" Jimmy quickly peeked into the room.

"Just one for you, Jimmy," Harry said, as he handed Jimmy a token, all the while wondering why his cigarette was almost to the filter. Had it been 7 minutes? He was thankful that he switched brands from Lucky straights.

Terry was never irritated by interruptions. He may have also been drunk at the time.

"The man turns to the cook and says, 'See? He said, Ruth, Babe Ruth!' The cook was fuming at the scam and yelled, 'Get the hell outta here!' and threw them both out on their butts."

Harry's cigarette and mind were both at the butt. Luckily, the joke was funny. He thought he'd heard it first on *The Carol*

Burnett Show. Harvey Korman and Tim Conway were sure things, particularly when they had the giggles.

Terry headed to the punch line, his face convulsing with a cartoonish grin. “Outside the diner, the dog and the man got up off the pavement and brushed themselves off. The dog then turned to the man and said, ‘Should I have said DiMaggio?’ ”

Marty was sitting in the chair next to the door and looked up at his friend Terry with a grin. He had been hearing the joke most of his life, at least the parts he could remember.

“Maybe you should try Phil Roof next time.”

CHAPTER NINE

JERRY AND FREDDIE

Jerry Tork stopped into Harry's office on his rounds.

Jerry was a success story at Saint Anthony. His abuse of corn-fortified products had led him through a multitude of nefarious and inconceivable predicaments. His nose had been broken more times than he could count, his eyes almost permanently blackened. Even his tattoos were pulling apart under the tension of age and stress. The heart tattoo with "Mom" in script was broken.

For all his weathered looks and barely accountable past, someone gave Jerry a chance. He was too busy and too tired to wax prophetic about the chances he had been given, but by the 1980s, his soft-spoken demeanor and loyalty to the task at hand landed him a solid place on the Catholic Charities favorite ex-client list.

He was offered a job, he accepted it, and he kept it. It was a rare confluence of life events that were often mutually exclusive at the Saint Anthony.

He was Jerry-of-All-Trades. He was not often seen, but his presence was known and respected. He fixed everything, including an occasional soul.

He looked into Harry's office on his way out the door, "I'll be back next week to look at that toilet upstairs. If it comes off the base again, we're in trouble." The bathroom was above the kitchen.

"Tell Jim to put it on his list. See you in a few days." It was unclear if Jerry reported to Jim, or vice-versa. Organizational chart lines in the trenches were mostly dotted. Harry wanted the toilet off his plate and on its base.

"Sounds good," Jerry said as he turned to Marty. "Hey, Mr. Martin Peterson."

"Hey, Jerry," Marty replied, his legs tightly crossed and his eyes fixed on *The Price is Right.*

Marty and Jerry knew each other even when they couldn't remember that they knew each other.

Jerry turned out of Harry's doorway and was met with a marginally toothless smile. "Hey Harry, the washing machine is broken again."

"I'll check it out, Freddie," injected Jerry, putting his hand on Freddie's shoulder.

"Thank you, kind sir," Freddie slipped out of the doorway, waiting to walk with Jerry to the washing machine.

"There's nothing wrong with the washing machine." Harry grumbled to Jerry.

"I know."

Freddie lacked the usual qualifications for Saint Anthony admittance. He did not have a multipage treatment history, and he had been to detox less than the usual 50-plus visits. He never traversed the typical maze of social services, law enforcement, rejection, and eventual destruction. He was on the edge of every evaluation.

Somewhere along the paths of the well-meaning, Freddie was forgotten.

It seemed to Harry that Freddie avoided regular alcohol consumption, "seemed" being an operative word at Saint Anthony. But Freddie had his liquid moments. It was rare when the wave hit, but when it did, it was momentous. It was possible that he was the only resident whose passage to entry may have been born of a single incident.

Harry knew that Freddie grew up in Rondo and that his family lost their home in the highway construction. He had three strikes already in life, none of which came from his own bat. He was Black and subject to persistent racism, he was borderline on every mental health evaluation, and he was poor. The alcohol arrived later.

The rest of Freddie's background was mostly unknown. He didn't need a backstory or a tall tale because everyone liked him as soon as they met him.

Marty knew about Freddie. He vaguely recalled a younger Fred or two from the old neighborhood, and one of them might have been Freddie. Marty also knew about consequences. If you take someone's house from under them, there are consequences. When the highway came for Freddie's parents, the ball rolled uphill faster, which meant it rolled down like an avalanche.

Freddie was never able to get a footing.

At the Saint Anthony, Freddie was home, a fact that pleased all who encountered him.

The bosses were unlikely to tear him away from it.

"OK, Fred, let's walk down to the laundry room and check out that old machine. If the powers that be ever got up off their butts, they'd get us a new one," Jerry grumbled.

"Got that right."

CHAPTER TEN

MARTY FUNGO

Marty took a full swing of the wooden bat, and the ball sailed over the rusty fence. He found the bat in a garbage can a few weeks before. The hairline crack in it was toward the fat end, so it still had enough swing in it. He brought the baseball from his room.

Terry stood next to Marty. "Now what are we going to do?" They were alone at Raymond Field, playing a baseball game with no pitcher and a roster of two.

"I was just testing the bat. I'll go look for it."

Marty walked from home plate to the fence in right field and quickly found the ball resting in between two empty 16-ounce cans of Schlitz Malt Liquor. He took note of the Blue Ox on the cans and wondered why a Wisconsin beer would have a Minnesota icon on its can. Perhaps Paul Bunyan was a big drinker. It would make sense that he would drink malt liquor.

"Found it!"

Terry couldn't hear him.

Marty emerged from the bushes tossing the ball in one hand and smoking a cigarette in the other. The elder, bony gentleman had a perfect rhythm of walking, smoking, and precisely throwing the ball up and down. His clean, white shoes miraculously escaped the right-field mud.

"You really pounded it," Terry said.

"I didn't even feel the ball." Marty was smiling.

"You looked like Jose Canseco—only without the hair, the body, the girls, and the money." It was a full year before the ascent of the Bash Brothers, but the Oakland rookie was a legend on Opening Day.

Both of Marty's arms could fit into Jose Canseco's shirt sleeve. His legs would fit in there as well. He could put his whole body in there and make it a sleeping bag.

Taking away Jose's muscle and the money, their swings were identical. "It's been a while since I hit the ball, I guess. It feels good to swing the bat."

Marty had been out of baseball for almost 30 years. The only thing he had been swinging since he last ran the bases was a mug of beer up to his mouth. Lifting the mug grew difficult and uninviting with age. Swinging the bat did not.

Spring baseball had been on TV earlier that afternoon at the Saint Anthony. The resurgent Twins were playing the hopeful A's. Marty and Terry watched the game together and enjoyed a protracted conversation about Jose Canseco and Kirby Puckett. It was hardly heated but about as contemplative as either of them would have expected from the other.

Terry was a Canseco guy, and Marty was a Puckett guy. "I just think Puckett tries harder," Marty said.

"But Canseco is a natural. His arms are like howitzers, and what is he, 6 foot 4?"

"Puckett looks like he's having more fun with the game. Canseco looks like a baseball player, but Puckett feels like one."

Terry suggested they continue the discussion on the diamond down the street. It was possible that Terry wanted to go to a bar. By the time they reached the field, any thought of a bar had been replaced by baseball.

Marty had not actually thought about playing baseball since he walked out of college in the late 1950s. He didn't storm out. He just left.

Back at the field, Marty felt alive.

A sizable cadre of neighbors were in their front yards, and they all stopped in unison when Marty walked back to the plate. Marty felt the eyes drilling on him, but he also wondered why they were all home in the afternoon. He was at the Saint Anthony, so his own presence was obvious. He felt their bodies tense, as though they were moving into a defensive position.

Back at the plate, Terry returned the stare, and their eyes retreated, as if threatened by the reality of their own intransigence. Fear and defense against "those people."

"Don't they have jobs?" Terry asked.

"I sort of wondered, but maybe they work nights." Marty always found the positive.

After avoiding a confrontation with the loose phalanx of neighbors, Marty stood silent for a few moments. He turned to Terry, smiled, and tossed the ball up for another swing. The bat broke in half, and the ball sailed over the fence and rolled into the sewer. Praying to Saint Anthony would not help.

The neighbors didn't pray to the saint, but somehow their wishes were granted.

Without the ball and bat, Marty and Terry walked back to the residence, continuing a disagreement that never ended. They took the long route past the Ace Box Bar, stopping in front of the bar, but not entering. Cigarette smoke and the odor of stale beer billowed out through the front door, and there was noise in the bar, but it was the daytime version, and the slurring could be heard from the sidewalk.

Back at the residence, Harry had his gruff on, but he was content. He was alive, he was sober, and he had a job. Life could be almost perfect, even with a bad attitude.

The usual suspects were paying their visits to his office, but Harry was without cleanups, altercations, or any other appointments that could deepen his scowl.

Nothing could be too smooth on Wycliff Avenue, as Harry quickly learned that the cook had to take the afternoon off without notice, supposedly for a family emergency. "Supposedly" was another operative word at Saint Anthony. Despite the minor possibility of tragedy, Harry took it as a positive. He was automatically green-lighted to order out for food, and he called in Magnolia's on the East Side for his favorite fried chicken.

"I'll take 12 buckets of fried chicken, 15 quarts of mashed potatoes, extra gravy, 8 quarts of coleslaw, and 1 BLT on wheat toast with chips," Harry said into the phone with the smile of a successful hunter-gatherer.

"Say Harry, where's Dave?" Freddie peered in, worried when equilibrium was jostled.

"He had to take the afternoon for some sort of thing. There's cold cuts in there for lunch, and I ordered Magnolia's for supper. You're on your own for snack."

"Oh?"

"Don't worry, Dave will be back tomorrow." Harry hoped. His green light lasted only one night. Tomorrow would be a peanut butter day.

Marty and Terry walked in during the conversation. The Twins were still playing on the 12-inch, black-and-white Zenith, and the din of Bob Kurtz's voice was trudging its way through the smoke.

"And Hrbek lumbers across the bag for his third home run of the season. Twins 5, A's 3."

"Hey," Harry muttered to Marty, who quickly took a seat in the metal chair across from Harry's desk, his yellow fingers treacherously dangling a Parliament.

In the social service business, the positioning of chairs mattered. On the side of the desk, the client and case manager were level. Standard practice. Across from the desk, the case manager was in charge, which was a no-no. Harry was not a case manager.

Marty was aware of the protocol.

"Hrbek," Marty whispered with a thin grin.

"Jeez, is that guy slow," Harry scowled, even though the Twins were winning, and it was a home run. Hrbek would go on to hit almost 30 home runs.

"I like Hrbek. He's local." Marty said.

The silence continued through more cigarettes, coffee, an RC Cola for Marty, and a cigar for Terry. Harry held out for his BLT, which would arrive just in time for him to take home, along with a clamshell of chicken.

"The Twins get one hit, one walk, and leave two on. We're headed to the bottom of the eighth, and it's still Twins 5, A's 3," Bob Kurtz's voice rose in a crescendo.

It had been a nirvana day for Harry. Twins game, Magnolia's chicken, and quiet halls without a single projectile. For icing on the day-old cake, Harry's nose wasn't even lightly itched by the touch of foot odor.

When Harry first heard the door clang open, he suspected someone was arriving drunk.

The door crashed as though someone fell through it. He smelled booze in advance of the visitor. "On comes the booze."

For Harry it was "booze" post-ingestion and "liquor" pre-ingestion. Booze had a thud that delivered a knockout punch, often literal, for both the drinker and the secondhand drinker, the latter being anyone in range of the drinker's breath.

According to the National Institutes of Health, alcohol in the mouth or liver reacts with other chemicals in the body to create "odorous byproducts." One of these is acetaldehyde, which is also a hangover culprit. Alcohol causes the mouth to dry out, thereby eliminating the opportunity for saliva to wash out dead skin cells. The result is a decomposing body in the mouth. Measured on the Halimeter, all of this adds up to oral *malodor*. For the chronic inebriate, saturated livers and daily alcohol swishing in the mouth result in chronic *malodor*. For the secondhand drinker standing next to a Saint Anthony resident, even in the same building, chronic *malodor* is some serious bad breath.

Harry found out quickly that it was not booze today. It was the Queen.

The Queen wore full-length, flowing dresses ensconced with floral scarves that emitted powerful scents of JC Penney signatures, all befitting a queen. Like everything in her life, she loaded it on thick . . . and people noticed.

"Shoot. It's the Queen. She was just here, for Chrissake." Harry uttered, quickly pulling his feet off the desk and squaring himself to an unknown stack of papers. He was not slacking off in any way, but it was the *modus operandi* of all Catholic Charities employees to look furiously busy when the Queen approached. Even the Queen's superiors stood at attention.

"O, tremble, for you hear the lion roar," Marty softly whispered. Marty knew he was quoting a story about a king, but Harry wouldn't know the difference.

The Queen barreled around the corner into Harry's office with *Wizard of Oz*–like fire shooting from her eyes and ears. It was one of those rare moments where Harry recalled the guilty feelings of his own post-drunk escapades. He immediately thought he had missed something. Did he lose a resident? Was there money missing? The latter was not even possible since money was never on-site.

"I hope she's not here about the chicken. People have to eat, you know. It's not even here yet," Harry nervously mumbled to Marty. The Queen knew all.

"I'm back, boys," the Queen said.

The Queen took a long, blank stare at the tiny Zenith. "What's the score?"

"5-3, Twins," Marty returned, so engulfed in the game that he failed to recognize that his cigarette was burning his finger.

"We'll see if they can pull it out this time. Last night was a mess. I do love Puckett, though."

She turned to Marty, "How is Marty Peterson today?"

"I am well, thank you."

She looked at Terry, who was holding a baseball glove, "What's with the baseball glove?"

"Marty and I were knocking it around over at Raymond."

The four of them sat in silence for what appeared to be a full minute. The Queen's nose was flaring.

"Where is everyone?"

"Not real sure. A handful hit the streets, a few might be in the kitchen, and I would imagine that the rest of them are in their rooms," Harry responded like a worried, but loyal, subject.

"What are they doing in their rooms?"

"I would guess watching the Twins game or maybe sleeping?"

"And the Twins take it nice and clean from the A's. From the Coliseum in sunny Oakland, along with the great Harmon Killebrew, this is Bob Kurtz. Stay tuned for Twins post-game . . . after these messages."

The Queen remained through another bout of silence.

"Is there anything you need?" Harry almost whispered, hoping that the Queen was merely stopping in to kill time.

"I was in the neighborhood again, and I thought I would let you know that The Padre and Mr. Long are going to pay a visit next week, likely for lunch. Tell what's-his-name to nix the cold cuts."

"What for?"

"I'm not sure, but it doesn't matter. They're coming here, and the place needs to be ready, and when I say 'ready,' I mean no puke, no shit, no nothing. And get some air freshener in here. It smells like feet."

The Queen knew that she could have called in the information. This time, she needed Anthony, the Saint.

"I have another meeting, so I'll check with you later. And where the heck is everyone? The place looks abandoned. Maybe you should get them to play baseball or something," the Queen bellowed as she hastily and formally departed the premises.

She did not have a meeting. The Queen got in her car, pulled around the corner next to a prefab building, and lit up a smoke. It was her first cigarette in over a month.

Marty creaked out of his chair, flicked the long-dead cigarette into the ashtray, and slowly walked down the hall with a sliver of a grin on his weathered face.

CHAPTER ELEVEN

FUN WITH MR. LONG AND THE PADRE

Office visits from CEOs are scary. The Padre was the terrifying CEO of Catholic Charities.

He was known in the community as "Monsignor," but to guilty Catholics and his employees, he was "The Padre." Everywhere, he was iconic. The Padre was far from the stereotypical outspoken priest.

The Padre enjoyed scotch, he loathed all sports except baseball, and he never affected even a touch of character. All of The Padre was the real thing. He was a midsize man with a hitch in his gait and a sinister Irish grin with an accompanying red nose. His attire was black priest pants, black priest shirt spotted with dandruff, white priest collar, and black priest jacket. For The Padre, it was less priest garb than mafia-wear.

He had been the ward boss at Catholic Charities for over two decades, building the organization from a soup line into one of the largest social service organizations in the Midwest. The legend of The Padre was a true story of a forthright priest whose disgust for lack of action on poverty was only surpassed by his disdain for those who talked about attacking poverty yet took no action.

The Padre never gave speeches about poverty. Instead, his speeches bellowed demands on what to do about poverty. In corporate boardrooms, parish halls, city halls, and nearly any room with money or power, The Padre could be found with a smile *and* a scowl. He spoke his mind without shtick, but with truth, profanity, fuming anger, and a call to action.

He was a charitable mobster.

When the city council was poised to deny a simple permit for a transitional housing facility, only steps from a church, The Padre stormed city hall. He started with his elected friends.

"I'm not here on the Jesus stuff. I want to know what you're doing to get this permit done. For Chrissakes, I'm not asking for money. I just want the goddamn permit." It was always about permits. The Padre had little trouble finding money.

"There's no way in your heaven I can get approval for transitional housing in that neighborhood. I need four votes, maybe five if the mayor is against it. I only have two right now, three including myself," the council member said.

"You'll find a way," The Padre's face reddened to a holy tomato. "You know I know your mother?"

The council member succumbed as though shoved physically into a corner. He knew it was the right thing to do. It was only two more votes, and he didn't want The Padre to call his mother.

"I get it, sir, I get it. Yeah, yeah, I know the challenge isn't here in city hall, it's for the people on the streets. I'll do my best to make it happen."

"Well, your 'best' better get me my permit."

"Yes, Padre."

After his elected friends, The Padre would proceed to the elected detractors. In his mind, The Padre didn't have enemies, just those waiting to comply.

"Either your brains or your signature will be on this permit."

"Of course, Padre." The council member knew *The Godfather* reference, but he also knew the Padre wasn't joking.

The Saint Anthony Residence was special for The Padre. It served a different brand of the forgotten, and he believed that, without interrogation, humanity deserved a roof and three squares. It was dignity, and anyone who disagreed would be crushed.

When the Queen, his *consigliere,* came to The Padre with the idea for the Saint Anthony, they rolled everyone in their way.

Solutions to poverty are expensive and politically difficult. For The Padre, everyone was in the way, but if he menaced like a mobster, dignity might have a chance.

"It's not personal, council member, it's strictly business."

Mr. Long drove a Cadillac. He had to drive a Cadillac because he was retired, he supported America's unions, he was wealthy, and he used to own a Cadillac dealership.

Mr. Long was the real deal. He was short, skinny, and always sported tight, tan skin from golf outings at historic clubs across the globe. He tossed the suits many years ago and could regularly be found in tan slacks and a Cosby sweater, even in the summer.

He carefully drove his always-new Cadillac low in the seat. From his days growing up hard in Chicago, Mr. Long never took his Cadillac for granted. He cared for everything as though it was a gift of humility.

Mr. Long was a devout Catholic, in that if there was ever Jesus in a car dealership, it was Mr. Long. He was America's great contradiction—a car dealer who did unto others as he would have done unto himself.

Mr. Long gravitated to The Padre's "Don't ask questions, just help" theology. Mr. Long went to mass, but his true church was among the poor.

Mr. Long was a charitable mobster without The Padre's gun of damnation. He was attracted to The Padre's cabal of angry do-gooders, and he joined The Padre with his own cabal of well-funded do-gooders.

When The Padre and the Queen were pushing the Saint Anthony, Mr. Long was in the background with a check—not the giant cardboard type to hand off with a handshake and a photo, but the folded kind passed across a table over a lunch of rare steak.

Donating the big dollars made a difference, but Mr. Long wanted to be close to the results. He wanted to talk with the homeless person whose life he changed. He wanted to hug the odorous, disheveled old man he fed.

Mr. Long did not drink because drinking nearly killed him. He was proud of his sobriety, though he rarely discussed it with anyone except priests.

Mr. Long served on the Catholic Charities Board of Directors. He disliked the board meetings, but enjoyed the to-do list conversation afterwards—the "meeting after the meeting."

The Saint Anthony Residence was on one of those lists.

The Padre and Mr. Long were partners in everything except scotch. The Padre happily rode shotgun in Mr. Long's Cadillac as they poked and prodded politicians and executives to do their bidding. The Padre led the charge, but his kind sidekick helped open the local checkbooks. After every scotch, every club soda, and every rare steak, someone was better off, somewhere.

Harry was worried about their visit. Marty looked forward to greeting his friends.

MARTY INTERLUDES

"All That Is Left"

By Marty Peterson, 1984

This old hotel
is my home
plaster breaking from the wall
and one window
facing an old parking lot.
This old hotel room
has good memories
on the old metal table
lies one leather glove
you left behind.
All that is left that I could find
of your presence here
one leather glove
breeds sentimental thoughts
perhaps someday you will return
and bring the other half
to make this room complete.
Echoes of your voice
are fine within this place
but leather gloves lie lonely
and echoes long to see your face.

CHAPTER TWELVE

PRE-GAME

Marty and Terry brought their gloves to the park in search of a pickup game. They didn't have a bat or a ball. They had finished breakfast and tobacco, and there was nothing left to do but watch TV or drink. Terry was out of money and Marty didn't feel like drinking.

When they arrived at the park, it was in some ways a typical spring scene. One section was filled with a mob of baby strollers and their accompanying caregivers, and another was lined with local neighbors commiserating on park benches about city hall's this-or-that. On the south field, there was a group of college-aged men playing a pickup softball game. School was out early for university students, and summer jobs had either not started or been acquired, leaving afternoons famously open for softball and day drinking.

The gregarious Terry was all about the integration. "Let's see if those boys need some tutelage."

Marty loyally accompanied Terry toward what appeared to be a scheme for free drinks. "You boys looking for some ringers?" Terry had a cigar hanging from his mouth. The boys were well into the afternoon and relished an opportunity for new conversation.

It was unclear to the students whether Marty and Terry were folksy locals or creepy old men. The boys were adventurous.

"Works for me, slick, hop aboard," the English major with a *Born in the USA* T-shirt affably responded. He was obviously the fun and adventurous one in the college crew. The rest of them appeared to follow his lead.

They had enough players for an acceptable ballgame.

The English major picked Terry, saying, "I'll take slick here. He looks like he might be the one."

"Not a chance. I'll bet my rent on skinny over here," the business major replied, clearly believing that Marty would break in two if he swung the bat too hard.

The game was on.

As competitors and friends, it suited Marty and Terry to be on separate teams.

They blended in nicely right from the beginning. Terry was offered the first can of Blatz and he gracefully acquiesced. Marty passed on the ale, but he was immediately accepted as a teammate, at least by the philosophy majors.

The teams battled it out for nearly two hours and two cases of beer. Terry shared cigars, and Marty shared wisdom.

"You know, I played baseball at the University of Minnesota," Marty waxed to a handful of the players on the bench.

"You think I believe that?" The business major was incredulous. It was not possible that the skinny guy with glasses was anything other than an old man from the neighborhood.

Marty didn't respond. The college boy had acknowledged the social disconnect. Marty knew he was downtrodden but never wanted to hear it. He could handle his own predicament. Nostalgia worried Marty, but he suddenly longed for the days of just boys playing ball.

The baseball aspect of the comment didn't annoy Marty at all. He would just have to prove it.

The loosely organized game was nearing its apparent end. It was the bottom of an unknown, but final, inning, and the score was tied. Marty's team was up to bat. Except for Marty, both teams were fully intoxicated.

Terry had failed to provide a single hit or any other positive softball outcome, but he was the life of the party. He went to college only briefly and never had the chance to elevate his social position on campus. The old man with the cigar regaled both teams with stories, true or not. It should be true that productive stats do not tell the full story of victory. The team needed a motivational leader, and Terry filled the roster. It made him feel like he mattered, but unfortunately it was a milieu he was all too familiar with—alcohol-fueled mayhem. His other milieu was playing second base, but he was unfamiliar with it.

The game had become serious. Frat-boy bragging rights had usurped stories of day-drinking escapades. Both teams wanted to win, with the business major leading the charge. He was, after all, a rugby player.

"OK, boys, time for some ass-shoving. Who's in?" The team responded loudly in the affirmative. Marty was silent as he lit up a smoke.

After a hard groundout from a biology major that hit a patch of flora and went into the hands of the shortstop, the business major stepped to the plate. Another business major was pitching. The pitches were down the pipe.

One out, game still tied, Big Man on Campus up to bat. Bragging rights on the line.

The business major took a giant swing on the first pitch and missed it by a mile, partially indicative of his go-big philosophy combined with intoxication and general overpromising. He took the giant swing again on the second pitch and it sailed to deep left, right into the glove of an English major. The business major loudly walked to the bench, trying his hardest to appear infuriated. He threw his cap to the ground and golf-swung a half-full beer can that exploded onto his gym bag.

Two outs.

Marty was at the plate. Earlier in the day, he had no expectation that a ball game could come down to his at-bat. He was still processing the moment and mildly stewing over the business major's comment. The bat felt good in his hands, transcending the feeling he had decades ago at Wilson High School.

His life and the business major drifted away. He was back in the game. He focused on the pitcher through his scratched glasses.

It didn't take long. The first pitch arrived exactly the way Marty wanted it, and his bat complied like a divining rod, launching the softball into deep center. The swing was effortless. The ball sailed over the head of the swaying fielder and disappeared into the bushes.

Both teams stopped. Marty didn't even start running.

The initial shock at the mammoth blast quickly turned to quiet awe, as the stupefied teams turned to celebration and converged on Marty at home plate. They didn't know what to make of the old man, but the hit was worthy of an extended celebration. Terry smiled as he tried to relight his wet cigar. He knew exactly what was going to happen before the game even started. Marty would own it.

Marty smiled as the head tapping and backslapping sent his glasses to the dirt. For a moment, he forgot who he was but remembered where he was.

As the crowd dissipated toward their conventional rungs on the social ladder, the business major turned to Marty.

"Hey Marty, sorry about not believing you. You're really something. It was a great game, and it was great meeting you. Maybe I'll see you around the neighborhood."

"Thanks. It was fun," Marty responded with a smile. Marty never got his name.

MARTY INTERLUDES

Old coaches are the stuff of legend. The older they are, the more legendary they become. If they reach the pinnacle, they get things named after them. With 31 years at the helm of the University of Minnesota baseball team, Dick Siebert was a legend. After 3 College World Series titles and 12 Big Ten titles, Coach Siebert dominated college baseball and shaped the character of a thousand players.

He also played 11 years in the major leagues, swinging the bat for the Brooklyn Dodgers, the St. Louis Cardinals, and the Philadelphia Athletics. In 1943, he was named to the American League All-Star team.

In 1979, the University of Minnesota named a baseball stadium after him: Siebert Field.

In Minnesota, anyone who played an inning for him could proudly announce to their grandchildren, "I played for Dick Siebert."

Marty Peterson had played for Dick Siebert.

Long before Coach Siebert appeared on his couch in Frogtown, Marty was marching through the baseball ranks at Wilson.

The Wilson High School colors were red and white. In the early days, the players would choose the team's name, which often changed. The Wilson team was occasionally known as the Red and White, or at times the Albert Street Gang. Someone wanted them to become the Pointers, perhaps after President Wilson's 14 Points at Versailles. It was roundly discarded. Marty liked the Pointers. A few wanted them to be the ubiquitous

Cardinals, but that failed as well. They were eventually dubbed the Redmen for their original red and white colors. Apparently.

The team achieved neighborhood greatness during Marty's senior year, traveling to the state finals in Rochester, Minnesota. The 90-minute drive seemed like a whole day. They lost to Minneapolis Washburn 11 to nothing, but they won a lifetime of friendships and memories.

They would have achieved city greatness just for the Rochester trip, if it were not for Herb Brooks. Herb and the Johnson Governors took the coveted state hockey championship that same year, etching the Governors into lore. On the diamond, Marty and the Wilson squad dominated Herb and the Governors. That year, it was about the rink, and Marty and the whole city cheered.

Marty played with poise. He had little fear and even less concern for celebrations and trophies. He was in the game.

In his prime, Marty's body was wiry and lacked physicality, a term that did not exist in the 1950s. Marty was lucky in that he was never strong enough or competitive enough to play football. He would have been destroyed. Baseball was natural.

After 30 years of drinking, the only differences between Marty's body of the '80s and his body of the '50s were his liver, his teeth, and his lungs.

Marty delivered solid base hits to a variety of landing zones in the short outfield. He had occasional power, but his beauty rested in his swing. He was fearless and singularly focused on making contact. On base, Marty almost never stretched a single into a double, and diving wasn't his thing. Later in life, he dove headfirst into just about everything, including the street.

Marty enjoyed conversations with first basemen. To the first baseman, it seemed a ploy to strike up a conversation and then bolt for second. Over time, most first basemen would know that Marty just wanted to chat, and they obliged. For some, Marty became a friend. He stole a base or two when given the sign, but his percentage was low.

Marty's game was revered by coaches and players. His consistent numbers at the plate, his reliable glove, and his lack of controversy made him ideal to coach and equally ideal to play alongside. And the swing.

"Love that swing, Peterson."

If stats were tracked as they are in modern baseball, Marty would have been on his way to The Show. He might have been short on the power desired by today's teams and their accountants, but his high school batting average was likely in the low .500s. Long before Canseco, Marty was a lock.

Of course, he also drank beer.

At Wilson, his beer enjoyment was nascent, which made him little different than a kid nabbing a can of suds on the sly with his pals. Like a nagging sports injury, however, it was the compounding habit that eventually made the difference.

Soon after the state finals, Marty and his mother found a legend sitting on the tattered couch in their Frogtown home. Dick Siebert knew baseball, and now he knew Marty. He didn't hear the beer cans under the couch when he sat down.

The brief visit yielded Marty a coveted spot on the University of Minnesota Golden Gopher baseball team. Marty never publicly shared his Minnesota baseball immortality.

He never said. "I played for Dick Siebert."

And he still drank beer.

Marty's days at the University of Minnesota were uneventful. He hit the ball, even with increasing talents on the mound. Lobs and fastballs down the pipe from Rondo pals were long gone. In their place were breaking balls and changeups. Marty continued to make contact, but he needed practice and at least some sort of drive. By that time, all he had were the ales.

One year into his University of Minnesota career, Marty left the team and the university. There was no storming out of the locker room or arguments with coaches. He just hung up his glove. No hard feelings, coach.

Marty was pounding beer by this point, achieving intoxication almost every day. He was not drowning his sorrows. He just drank.

After the Gophers, Marty enrolled at Saint Thomas College in Saint Paul. He took a handful of classes, and he even played briefly on their baseball team. Fastballs were fast, and breaking balls broke, but not nearly to the velocity or vector of the Big Ten. Marty excelled on the team, and he enjoyed it, but tuition and lack of drive ended college, thus his baseball career, after only one year.

He still had the swing, and while countless others would ruminate that they could have been "someone," Marty didn't even think about it. Instead, he drank beer. Gallons of it.

CHAPTER THIRTEEN

EXPANSION TEAM?

Harry spent the morning polishing floors and spraying hallways with air freshener. His best effort was temporary, as the *malodor* of poverty may be as pervasive as poverty itself. Harry kept a case of Glade air freshener in his office. He had to be careful not to show it around, as desperate alchemists would promptly abscond with it and derive its intoxicants. He never took risks, so he kept the box under lock and key, which meant the canisters were hidden in a garbage bag in the office closet.

Harry waited patiently for The Padre and his entourage. He could not decide if he was nervous or nauseous. Hundreds of local officials had been through the facility to observe the philosophy. Harry had shining moments and not-so-shining moments on the tours.

"Is he dead?" The wealthy donor asked Harry, staring at a resident lying face down in the laundry room.

"No, he just had a rough morning. Must be some sort of bug going around."

Despite the occasional seepage of vomit from under a door or the belligerent resident who chose rubbing alcohol for his aperitif, the Saint Anthony was predictable. Visits from dignitaries challenged predictability, which upset Harry's stomach.

Harry sat in his office, nervously waiting for the motorcade. Marty walked in quietly and took his place in the metal chair.

He lit up a cigarette. "Do you need help with anything?"

"No, it should be an in-and-out affair," Harry replied, with one eye staring toward the egress window.

"Weren't they just here two weeks ago?" Marty recalled. He had a cup of coffee with The Padre and Mr. Long in the cafeteria. It was a fond recollection, even though he also remembered the smell of scotch on The Padre's breath.

"News to me. Maybe it was after my shift."

Harry lit up a cigarette. He wanted the smoke to dissipate before the meeting, but he also knew it would be additive to the Glade. The Padre smoked for 30 years before finally quitting, so he was attuned to the smell and philosophy. Mr. Long was a recovering alcoholic, so he must be OK with it, Harry assumed.

"Do you want me to hit the road?"

"Stick around. The more the merrier." Harry needed Marty. It showed that he was among the people.

"Why are they coming today?" Marty coughed in a cloud of Parliament smoke.

"I have no idea."

That was the problem. Harry usually knew the reason for an announced visit. He couldn't worry about the unannounced ones. This time he was stumped, and it concerned him.

Luckily, there was a Twins day game on TV.

"And Gaetti rips it down the line . . . foul," Bob Kurtz said. Most baseball announcers could fit their tonal tendencies within the undulations of a roller coaster. For Bob Kurtz, it was usually a rapid decline to disappointment.

Marty analyzed Gaetti. "He's not exactly big, but boy can he pull the ball."

"In other words, he's good at fouls," Harry coughed through a smoky exhale. The baseball conversation was a diversion.

In 1986, Gary Gaetti would lead the Twins in RBIs and homers. He also had the best mullet.

It was 1:45 p.m. and Harry was nervous. If they showed up late, the alchemists would be returning from their afternoon escapades. He could have a sober house, or a house full of jolly drunks that had changed into angry drunks. The potions turned them into monsters. Another option would be that the residents had not yet shifted to alchemy, and thus were angry, sober, and capable of rational complaints. Harry just wanted to get the visit out of the way.

The lunch rush was over, and the residence was beginning to smell like a combination of feet and burnt cheese.

Terry leaned into the office and sat next to Marty. "I'm walking down to Raymond to toss the ball. Maybe the college boys will be back." Terry had a color TV in his room, but he preferred the company, and he didn't want stragglers in his room.

"Let's head out in a bit. I want to say hello to Mr. Long," Marty responded.

Terry also knew Mr. Long. Terry liked that he was a mucketymuck in name only.

At his core, he was also a salesman.

Mr. Long knew about half of the residents by name, but he was closest to Marty. Their relationship was intricate. Marty knew all about Mr. Long's life, family, and struggles. Mr. Long knew all about Marty's life, family, and struggles. They knew each other's nature.

The building was quiet.

"That's the end of the third with the score still tied. Twins 2, Tigers 2. We'll be right back."

Freddie walked past the door without stopping. Even the Professor failed to appear with a quip. Harry had not seen the Professor in days. Thankfully, he had also not seen Carl.

Above the sounds of the TV, Harry could hear anything. The toilet overflowing particularly bothered him. Everything else was part of the job.

This time, it was gravel. Harry jumped to attention and nervously peered out the egress window. It was not a Cadillac.

He quickly grabbed two cans of air freshener and fast-walked down the hallway with a can in each hand, spraying as though fumigating for mosquitoes at a drive-in movie. At the end of the right-angled hallway, he turned into the laundry room, put the cans on the shelf and briskly walked to the office. He knew it was the Queen, and he knew that she always sat in her car for a few moments after turning off the engine.

The car door slammed and the sound of shoes on gravel was almost as pronounced as the one-ton vehicle. The Queen was in the house.

She looked around the office for obvious failures. "Are you ready? They'll be here in a few minutes. It smells good in here, by the way. I hope it lasts."

The Queen knew there was no solution to the systemic odor of male poverty. Family homeless shelters smelled like diapers, and male facilities smelled like BO. She was pleased that Harry had thought so far as to make a temporary effort. It ultimately didn't matter.

She looked at Terry and Marty, offering little more than a physical acknowledgment.

Today, the Queen needed to be the Queen. She knew that The Padre and Mr. Long often visited the residence, but it was rarely formal. Today's visit seemed official, which put everyone on edge.

The Twins game was in the fifth.

"Are they coming?" Harry carefully asked.

"I said they would be here in a few minutes," the Queen snapped, knowing that The Padre and Mr. Long had a late lunch and would be arriving together. She was thankful they were not having lunch at the residence. The bill of fare was lukewarm meatloaf and potato salad that had accumulated water on the bottom of the foil pan. Ingestion by the untrained would be at their own peril.

Just as the Queen was moving to tell Harry to take a walk around the block and perhaps not come back, gravel interrupted the tension.

It was a Cadillac.

Harry nervously watched as two sets of legs hit the ground, one short and decked in plaid pants and brown loafers, and the other longer, clad in dark pants and hard black shoes.

Harry knew that he would not be fired by Used Car Jesus or the charitable mobster, but his whole life was tenuous, and he was worried. Everything could go wrong. There could be a fight. Someone could throw up. Worse, there could be another stretcher.

Harry heard the residence door open and close, then quickly turned out of the office to greet them. Marty and Terry watched the game while the Queen took a seat at Harry's desk, sighing as she sat in the uncomfortable metal chair.

Harry greeted the two statesmen with a smile that revealed

his uneven yellow teeth, “Gentlemen, welcome to the Saint Anthony.”

“Mr. Opus, I presume,” The Padre said, pretending to meet his longtime staffer for the first time. The Padre remembered Harry’s drinking days.

Mr. Long was pleased to be in the building to greet friends, “Hey guy.”

They gathered at the end of the ramp and shook hands. It was unusually formal. They turned as a group and walked toward the office.

“The place looks good. What’s with the air freshener?” The Padre grumbled.

The Padre and Mr. Long were pleased to see Terry and Marty watching the Twins game. The Padre liked Terry. They were both local provocateurs, each with their own methods and motivations.

They offered a sinister smile of respect, as though they had just executed a caper. “Mr. Terry, sir, I trust you remain in various levels of trouble,” The Padre opined.

“Of course, Padre, of course. And you as well?” Terry countered.

“Of course, sir, of course.”

Mr. Long went right to Marty, and they hugged. The two frail bodies almost broke in half. “Mr. Marty Peterson, sir, how are you, guy?”

“I’m good, sir,” Marty returned.

“That’s it for the seventh and it’s still tied 4-all. Top of the order for the Tigers when we come back,” Bob Kurtz chimed over the Zenith.

At that moment, all four men turned toward the tiny TV. All but Mr. Long were lifelong fans. Mr. Long didn’t watch TV, but he looked at the 12-inch black-and-white model, thinking about Marty.

The Queen brought them to attention, “Gentlemen, welcome to the Saint Anthony.”

“Allison,” The Padre returned.

“Hello,” Mr. Long said as he walked over and gave her a hug. He looked like a small child in her prolonged embrace. They both smelled of perfume after the hug.

All heads returned to the Zenith.

“I wish the whole team would play like Puckett, although I do like that scraggly Gaetti,” The Padre offered, knowing little about the game in progress but a fan of Kirby Puckett. The Padre appreciated the diversion that sports offered the downtrodden. It was something they could root for other than salvation.

The Queen moved to the task. “Let’s go. I have another meeting.” The Queen regularly commanded her CEO.

“I’ll stop back before we leave,” Mr. Long said to Marty.

Harry was pleased that, up to this point, nothing was out of the ordinary. The halls were quiet and briefly covered with the scent of Glade Lavender.

The reason for the visit was still unknown. The Queen knew that The Padre could occasionally make up a reason to throw staff into a flurry of orders and frustrations. She was unfazed.

Any other staff person would be nervous. If the CEO visited for no defined reason, it could only mean one thing. Someone is going to get fired. But she knew the Patron Saint of Lost Causes. She also knew that Mr. Long would never come to a termination.

The Queen was kindred with The Padre and Mr. Long. They believed in justice. It sounded a touch socialist, something to which the Queen and The Padre—not the car salesman—aspired.

In the kitchen, Harry took coffee orders, even though they were out of cream, sugar, or anything else to cover the power of Saint Anthony coffee.

"How is my Jim doing?" Mr. Long asked the Queen, cringing over his coffee.

"He is quite well, actually," the Queen returned, unclear and unconcerned if anyone but Harry knew they lived together, conjugally or not. She wondered where Jim was, and Jerry for that matter, as they all seemed to be at the facility at some point during the day.

Jerry was a larger mystery to the Queen. They rarely crossed paths, but the Queen liked him. It must have been something about the worn-out and lanky.

The conversation took off about facility needs, resident updates, and the general comings and goings of the guests. Never call residents "clients" in front of The Padre.

Harry was relieved that, midway through the discussion, he still had a job. The Padre seemed frustrated.

"Where the heck is everyone?"

Harry and the Queen wanted to say that they were all at the library, which was entirely possible, although they would not be checking out books.

The Queen jumped in with force, "Probably in their rooms sleeping or out in the neighborhood getting drunk."

The Padre knew this. If they first have food, then they should have shelter. If they have shelter, then they should have opportunity. He didn't care about taxes, bootstrap theories, or multifaceted causalities. He was set with life and liberty, but what about the pursuit of happiness? For The Padre, justice was happiness.

There had to be something to do other than getting drunk.

The Padre was moving toward a directive. "There ought to be something going on around here."

"I guess so," the Queen mumbled as the group walked back to Harry's office. Mr. Long was silent. He knew it was his job to get money, not make decisions. Harry was also silent, thinking that he had escaped termination.

Marty and Terry were still in the office. They were wearing baseball caps, and there was one glove on the floor with a ball in it. Marty had found the ball in the bushes.

The Padre looked at the TV. "Who won the game?"

"If you can believe it, the Twins pulled it out in the bottom of the ninth. Home run by Gagne," Marty softly responded.

"I'll be damned."

The room fell silent. There was a wisp of smoke in the air from Marty's cigarette that everyone looked at.

"What's with the glove?"

"We're headed down to Raymond Field," Marty said. Questions at the Saint Anthony were often taken as inquisitions. Marty knew that The Padre was genuinely interested.

"Maybe you should get a team together here," The Padre said, not yet demanding.

"That'll be the day." Harry said, immediately regretting his comment.

The room was silent.

"Anything is possible, I guess," the Queen softly interjected.

The Padre and Mr. Long left the residence for the Cadillac and scotch and soda, in separate glasses.

There was little accomplishment from the visit other than a commitment to fix the toilet, but it was the best thing they did all week.

- -

The gravel ceased crackling in the parking lot, and the foot odor wafted back into Harry's office. No matter how many cigarettes were consumed, the odor remained. Harry wished more people smoked cigars.

Marty and Terry left for Raymond Field as soon as the Cadillac kicked up gravel.

The Queen slumped in the corner metal chair. Returning to the office would be an unwelcome rush-hour adventure. Harry wanted to leave, and it quickly became a stare-down.

"I thought it went well," said Harry, struggling to make conversation.

"It did. Nice work." It was all the Queen could muster for a compliment. Harry knew his work was finished. He did not get fired.

Harry blinked first. He closed his desk, exchanged pleasantries, greeted the night staff, and exited the facility with precise timing. He was on a bus schedule.

The Queen stared at the TV.

Over the next hour, a handful of residents trickled in as the dinner hour ended. Marty and Freddie would usually be first in the dinner line, but this time it was only Freddie. Mealtimes for the others depended on the time of the month. Tonight's meal of spaghetti and bagged meatball product put most residents to sleep. Those who were awake watched *Hardcastle and McCormick.*

The Queen did not eat dinner. She knew that most beef at the residence arrived on the second stop of the delivery truck. The first stop was Stillwater State Prison.

Just after dinner, Marty and Terry entered the building. They looked like two Little Leaguers who had just finished bowls of celebratory ice cream. Marty's pressed blue jeans were spotted with dirt. His shoes were bright white, without a spot. Terry was smoking a cigar, his high-crowned cap standing even taller with the pride of victory. As they went down the ramp, they were bumping into each other like giddy schoolchildren. Normal eyes would assess that they were drunk.

They quickly noticed the Queen.

Each of them tried to get a word in edgewise. The staff person was curious to their chemical state, but he was mostly focused on *Hardcastle and McCormick.* Managing drunks was Harry's job. The night manager's job was to keep people from killing each other or themselves.

"Where have you two been?" The Queen inquired, readily assuming her position of authority.

"Just knocking the ball around over at Raymond," Terry replied. "Marty here punched one over the fence again, definitely more Canseco than Puckett."

The Queen was mostly certain they were talking about baseball. Did people still play stickball? She was too engulfed in happenings of the middle-aged destitute to know anything about the trends of 1980s youth.

Before she could obtain a game recap, Marty and Terry departed for dinner.

With no one left but Milton C. Hardcastle, Skid McCormick, and the night staffer, the Queen left the residence, had a smoke in her car, and drove home.

Back at home, the Queen and Jim were watching TV—not anything in particular.

Reruns of *Cannon* sufficed. The Queen enjoyed the stocky, feisty Cannon in his old Lincoln Continental.

Cannon bellowed through the tube as he pulled out his comically tiny revolver. "I don't scare!"

"I had The Padre and Mr. Long over at the Saint Anthony today," the Queen said, appearing to talk to Cannon.

"Ol' Marty and that sinister Terry came back after the visit and apparently had played in some sort of baseball game," she revealed, thinking that she knew something Jim did not.

"Yeah, I told you those guys get together and play pickup ball over at Raymond—you know, over by Highway 280. They're actually pretty good. At least Marty is. Marty played for Dick Siebert over at the U of M. He really knocks the ball," Jim coughed through a Camel, knowing that he was repeating himself.

The Queen didn't know all the baseball details. She knew Marty as a phenom in a different category. Nice guy with a league-leading record of alcoholism.

The TV stayed on for another hour or so. Jim dozed off almost right away, and the Queen stared blankly at the screen, crafting what would become an impossible scenario.

CHAPTER FOURTEEN

BOYS DROOL, QUEEN RULES

The next day, the Queen sat uncomfortably in her office. When the Queen was unsettled, she was angry and she talked to herself, "I'm sick of this shit."

She got up from her desk and walked out the door.

There were inspirational placards on the walls with treatises of hope, but the Saint Anthony did not have a schedule or mission focused on sobriety. A few residents attended AA meetings, but the visits were short-lived. Some of the residents themselves were short-lived.

There was little to do other than drink, look for something to drink, drink again, create something to drink, and then drink.

The Queen pulled into the parking lot thinking she was Frank Cannon.

"I don't scare."

She pushed open the large car door and heaved herself out of the low-rider. She left her oversize rucksack on the front seat of her car, a no-no at Saint Anthony. She knew it and she didn't care.

Jim stood at the front door as directed.

Earlier that morning, the Queen sat down in the kitchen with Jim, fed him a heaping plate of scrambled eggs and sausage, and demanded that he tell her about the softball games. If the sausage didn't puncture his weak stomach lining, then the Queen would. Jim told all as bits of sausage greasily mingled with Camels.

He didn't think it was a big deal. Marty and Terry walked down to Raymond Field a couple of times per week and played pickup softball and baseball. Occasionally, another resident or two would join them, and sometimes a few strangers. It wasn't a team, but they had fun, and it seemed to bond whoever played. The only other bonding came over shared bottles.

The Queen met Jim at the front door and spun him around toward Harry's office. Jim had warned Harry that the Queen would be approaching with some sort of mandate.

Suddenly, the meeting was formal.

The Queen had been angry now for the whole day. Her eyes and her perfume became a flamethrower. She cut the pleasantries. "I think it's time we get some movement around here."

Harry lit up a smoke as the Queen threw fire at both Jim and Harry.

"I know about the softball down at Raymond, and I think we should make something out of it."

"What do you mean?" Harry coughed.

"I mean, we should get a softball team organized. I'll get them the games."

Harry was in disbelief at the prospect of 55 chronic inebriates formalizing anything other than a meeting around a bottle of gin. He went along with it.

"Works for me," Harry said.

The Queen expected rumbling. It was not like she was asking them to fix a toilet. She demanded that they put together a team of drunks to play softball. It had disaster written all over it—forfeited games, fights, rude behavior in front of actual citizens, and just the general embarrassment of odorous drunks trying to play softball.

It could destroy the facility in more ways than one. The Queen wasn't afraid of another urination issue.

Harry was unable to formulate anything but compliance. It was his survival. Jim was playing his usual role of loyal subject. He was smart.

The Queen wanted all plans to be foolproof. Jim and Harry would assemble the team, set the rules, organize the practices, and execute game-day operations. The Queen would locate opposing teams and trick them into playing. She may or may not tell them the whole story.

At that moment, it appeared simple. So was her final demand. "That's it, get it done."

It was how the Queen rolled. From her first realization that she could be sober and powerful to her position as "Lord of It All," the Queen took few prisoners. She was now the GM of America's first organized softball team of chronic inebriates.

The Queen loved bosses, and she wanted to be The Boss.

And she would need to be The Boss because, in America, weeknight softball players drank Styrofoam buckets of ice-cold light beers. The Saint Anthony team would have the first cooler in history filled with Mad Dog 20-20.

Pray to Saint Anthony and you will find it.

MARTY INTERLUDES

Spring, 1990

Marty and his job-service case manager sat in a corner that Marty had fashioned into an office. The case manager started as a VISTA volunteer at Mary Hall Shelter and hung on for a real job after a year of gratis labor and a break in student loan payments. The pay was enough to buy a pair of khakis at Target and an occasional pitcher of beer at O'Gara's Bar and Grill. Even after volunteering and well into a real paycheck, he was still a preeminent leech. He went to *Top Gun* at the cheap theaters, and he was a Goose guy.

Conversations with Marty were worth all the money the case manager could have made in a three-piece suit selling thoughts at a call center. The making-a-difference part was worthless at parties, but he didn't care. He was exactly where he wanted to be at 23 years old.

The Union Gospel Mission Thrift Shop was an interesting and productive afterthought from George Verley, the director of the mission. Located on the edge of what had become the mission's campus, the shop was in a dilapidated, rectangular shed, its walls patched together by metal sheets and secured by a metal roof.

George was thankful that city inspectors believed in his mission—the mission's mission—as the makeshift facility likely had a range of code violations. So did its patrons.

Run-down clothes, run-down building. Marty Peterson presided over both.

Over the past several days, Marty told the case manager a story about a game. He even had a photo of a ragtag team, and Marty was in the front row. Marty's appearance was largely unchanged. It had only been a few years since the team took the field, but the destitute tend to age faster, so one would expect his frailty to be more pronounced. The case manager at least expected new glasses. Except for a piece of Scotch tape on both hinges, they were the same thick, foggy glasses from the team picture. The job-service program would spring for a new pair of specs.

Marty sat comfortably behind a metal desk, glasses askew and a cigarette in his yellowed hand. With an entire library of books and a store full of clothing in the warehouse behind him, the case manager imagined how long it would take for the cigarette to reduce the facility to ashes.

"It was a fun summer, I must say," Marty said. "It passed the time."

"I can't believe guys actually showed up and played." The case manager was incredulous. He believed that Saint Anthony residents were largely zombies, and that Marty was an anomaly.

"Nobody believed we could actually get out there and play, and we showed 'em good."

As he told the story in bits and pieces, a few patrons entered the thrift store. One of them was a woman looking for kids' clothes, and the other was a man seeking treasures. The hunter was looking through piles of books, settling on what looked to be an old copy of *Heart of Darkness.*

"I had a first edition, but I gave it to the U," Marty told the treasure hunter, who looked disappointed. Most of the books in the store were assembled through donations. Marty put a few books on the rack from garage sales he visited in his free time. He wasn't lying about the first edition. Legend had it that Marty made a sizable donation of first editions and other rare books to the library at his alma mater.

"I always wondered where Terry went. He just left one day, and that was the last I saw of him. We had fun. He wasn't much of a ball player, but he was fun," Marty whispered. "I think Freddie is still over there. I should go see him."

The case manager chimed in with his baseball prowess. "I was never much of a player. I was a superstar in T-ball—hit a home run almost every time. Then they started throwing the ball at me. I felt like Don Baylor, but I wasn't trying to get hit."

"I loved the game. As long as there was no snow, we played. I think we played once in the winter, but all you could see were the laces," Marty said with a nostalgic smile on his weathered face.

The woman asked about two matching sets of brand-new infant jumpers. "Can I get both of these for $2?"

She was a New American. In the '80s in Saint Paul, immigrants from East Africa were only slightly less rare than first editions. Marty believed everyone had a pathway that should be paved with kindness. In the rough world of the Union Gospel Mission, he was unabashed about saying so.

"How about you take them both for nothing?" He smiled at the woman. She appeared confused. She handed him two dollar bills, and he folded them back into her calloused hand.

Marty returned to baseball. "We had a team back in the neighborhood that was really something: Jim Senske, Ron Causton, Terry Schreiber, and a whole pile of guys. Made it to the state tournament in Rochester. We were like the Yankees."

The case manager sat quietly. The story was fascinating, but it seemed less about baseball than it did about something else.

"Those guys went on to some great stuff. Jim is a baseball coach in New Ulm. He coached Terry Steinbach and, I think, some other pros. Ron is coaching and teaching here in town at Highland High School, and Terry started a famous acting school in New York City. I would love to visit him someday."

He was proud of his friends, and he knew their details.

Marty's details were still out there, but it was clear to the case manager that baseball was an anchor for the tired soul.

The case manager often rolled his eyes over incessant yarns of America's pastime as an elixir for life's ails.

Now, he was starting to believe it . . . and perhaps need it.

CHAPTER FIFTEEN

BIG SWING

The Queen's car barreled out of the lot, the white sidewalls evenly spitting gravel.

Harry and Jim sat in silence for an extended period. They filled the office with smoke. "It's going to be hard to control," Harry started. Harry's apprehension emerged quickly after the gravel settled in the parking lot.

"We'll figure it out. Queen is right, the guys need it. This place needs a spark," Jim returned. Jim was slowly and quietly doing the Queen's bidding, but he believed in it. The team embodied everything Jim was about since he emptied his last bottle and threw away his last needle.

Don't forget the forgotten.

Harry and Jim had organized only a handful of group activities over the years, mostly barbecues in the parking lot. The cookouts would go either way, depending on the time of the month. All it took was one resident to start kicking over chairs and throwing hamburgers like Frisbees. It would escalate and soon carry over to the neighborhood or to a resident alone in an alley with a can of Lysol.

Normalcy was occasionally worth the risk.

A softball team would be different. The games would involve interaction with the outside world. They could be on the same playing field . . . or they could make a stereotype come alive.

"I hope this isn't a *Longest Yard* thing," Harry said, "Because that makes me one of the guards."

"Not even close, unless you think that the general public are the bad guys," Jim said. "Depends who's askin'."

Everyone at the Saint Anthony saw *The Longest Yard.* They cheered as Burt Reynolds assembled a football team of inmates that clashed on the gridiron with evil prison guards in an iteration of *David vs. Goliath.* There was even homemade hooch.

Saint Anthony was not a prison. Residents did not feel like prisoners. They were not treated poorly, and they did not struggle with the "guards." A handful committed heinous acts, but they didn't have to hide the raisin jack in the toilet, and they were all free to leave.

Saint Anthony residents were not imprisoned, they were forgotten.

The Queen and her underlings knew this. They also knew that forming a softball team at one of the nation's only homes for chronic inebriates was a shot at the big leagues of perception. Victory on the scoreboard did not matter. If the team went the distance without vomiting or fighting, they would be in the win column.

The two men sat quietly until dinnertime. Jim offered Harry a ride home, but Harry wanted to stick to his routine. He wouldn't even take a ride to the bus stop.

Jim stayed for another hour after Harry left, but he skipped the dry meatloaf. As he walked into the parking lot, Marty and Terry were playing catch in the street. Freddie was sitting on the curb cheering.

"C'mon Jim, how about gettin' in the game?"

"Not tonight, Freddie, but just you wait, because ol' Jim is gonna go home and get his big ol' bat ready."

"Hot damn, boy!"

Jim didn't have a bat, a glove, or a ball.

CHAPTER SIXTEEN

CAPTAINS AND MANAGERS REPORT

The next day, Jim put the Saint Anthony first on his list of rounds. The Queen's timelines were inviolable.

A commercial for Calvin Klein Obsession was on TV when he stepped into Harry's office. "Oh, the smell of it."

Harry quickly announced his baseball pedigree to Jim. "I played baseball my freshman year in high school, but that was about it, I think." Harry sort of believed it but couldn't remember it as fact. He was aware that memory and truth were processes of his recovery.

Jim was fixated on the Calvin Klein ad. He was wearing a Hawaiian shirt, jeans, and a Twins baseball cap.

"Let's just get a team together and see what happens. We'll do it regular and start with captains." Jim was impressed with himself.

"Good idea," Harry smiled, writing down Jim's idea, as though he'd been ordered to record the proceedings.

Harry considered the leadership role. It meant risk, which he was averse to. His life had leveled to a point of unusual comfort, but not offering leadership was even riskier. He could get fired.

Harry also wanted to have fun. His scowl had been on such a long run that even the scowler himself knew that he needed a break.

“The obvious choices are Marty and Terry for co-captains,” Jim said, as though he scoured the minor leagues and analyzed stats. He was still thinking about Obsession, not because the Saint Anthony smelled like a dugout.

“Right,” Harry returned.

The first of the month was almost in the rearview mirror, and Marty and Terry were nowhere to be found.

By dinnertime, Jim had moved down his to-do list and departed, and Harry was contending with the time of the month. Neither of them had a choice. Some of the residents had pushed it fast and hard, and some were making a day of it. Large-scale vomiting incidents were unusually prevalent, but luckily it was the sleep-it-off kind that did not require paramedics or a negotiation to avoid drunken pugilism. Two drunks swinging at air could be imagined by some as humorous. For Harry, it was sad and annoying, so he was thankful to avoid it. Sometimes, he preferred the paramedic, and he wasn’t proud of it.

Harry knew that Marty and Terry would be back for dinner. Some residents would take their monthly allowance and spend it on both drinks and food, attempting to fit into the mainstream if at least for a day. For those who drank and ate with their money, banishment from the eatery was commonplace. Restaurants were less tolerant than bars.

Marty and Terry were long past the desire to enjoy fine foods. Marty never enjoyed restaurants, while Terry had worn out his welcome at most places, so much so that he forgot his once-fancy palate. Smoked whitefish in Duluth was replaced with pressed turkey loaf in Saint Paul.

Marty and Terry entered the building at the same time. They had been on their separate ways most of the day, but they knew how to time dinner.

Terry was slurring. "Hey Harry, whaddya know?" He had taken the cocktail roller coaster on a spin for the ages, and he would feel the pain.

Harry knew that Terry was drunk, but Harry also knew how to navigate a boozed-up conversation, and it was particularly easy with Terry. The only annoyance was Terry's elixir breath. He smelled like a 1930s old man—coffee, cigarettes, and cologne. Harry lit up another cigarette to soften the blow. He had been smoking straight for about a half hour as the residents arrived.

Marty sat quietly, drawing from a Parliament. His powder-blue jeans were unscathed.

Marty's day was at the Ace Box, and his drink was coffee. He also bought a carton of cigarettes. "I want to chat with you two about something fun," Harry said, knowing that his use of the word "fun" was irregular.

"Shoot," Terry said, a touch too intoxicated to notice that Harry said "fun."

Trying to be formal, Harry set down his cigarette. Terry and Marty noticed the effort and found it humorous.

Harry's voice wavered. "The Queen wants you guys—us—to put a softball team together." Harry had a new viewpoint of captainship. Marty and Terry would do all the work.

"Works for me," Terry quickly responded. He was starting to nod off.

Marty lowered his cigarette and looked into Harry's eyes with a short smile. "Who else is on the team?"

"No one. It's up to you to get it together. I have to report back to the Queen and Jim."

“Wesley can play, so can Freddie,” Marty said.

“Are you serious?”

“They come to Raymond Field with us. Who are we going to play?”

“I don’t know. Get the team together first.” Harry did not have a clue as to who they would play, when they would play, or any other aspect of the whole darn idea. It was now a darn idea. The realization hit him in the face like a line drive.

Terry abruptly came back to the conversation and appointed himself Assistant GM, saying, “Sounds good, ol’ Harry, I’ll have a talk with the guys.”

Harry felt stressed. He quickly packed up the office for the shift change, almost forgetting to lock up the petty cash drawer, which was still empty.

Marty and Terry were last in line for dinner.

Dinner was baked chicken. It was surprisingly good, but on the first of the month, it was not the cleanest choice for the seasonally uncoordinated. Efforts to devour the meal were aggressive. Luckily, it was just greasy and time-consuming enough to incite fatigue.

The salad bar was the same every night—iceberg lettuce, red onions, whitish cheese, shredded carrots that no one ate, off-tasting cucumbers, and an array of warm dressings. The only certainty about salad at the Saint Anthony was that it gave residents bad breath on top of already-bad breath.

Marty and Terry went through the remains of the buffet. The cafeteria was a zone of silence. Even the most raucous early-month parties that took place in neighborhood alleyways became subdued once back to the residence. At the first of the month, residents were either too intoxicated to speak or even fight, or they were in a state of sadness for having spent their $45 in one afternoon. The cafeteria, on any day, was a place of introspection or, for many, a penultimate moment of satisfaction before the arrival of stupor.

Heads were buried in plates, sometimes literally.

Today, Marty and Terry had a dinner meeting. It was as formal as they had ever been at Saint Anthony.

Terry's first-week-of-the-month intoxication had apparently dissipated.

"Alright then, who should we put on this team?" Terry asked, assuming that he was going to be the leader.

The first decision was easy and unspoken. Harry as manager was out of the question, which pleased them both immensely. It would please Harry as well.

Marty's thoughts were in high school. He cared little about conquest. He just wanted to play ball. Picking the team was fun, but already he wanted to get on the diamond.

"Not really sure. As I said, we both know Wesley can play ball," Marty whispered.

"All right then, he is on the team. We should get some paper and write this stuff down."

Terry left the cafeteria and returned quite a bit later with a grease-stained yellow tablet that had his and Marty's names on it. Marty didn't mind the unusual wait. He had all the time in the world.

He hoped Terry didn't sneak a bottle into his room.

"OK, I'm back. I ran into that goofy Professor. No way he is on the team. I know this team will be rough around the edges, but we all have limits, right?"

No one annoyed Marty, but he got the picture. "No arguments here." They saw the challenge, and they saw themselves right in it.

Even if residents played in high school or college, vomiting in the middle of an inning was not a recipe for victory.

Just showing up on time could be the greatest challenge. A team bus or a chartered jet was not in the budget, even if there was a budget.

They discussed the positives. With breath worse than dragons, players would be afforded extended leads off first base. Unfortunately, they would be so slow on the steal that they would never make it to second.

Imagine if Rickey Henderson had bad breath.

It was also possible that disgust with the team's appearance and mannerisms could elicit fear that might prove advantageous. Would an opposing player really want to tag another player out who smelled like a garbage can?

They continued to talk through theories and possibilities. "Who else?" Marty asked.

"I assume Harry and Jim will be on the team, right?" It was an assumption, but they needed players, and they needed at least a few of them sober.

"That was my thought as well."

Thirty minutes into their managerial careers, Marty and Terry had Jim, Harry, and Wesley, apparently. That was five, including themselves. They needed at least four more to make a team that would take the field. Bench players were not a consideration, but it was obvious they would need subs.

Marty was already digging deep. "What about Jack?"

"You're kidding. That old codger is no more than a common hobo." Terry disliked stereotypical hobos—the funny, crazy homeless guy with the bags of newspaper and cardboard bed. Jack's realization of a stereotype offended Terry. It made Terry's own predicament a reality.

"OK, probably a good idea to skip Jack. Skip Carl too."

"I saw Jerry the other day over by the field," Marty recalled. "Not sure if he can play ball, but he might be interested."

"Which Jerry?"

Jerrys abounded at the Saint Anthony Residence. There are a thousand studies, surveys, and theories on the causality of homelessness. None produced a bar chart on the weighted average of given names versus poverty. If they did, Jerrys and Jacks would dominate. Festus and Thornton wouldn't make the list.

This Jerry was just a Jerry. He was not funny. He was not outgoing. Marty and Terry did not know him. Harry only knew what was on his intake form. They knew he was easygoing and that he never caused any issues with Harry or other residents. He seemed to track the cycles of the month with some predictability, which had to be acceptable for this team or they would forfeit every game.

Jerry had the one quality that made him an easy choice. He was reliable.

Marty and Terry knew that talent requirements did not necessarily call for 85 mph fastballs and 4.5 speeds in the 40-yard dash. It was the Saint Anthony Residence, and it was softball. Men and women across America played softball once a week, occasionally under the influence of barley drinks and tobacco products. Anyone could play. Baseball is not America's sport. Softball is.

Talent was optional. Showing up was everything. "Jerry makes the team."

Terry wrote down the new addition. He did not know any last names at the Saint Anthony, except Marty's.

Marty, Terry, Jim, Harry, Wesley, and Jerry. Not the Professor, Jack, or Carl, for now.

- -

The next morning, Marty and Terry were in Harry's office immediately after breakfast. It was earlier than normal, and the mood was different.

Marty sat with his legs tightly crossed, smoking a Parliament, and Terry was working the Jumble Puzzle in the *St. Paul Pioneer Press.* Harry conducted tasks of the early days of the month, largely bottle returns and the search for missing residents.

Jim arrived midmorning, continuing to acknowledge the Queen's implicit demand. He also had his regularly toted to-do list in the back pocket of his low-riding jeans.

Jim turned the conversation. "Where are we at with this ball club?" Jim relished his use of the word "club."

Terry chimed in, "We have Marty here, you, ol' Harry, Wes, Jerry, maybe Charlie, maybe Eric, maybe Ray, maybe Freddie, and me. That's one for the bench." Terry failed to note that he only really had himself, Marty, Jim, Harry, maybe Wesley, and maybe Jerry. Terry thought to himself that he needed to stay sober to retain a roster spot and not be relegated to the list of alcoholic roster uncertainties.

Could he really count himself?

"You're gonna need more than that," Jim said.

"I'm not worried. We're just getting started." Terry's confidence followed his role as the resident provocateur.

No one in the room thought that any of the expansion draftees would decline the opportunity. What else was there to do except drink? The inability to answer that question, the very reason for residing at the Saint Anthony, escaped everyone for the moment.

It was agreed that Marty and Terry would deliver the news to their new teammates. Harry would be their assistant, per Jim's prolonged stare. Players would have to be reminded every day that they were on a team. There would be no tryouts and no cuts because everyone except Marty would have gotten cut.

Jack leaned into Harry's office. "Hey Harry, can I get a token? Who's the creepy guy?" He was looking at Jim, who he had known for over a decade. Jack was physically standing, but he was long gone. He was holding a garbage bag full of cans that was leaking onto the floor.

"Okay," Harry replied and handed him a token.

The early days of the month were lingering. Spring had arrived and, along with it, a cornucopia of available cans and other recyclables. It would be a challenge even to locate ball-players, let alone explain the opportunity to them in a manner they would comprehend.

Harry watched the garbage bag leak all the way out the door. "Guess it's that time of the month," Terry smiled.

In Minnesota, snow in industrial areas eventually acquires a homely shade of gray, mostly due to passing vehicles. The gray snow attracts a sizable amount of garbage, much of which includes the highly sought-after aluminum can. As the snow melts, glistening cylinders of opportunity are revealed. A brisk spring walk and a visit to the recycling plant offer the enterprising resident a bonus day of inebriation—sweet nectar of the dirty snow.

Marty and Terry knew the trade well, and they went scouting for players around the usual trash cans and the recycling center.

Unfortunately, the recycling center was only a block from the Ace Box.

Later that afternoon, Marty found Wesley in the laundry room, leaning against the washing machine for no apparent reason. Wesley was not intoxicated.

"Hey Wes, we're getting a softball team together. Do you want to play?"

"Yuuup," Wesley responded and quietly went about his business, which was unclear as always. He was gone before Marty could explain any of the details.

In one slurred word, Marty felt like he was on a roll.

By the time Marty got back to Harry's office, Terry was already making his move.

"What can I do you for, gents?" Ray said to Terry and Harry.

Every group of men needs at least one "Ray." Rays are mechanical and useful. They are quiet but engaging at an engineer-like level, always using a freshly sharpened pencil to solve quandaries. Their long fingers work oiled machines. They wear dark clothes, hard boots, and black-rimmed glasses.

This Ray was affable, and he rarely fell into any of Harry's categories of difficulty, notably vomiting. He was middle-aged, neat in appearance, and possessed acumen for numbers that would provide little use on the ballfield but at least indicated some level of comprehension. He picked up the taste of beer in his brother's auto shop, and it soon became irresistible. He drank to excess several times a week, but instead of throwing up, he talked about *Star Trek*. Unusually, in a literal breath of fresh air, he did not smoke.

Unlike most residents, Ray believed that he would leave Saint Anthony. He was unaware of his chronic alcoholism and its attack on his ability to be self-sufficient. He apparently forgot about denial.

Harry had never administered a Rorschach test, except in a drinking game 20 years earlier, but he could judge most individuals. Ray would not rock the boat.

Terry liked Ray, but there was something about him that made Terry nervous. Rumor in the residence was that Ray enjoyed more than alcohol. For all the destructive elements in the building, drugs were an absolute no-no.

Terry took a chance and asked him to be on the team.

Standing in Harry's doorway, Ray looked like a smart Frankenstein's monster—tight black jeans, large black shoes, and an imposing cranium.

"Sounds like a hoot. What's the plan?" Harry gave him the background.

"You realize that I was on the Quiz Bowl team in high school?" Ray responded, not in the least bit allowing for any admission of athletic embarrassment, but rather with well-placed pride.

"So? That doesn't mean you can't hit a soft round orb with a wood cylinder," Terry retorted, surprised at his quick scientific wit.

"If the rest of these knuckleheads can do it, I can do it," Ray responded. It was unusual for Ray to be condescending. It revealed a competitive nature that Terry liked.

"So, are you in or are you out?" Terry thought he had made the sale.

"You should do it. I'm on the team," Harry added.

"I'll get back to you," Ray responded with a smile, and then went out the door to the alternative world he existed in during the first part of the month, greeting his friend Marty on the way out with "Hey, Marty."

Ray would be on the team.

Walking with Ray out the door, Harry caught the smell of vomit and headed toward the cafeteria to investigate and eradicate.

The quiet day turned the other direction. Issues flowed like a river of booze. Harry had the bathroom cleaned no less than three times and there was a near-fight in the laundry room. For the first time in over a year, Harry had to contend with an errant defecation. Those were always fun.

After Wesley and Ray, round one of the draft was called due to inclement addiction. It was shaping up to be a long season in Saint Paul.

CHAPTER SEVENTEEN

LIQUID LULLS

A few days passed; the early part of the month was finally over.

The entire building had a hangover. The halls were barren, and the cafeteria was eerily quiet. The building seemed to close in on itself like a pounding headache. Coffee expenses would spike but were offset by savings in cleaning supplies. Residents shifted down the halls to the shared bathrooms with narrow gaits and tired eyes, as though they had returned from a week of hard labor.

Even the most docile and high-functioning of the residents would wear their admission tickets to the Saint Anthony on their tired faces.

Thankfully for both staff and residents, the Twins were on a long road trip and on TV almost every day. It reminded at least a handful of residents that something else was happening other than drinking.

As the middle of the month settled in, the air eventually cleared, and brain cells rejuvenated to a midpoint of function. It was now mid-May, the Twins were off to another mediocre start, and the residents were out of money.

Instead of alchemy, Marty and Terry rode out the benders on coffee.

"Hey, Harry," Marty said as he walked into Harry's office. He took a seat in Harry's office and lit up a Parliament out of a fresh pack.

After a cigarette and a half, Terry entered the office.

"Hey, Harry," Terry whispered, and sat in the corner metal chair. "I saw Johnny Luck the other day, and he said that he would play." Terry had seen Johnny the day before at The Cromwell. He didn't talk about what else happened at the bar.

"I saw Ray at the hardware store, and he said he was in as well," Marty added. Harry wondered what either of them was doing at a hardware store. Marty wondered what he was doing there as well.

"We're in business. We have me, Jim, Marty, Harry, Johnny, Ray, and Wesley," Terry continued. "That's seven."

The past few days disappeared. This was the real business as usual at the Saint Anthony.

The consequences were already in the building.

Harry was pleased that Terry and Marty were taking the reins. He sensed guilt emanating from Terry. Regret was rare and welcome in a facility considered to be the end of the road.

Perhaps Terry could make a hard U-turn on his life.

"I got Jerry. Pretty easy, actually," Harry added, regretting that he said it was easy. He wanted everyone to think he was laboring over even the simplest of tasks.

"What about Eric?" Terry asked.

"Can't find him," Harry responded.

Terry turned to Marty, "Which means we only need one player. Like I said, we're on a roll."

MARTY INTERLUDES

"Nine Edge"

By Marty Peterson, 1984

When at last the feelings moved
turn back and live with the memory
or move
into slow growth
let it happen
unrestricted
a line has been drawn
on the edge of a cliff
fall one way
into memories pit
or slow journey
into a new day
with love's slow way

CHAPTER EIGHTEEN

REALITY—NOT BOTTLE—CHECK

The next day, Jim pulled into the Saint Anthony parking lot in his 1979 Grand Marquis, inching the front end as close to the wall as possible. The vehicle enveloped the parking lot with carbon monoxide, which, if anyone were thinking about it, could have provided a brief and low-cost high to those who lingered.

Jim exited the bright-red vehicle almost parallel to the pavement, coughing up the carbon monoxide from his cigarette in an unusual marriage of tobacco and union-made combustion.

After regaining a 90-degree angle to the pavement, the thin man made his way down the ramp to Harry's office. He pondered why anyone would build a first floor on a sublevel. He took note of the usual odors and turned into Harry's office. Marty was in the corner metal chair smoking a Parliament, and Harry was at his desk attempting to change receipt rolls in a 10-key machine.

"Hey, Jim," Marty said.

Harry seemed concerned. "What brings you down here?"

"I need to check in on some things. And I need an update on the team," Jim answered, not in the least bit feeling as though he had let the cat out of the bag about a surprise inspection.

"And the Queen says that she's working on a game—maybe as soon as next week."

Harry and Marty looked at each other. It was difficult to see Marty's eyes through his thick glasses, but they went as wide as they had been since he arrived at the residence. Harry's brow had furrowed, but he forced it back to its usual position of indifference.

"The team is coming along fine," Harry said to avoid guilty silence. "We have you, me, Marty, Terry, Jerry, Ray, Wesley, and hopefully Johnny Luck. That's eight, or rather seven and a half."

"Maybe six and a half," Marty whispered, unusually critical.

"Ray plays sports?" Jim knew Ray from a few odd jobs he hired him for over the years. Jim knew about Ray's mechanical skills, and while he was careful not to rely on residents to complete jobs, Ray was the one resident who could fix a washing machine, a residence necessity.

"Not sure if he is playing, but he is on the team," Harry replied.

"He'll play nicely," Marty added. Marty was confident, less in Ray's ability than in his own ability to coach him.

"You still only have eight, or seven and a half. Did you get equipment?"

Harry and Marty looked at each other. They both realized that there was more to do with their little ragtag team than they thought. A lengthy silence fell upon the office.

Jim left Harry's office and walked around the building on made-up errands.

That no-turning-back feeling filled the office, which was particularly unusual since the direction was forward.

"Oh boy, we have some work to do." Marty said through the smoke, not moving the position he assumed over an hour ago.

"I would say so." Harry innately put the task on Marty.

"We could knock on doors," Marty offered as the first strategy.

"Or we could fake it and get some VISTA volunteers from the Dorothy Day Center. I can douse them with whiskey to get them up to speed," Harry said.

"They should smoke as well."

"Alright, we have a plan. Now we just need a bat and ball."

"And gloves."

After chatting through a few smokes, Marty and Harry agreed that the task was not as daunting as they believed only minutes prior. It was an operative principle of the Saint Anthony Residence. If you wait long enough, the problem might go away.

Their second agreement was to summon Terry. Terry had been absent all morning. He may have been in a chemically enhanced sleep. Harry knocked on his door, which was about halfway down the hall on the interior side. After progressively louder knocks, Harry considered the master key.

Terry opened the door. His odors, greenish face, and omnidirectional hair told a wallowing chemical story of the previous night. He swayed like a willow, and with one hand, he put a finger up to his mouth. "Shush."

With the other hand, he extended five digits. "Five."

After about 30 minutes, Terry arrived in Harry's office, stub cigar in his mouth, hair coiffed with unknown oil, and a clean shirt tucked neatly into pressed polyester dress pants.

Harry knew, with a little bit of time, his guests could clean up nicely.

The mood was rare. It was as though Terry missed a meeting, and it wasn't around a bottle of vodka. The acknowledgment was powerful.

Business catchphrases at the Saint Anthony were opposites. Core competency is a pathway to destruction. A deep dive is into the parking lot. Failure is not an option because they have already failed.

For the first time since he introduced himself to Harry and bummed a cigarette, Terry knew that failure was not an option, actually.

He was rife with guilt for joining a rogue Saint Anthony crew the prior evening, where everyone drank cocktails of Kool-Aid and rubbing alcohol. The alley circles were out of character for Terry. He knew he had not let the team down, but he knew that he was capable of it, which troubled him. He needed to assert contrition.

He had a life's worth of apologies he could offer, but Terry had not apologized with sincerity since he started drinking in high school. Today, it was short, but he needed it.

"Sorry about that, gents."

Marty and Harry gave Terry a recap of the day's events, along with their to-do list for the team. Terry cautiously positioned himself back in the role of Assistant GM.

"OK, let's finish building this team before we move to the matter of equipment," Terry said, knowing that equipment was the least of his worries.

Jim had a different plan.

Jim pulled the Grand Marquis into the Queen's parking spot at the main office. The dock attendant, an old and stodgy transitional housing resident with a made-up job, was an automatic friend to Jim. Jim tossed him the keys.

"What can I do you for?"

"Back in 30, Mr. Joe."

Jim was out of place in the carpeted headquarters.

"Hey," he peered into the Queen's office. The Queen nearly jumped out of her chair. She was at her desk engulfed in an array of paperwork, empty coffee cups, and doughnut crumbs. The perfume was as powerful as the Queen herself.

She smiled at Jim. "What brings you up here?" She thought it might be a first-ever romantic visit—a surprise lunch or a cute hello from someone who looked like a Sasquatch.

Jim talked through his concerns for the team's success. Equipment and games were on the list. He forgot about uniforms.

The Queen walked with Jim down to The Padre's office to rally the forces.

The Padre liked Jim. He was a rough-around-the-edges, come-back-from-the-depths guy. "Mr. Jim, what brings you to the Captain's bridge today? The ship is sinking, you know," The Padre announced.

After a few minutes of conversation, Jim had hammered out a collective bargaining agreement.

The phone rang as Jim walked out of The Padre's office. It was the Chief of Police. "Hasn't he heard of *habeas corpus?*" The Padre's priest-Latin served him well at times.

"Of course, Padre, I'll take care of it."

"Thanks, Chief, let's get lunch soon. I'll buy." The Padre never picked up checks.

CHAPTER NINETEEN

TEAM MEETING: RULES? THERE AIN'T NO RULES

A few days later, the team count hovered at seven and a half players. They could still turn back and not call it failure.

In modern baseball, teams are comprised of thick legal contracts gathered in secure file cabinets in law firms, where oversize pictures of stately partners adorn the walls. A player in the cabinet can be on a team without ever meeting a teammate or throwing a ball.

The Saint Anthony players had to show up for roster check.

It was now the middle of the month, so the time was opportune for a team meeting. It was clear that during the downswing between cash-infused mayhem and creative alchemy, there existed respite and opportunity. The cafeteria line was longer, evening snack time quietly bustled, and the halls were like a college dormitory—only silent and without the hopeful anticipation of incoming freshmen.

Marty and Terry holed up in Harry's office. The usual parade of residents made periodic visits for conversation and desperate requests. It was a time to regain brain capacity after the early days of the month. As hours passed and guilt slowly released from the pores of weathered bodies, heart rates would return to normal, relatively.

The team intermittently slipped into conversation.

The Twins were playing a day game, which nicely suited the Saint Anthony, particularly at this time of the month.

Bob Kurtz's voice crackled through the rabbit ears on Harry's faltering TV. "That's the end of the third in Chicago. A solo homer from Tom Brunansky, and the Twins are back on top. Twins 2, White Sox 1."

Marty was staring into the TV. "We should probably get that team onto the field for a practice."

"You only have eight players," Harry grumbled through a Marlboro Red.

"We only have seven players," Terry corrected Harry.

"Let's get everyone rounded up today sometime. Maybe more will show up," Marty replied, taking a leadership role.

"What about Eric?" Terry asked Harry.

"Haven't seen him." Harry buried his head into his neatly folded newspaper. He looked at the classified ads and the obituaries every day.

Harry did not delve into theories about Eric. He was afraid that Eric was either in another city or dead, perhaps dead in another city. Harry continued to check shelters and his connections at the police department. Eric did not have family who would acknowledge him, so he could easily be in a county basement waiting for the government to identify him and pay for his unmarked burial.

Eric's room was sparse, and whenever Harry visited, it was as though Eric just stepped out—desk lamp on, bed ruffled, and an ashtray with a single cigarette ashed to its length. He seemed focused on being transient. If Eric did not come back by the end of the month, Harry would tap the waiting list for a new resident—and maybe a new ballplayer. On his last visit to Eric's room, Harry turned out the light and emptied the ashtray. He did his best not to make it commonplace.

The waiting list at Saint Anthony was largely hypothetical. Walking out of detox for the 20th time, the habitual drinker would not think to himself that it was time to hightail it to the Saint Anthony. Even so, the county would keep a list, and Harry would do his best to work off its fluctuations.

Marty was not selected off a list. His county worker saw an opportunity and immediately took it.

Harry would use the list for Eric's replacement. He would know for sure in a few weeks, the unofficial "he's not coming back" timeframe. Vacations to the coast and sabbaticals were nonexistent. After two weeks "missing," a resident was gone in more ways than one.

"Let's gather who we have after dinner," Terry announced. Marty and Terry left Harry's office to assemble the squad, uncharacteristically leaving behind a four-run Twins lead as Ron Davis took the mound with two on and one out.

Sending a message to residents was not a simple task. There was a message board in the cafeteria that was overfilled with fingerprinted temp-work announcements and FBI most-wanted posters. Paper items under doors were kicked around, then adhered to the bottoms of shoes and relocated. Harry posted notices in the bathrooms above the toilets, a noble attempt, although to no avail since most heads at Saint Anthony sagged downward in both the seated and standing positions. The only effective way to send a message was to do it in person.

Marty and Terry worked the building, informing team members that there would be a team meeting after dinner.

Luckily, most of them were in the lull of the middle of the month, lying on beds tightly made with donated blankets that if laid out in unison would resemble one of those memorial quilts. Rituals were important, and making the bed was one of them. Spending their money early was another.

Terry and Marty were lucky there was still time left in the Twins game, which made for a host of viewers seated comfortably in their rooms, cigarettes dangling from their lips. Half of them had 12-inch black-and-white TVs, and the other half had transistor radios.

They found everyone, except Eric and Jerry.

Back in Harry's office for a few smokes, Terry and Marty outlined the meeting. "What are we going to talk about?" Terry asked Marty.

"I don't know," Marty responded.

"I don't know either," Terry said, seeing an opportunity to be a salesman. "I'll figure something out." They headed to the cafeteria.

The meeting was slated for 6:30 p.m. It could not interfere with primetime television.

Without *The A-Team,* there would be mayhem.

Ray and Wesley made their way into the kitchen, each taking a stale cake doughnut with sprinkles. The sound of the second-hand Hobart rattled in the background. Ray carried his hideously large gas-station coffee cup, which he promptly filled to the brim with stale coffee.

"Evening gents, when do the girls get here?" Ray asked.

"I couldn't get ahold of your sister, so I guess it's just us," Terry fired back.

"Nice, Terry, nice." Ray smiled and took a seat.

Ten minutes later, Johnny Luck surprisingly appeared, wafting scents of homeless alcohol—the unclear medium between shaving lotion, gingivitis, and Ripple. The odor was either coming from his mouth or his pores. He appeared coherent and indicative of the challenge the team would face.

Everyone was smoking, except Wesley and Ray.

Terry took control of the silence. “Does anyone know if Jerry is in the house?” His question was met with rotating heads.

“Someone go knock on his door. What about Harry and Jim?”

“Harry went home,” Marty responded, knowing that Harry knew about the meeting but would never attend anything too far off the edge of the working day.

Terry felt his stomach twitch with the thought that he forgot to invite Jim to the meeting.

“Jim?”

The crackling of a burning cigarette amplified the silence. Ray returned to announce that Jerry was nowhere to be found, but that a Grand Marquis had rumbled into the parking lot.

Terry looked toward Marty and back to the group, “All right, then. Welcome to the Saint Anthony softball team.”

Marty and Terry quickly assumed control of the businesslike meeting. They outlined rules and a possible schedule for the summer, all of which were fabrications. The goal was to avoid embarrassment. Winning would be an afterthought.

Terry fungoed the drinking topic.

“As to drinking, consumption will not be allowed on or near the field, and we would appreciate it if you would refrain from imbibing before games.”

He avoided the appearance of a counselor and instead projected himself as a fiery baseball manager, with rules that should be followed if they were to achieve fame and fortune. Like the baseball manager, he knew the real story.

No one responded. It may or may not have meant compliance.

He didn't realize that this was his first attempt, in his entire life, to articulate to anyone that drinking would impact success.

The players listened intently through full bellies and lingering buzzes. It may also have been a simple interest in being a part of something—recapturing the camaraderie and hope that a team once brought to their lives. Team was a concept lost in the uneven mire of alcoholism.

Residents gather around bottles, but once the bottle is empty, the team is gone.

Jim stood in the corner of the room with a feeling that had been lost in him. It wasn't a hangover; it was hope. It had been ingrained in Jim that the former was the prevailing truth at Saint Anthony, but this time he felt different.

Even though they were short a man, not including Harry, the cafeteria looked and smelled like a locker room.

Marty sat next to Terry for the duration of the meeting. Every manager needs a sidekick, and Marty was comfortable in his role as the baseball advisor. Like their lives, titles and responsibilities rotated daily.

Sitting quietly, Marty knew that he would lead on the baseball end. He rarely recognized his own abilities, but it was obvious to him, this one time in his life, that he was the only person in the room with skills. Someone had to conduct practices, select positions, and generally ensure the smooth operation of a ball club. While Marty's demeanor would suggest otherwise, he had little choice but to assume a leadership role. This time, he wanted it. He was on a team again.

"And therein lies the rule of operation, gentlemen," Terry concluded. "Now I'm turning this meeting over to Marty, our own University of Minnesota star baseball player and generally great American, and I mean 'generally' with the utmost respect."

"Thanks, Terry. Not sure about the star thing, but I am ready to help." Marty's large glasses floated to the end of his gin-blossoming nose.

"Right now, we have no assigned positions. Does anyone have a preference?" He was not commanding enough to elicit a response.

Wesley yelled out from the back of the room, "I need a glove!" The room collectively echoed the same in a chorus of head turns and nods.

"Equipment and all other items will be provided," Terry interjected. He had no clue as to the whereabouts of any equipment.

"What about jerseys?" Ray asked, hoping he would not be required to don anything other than his trademark black T-shirt. A front pocket for his pencils would be helpful, though.

"Those will be provided," Terry proclaimed, relighting a stub cigar. He didn't know about the jerseys either, but he was on a roll.

Marty continued, "Okay, once again, does anyone have a position preference?" He asked with a slightly more commanding tone. The room was silent.

"All right then. Positions will be assigned after the first practice," Marty said. He was just hoping the team would stay together beyond the meeting.

Reality set upon the room. Marty and Terry knew that their conversations of a team would not only require effort, but also a semblance of order, a trait that needed to be dusted off and tested for operational efficiency. The alternative would be to walk down the block and get drunk.

Tonight, even if it was a glistening, ice-cold bottle of premium ale, they would have chosen the team.

For the rest of the team, it was already toward the end of the middle of the month and most everyone was fresh out of funds, likely rendering the choice of beverage to be a plastic bottle of rubbing alcohol.

Terry adjourned the meeting.

"There you have it. That wraps it up for tonight, gents. Look to the bulletin board for our first practice and for any other pertinent announcements, opportunities, and generally interesting tidbits."

The Saint Anthony team was ready to play ball, such as it was. Now might be a good time to pray to the saint.

Marty, Terry, and Jim were alone in the cafeteria. Jim stood in the corner with a cigarette in his yellow hand, its ash nearly as long as its remaining life.

Wesley peered through the doorway, "Y'all talkin' about gloves? Just a reminder that I need a glove."

"Yes, Wes, we will have a glove for you. Left or right?" Terry replied, smart enough not to remind his chronically alcoholic teammate that the conversation had already taken place.

"Right," Wesley replied, his brow twisted from lack of confidence in which arm was for throwing, and which was for drinking. His baseball glove would be the opposite of his drinking glove. This, he knew.

"Right it will be," Terry announced, and Wesley retreated like a ghost.

"I think we have some work to do," Terry realized. "I'll get on the equipment thing. Right, Jim?" With Jim as his partner, Terry knew they could get just about anything, legal or illegal.

"Right," Jim nodded with a sinister smile. His cigarette was still in his hand, miraculously all ash.

"I'll try to come up with a roster, at least on paper. Showing up is another question," Marty added, knowing that for the first go-around, he would be throwing darts. He noted to himself that he questioned the commitment of his chronic alcoholic teammates, but they all lived in the same house.

"OK. Let's rally here tomorrow after lunch to set up the game plan," Terry seemed to order. If it was not procrastination, it certainly appeared that way. All steps were slow at the Saint Anthony, even the literal ones.

Jim barreled out of the lot to pick up egg foo young and watch TV, and Terry and Marty were back sitting in Harry's office, their faces glowing in silence from the black-and-white television. The night manager was clueless about the team.

The Twins game was over, so *The Love Boat* was being watched in both homes.

- -

Assembling a sports team with the collective years of addiction in the triple digits would be a challenge for anyone, even the greats—Tommy Lasorda, Earl Weaver, Billy Martin, and so on.

Now Marty was at the helm.

The key to success, which Marty, Terry, and Jim acknowledged, was that the pressure level needed to be on simmer. As soon as a modicum of stress enters daily life at Saint Anthony, the next step is to slip quietly into obscurity under the warm confines of a bottle.

Pressure was what brought them there in the first place. A quiet routine is what kept them there. It occasionally kept some of them sober.

Tommy Lasorda would be sitting by himself in the dugout.

Marty was the perfect manager. He was one of them. He wore the stripes of destitution and struggle, and his calm demeanor engendered trust and acceptance. The team was not about Marty, nor was it a statement for alcoholics across America. It was just a softball team. No pressure and almost no rules. Everyone was already in some form of clinical depression, so nothing Marty might do would make it any worse.

It was unusual to him, but Marty slowly began to feel leadership stirring within him, and he wasn't afraid.

In 1986, the Dodgers finished fifth in the National League West Division. They could have used Marty.

MARTY INTERLUDES

Lunchtime, 1990

At Mama's Pizza in Saint Paul, Peachy, the owner, recommends bibs.

"I was over at the Christ Center today," Marty said, as he took a bite of his Italian sausage. It was an enormous patty that was covered with mozzarella and marinara, stuffed in between two thick slices of bread, and covered again with mozzarella and marinara. Marty was moving through the sandwich from the top down, and he had reached the sausage.

"What was going on over there?" asked the case manager, as he enjoyed the same sandwich, attacking it sideways.

Luckily, they followed Peachy's recommendation.

"They had a meeting with some of the new guys, and Larry wanted me to talk with them."

"What did you say?"

"I told them about losing my job at the post office."

"And?"

"I said that drinking was the issue." Marty offered few details.

Marty's alcoholic life was mysterious. The case manager needed to know at least some of the details for the file, but they were difficult to uncover.

Marty often wrote poems about his feelings, but he rarely talked about the feelings or the poems. He was unabashed in his admission of the destructive powers of alcoholism, but his method of processing was internal. The case manager only knew that Marty was aware of his addiction. It was a start.

"I think one of the guys in the Christ Center group was at the Saint Anthony, but he wasn't on the team." Marty continued.

Marty changed the subject to the team. The case manager wanted to hear stories about the team, but his job was to learn about the "why" of Marty's addiction.

He wasn't a chemical dependency counselor; he was a job services case manager. So, he needed Marty to talk about the things that took him off the path of self-sufficiency. Marty had been sober for over a year, but he was only one mishap away from turning in the other direction. The case manager needed to understand the full story to keep him on the right path.

Self-sufficiency was the catchphrase of the 1980s.

The sandwich was the size of a small child. It was nearly an hour before the plates were clean, and the case manager still did not have enough file notes to formulate a solid plan for his client. Marty just wanted to talk about the team.

"What did you like most about the team? Winning games or time with the gents?" The case manager was delving.

"I think it was time with the guys. I don't think I really ever had that since high school. Back then, I felt like I was part of something."

"You two young men finished? Looks like you had a grand ol' time," the motherly server said, as she removed the plates. It looked like Marty and the case manager had had a fight to the death in the booth. There was marinara everywhere.

Marty kept coming back to the team. He was unusually talkative. As they sat in the booth with their bibs still on, he could see that the team was Marty's path forward.

Baseball carried him through his youth, and a softball team may have righted his path. "I miss that old Terry. He was something. Larry thinks he's dead."

"I'll see if I can look him up somewhere, maybe arrange a team reunion."

Marty and the case manager sat at Mama's for another hour. The server brought tiny ice-cream cones, and Marty never stopped talking about his teammates or his time on the diamond in Saint Paul.

The team was interesting and fun for the case manager, but now it mattered to his job. Later that evening, the case manager wrote in Marty's case file: "Had lunch and talked about marinara and baseball. A softball team saved Marty's life."

CHAPTER TWENTY

PRACTICE OVER PLASMA

Over the years, the residence held its share of PhDs and teachers. There were also artists.

Terry was neither an academic nor an artist, and when he sat down at the wooden carrel in his room to draft the practice announcement, he was at a loss. He was not illiterate. There were few at the Saint Anthony who could not read or write. Most residents read voraciously, whether it was a dog-eared book from the office library or the label on a can of cleaning fluid.

Terry was too busy talking to read.

With a piece of old stationery and a pen he lifted from the weekly rate hotel on University Avenue, Terry scribbled an announcement.

Softball Team 1st Practice. Thursday at Raymond Field. 4:30 p.m. Ask Terry or Marty.

He walked over to the kitchen bulletin board and placed it in the middle, adjacent to the notice from the Plasma Center.

He looked at the notice and lit up a cigarette. The stationery was from Terry's old company. On the top of the sheet, it read *DRYCO,* along with his name.

Terry stared at the announcement through the entire cigarette, recalling his first box of stationery. He couldn't afford a watermark or even a single fiber of cotton. It didn't matter; he had a business, and he was on his way.

Terry's mind was moving to what went awry when he was interrupted by an odor that traveled up his nose and down his throat.

"Hot damn! You boys playing softball? I'll take a swig of that!"

Terry wiped the spit off the back of his neck and turned around. Jack was heavily intoxicated and hardly able to stand. He had two sandwiches in each hand, and his white tank top was covered with mustard.

"Sure, Jackie. Love to have you on board." Terry ultimately wanted to shake Jack, and he knew that he would forget about the conversation. If he made it to his room and didn't die, Jack wouldn't come out until the practice was over. It was easy to be irritated by Jack but nearly impossible to be angry. He was simply too sad.

Jack passed out in the cafeteria. He would eventually be dragged to his room by the night manager.

Back in Harry's office, Marty was watching TV, legs closely crossed and a thin smile on his face. He had been a frail, contented elder for his whole life.

"I posted the practice notice, so we are game on for Thursday," Terry said, as he put out his half-smoked cigarette and lit up a large cigar.

"Okay," Marty quietly returned with a grin of yellowing, broken teeth, his smile wide enough to offer a glimpse of the bridgework he picked up from a volunteer dentist.

Thursday was another perfect spring day—one of those damp mornings that grows into Mother Nature's reward for a brutal winter. Nice weather is always noticed in Minnesota and always talked about.

At the Saint Anthony, spring mornings brought the feeling of a new start—fresh air filling the dry halls and bright-blue skies illuminating the dimly yellowed rooms as invitations to embrace a new day. Spring would even cover up the foot odor, if only for a moment.

Springtime sometimes even spurred an occasional resident to the local job fair or to an AA meeting. For most, the season's crisp, fresh air made it easier and considerably more enjoyable to pick up aluminum cans or walk to the liquor store.

Marty and Terry entered the dining area at the same time. Most of the longer-term residents showed up at the onset of mealtime for no apparent reason other than habit.

Marty and Terry sat at the same table. They never reflected on it, even in a chemically induced moment, but they needed each other.

It was not a typical day. Practice was at 4:30 p.m. It felt like Little League, the dread of practice mixed with the bright anticipation of playing a game. Nobody likes practice, but everyone wants to be on a team. Terry and Marty had the feeling. They had something on the docket, and it did not involve drinking. It reminded them of younger and considerably more hopeful times.

"I hope Jim remembers the equipment," Terry initiated, attempting to recall whether arrangements had been made. He was worried that his dual role of general manager and provocateur could be severely compromised if he did not produce a few gloves, one bat, and one ball.

"I am sure he is good for it," responded Marty, knowing that Jim was a man of integrity and diligence. It was the least of Marty's worries.

"I haven't seen anyone from the team in a day or so," Marty continued, mumbling through a fresh Parliament. "I saw Wes at late-night snack a few days ago, and that was it."

"Well, sir, it might just be you and me out there today taking on the world, like Mantle and Maris tearing up the league," Terry responded. He had to be prepared for disappointment, which for his entire life was approached with avoidance, humor, and alcohol.

A no-show team would have been a crisis in any other clubhouse. There was also the question of an opponent.

Contingencies and white-board diagrams were nonexistent. The moment was lived for, sadly in this case, and any sort of planning was done in a fluid manner—sometimes literally. It would all work out, even if everything crashed beneath it.

Marty and Terry finished their doughnuts and hoped for the best.

The sun rose high over the residence, lightly warming its tattered roof amid a cool spring breeze. It was a day for stadium planners and true lovers of the game.

Neither Marty nor Terry, and particularly not Harry, had considered the weather's impact on the likelihood of a full team. The pressure to seize the day and "get outside and enjoy the weather" was a rare philosophy for the residents.

Marty was never a happy drunk. He was not a sad drunk either. He failed to allow emotional access for even the most severe crisis. The world simply did not bother him. In analytic circles, his philosophy did not mesh with his need to stack empty cans of Schlitz in a pyramid, but it guided him to an apparently peaceful existence.

On this practice day, he grew nervous to the point of wanting to drink, which unsettled him. Equipment, attendance, and responsibility weighed heavily. The blue sky made a difference. A ball and a few gloves would help.

At 3 p.m., Marty and Terry instinctively converged in Harry's office. Unlike the MLB clubhouse, there were no deli trays, clean towels, or tubs of Bud Light. Harry was at his metal desk and the TV was humming a rerun. The inviting spring breeze cut the smell of smoldering cigarettes in overfilled ashtrays.

Marty sat in his usual chair and lit a Parliament. Terry stood in the doorway.

Harry had an unusual wisp of a smile protruding through his salt-and-pepper beard. Back in the day, he had been a terrible poker player, largely because he was drunk, but also because elation was so unusual to him that it was obvious.

Harry nonchalantly pointed to the corner. "Jim stopped in early this morning and dropped off that box."

Terry walked to the corner of the room and stood over a large box with "Listerine" marked over it. He remembered the box from when Jim dumped 50 bottles of donated mouthwash. He knew exactly what it was. He wanted to take credit for a nefarious skill in acquisitions, but he knew that he was lucky. He peeled open the top, revealing an array of baseball gloves and softballs.

Harry smiled. "He said he would meet you on the field with the bats."

Standing over the box, Terry looked to Marty, smiled, and with his best Mel Allen, said, "How about that?!"

Marty's eyes opened wide through his thick, fingerprinted glasses. "How about it? Let's play some ball."

PART THREE

TAKE THE FIELD, BUT NO STEALING

CHAPTER TWENTY-ONE

PITCHERS & CATCHERS REPORT

Marty and Terry slowly pulled the old red Radio Flyer wagon in a happy zigzag to Raymond Field. The wagon was filled with gloves and softballs. There was also a Wiffle ball. They stammered even when sober. To the untrained eye, they appeared intoxicated, but in fact they were merely tired old men with a combined 60 years of generally falling flat on their faces. If there was an association of Tired Old Drunks, they would have a class action against the liquor industry for the lingering effects of concussions, torn ACLs, and a host of other falling-down-drunk maladies.

Back at the residence to ensure key parties rolled out of bed at the appropriate midafternoon time, Harry was excited. Jim had arranged for an early shift change so that Harry could join the team. Excitement was a change for Harry, and for the first time since he lifted himself off a urine-soaked floor at the detox center, he accepted it. It was also the first time he had smiled when he was alone.

By the time Marty and Terry arrived, the sun was casting long shadows on the infield gravel.

The diamond was nicely groomed due to the cadre of Little League dads needing an excuse for ales. They were foolish to think that their spousal authorities were clueless to the fact that a one-hour job actually took three hours. In fact, their wives were onto the scam and considered their departure a blessing.

The grass was thick for a public field, the base paths were free of valleys, and the mound was a perfect circle with a scrubbed-clean pitching rubber. Even the batter's box lines were neatly in place, and baselines were perfect to first and third.

Marty and Terry felt as though the field had been groomed just for them. It didn't occur to them that a team of 12U sixth graders would arrive at 7 p.m. to find their beautiful field reeking of vomit and cigarette butts.

Practice was scheduled for 4:30 p.m., but Marty and Terry were on the field by 4. Time was oddly perceived at the Saint Anthony. Despite failure's association with tardiness, the inability to reach a target time on either side of the clock was the issue. Early arrivals were common, but instead of remaining until the target time, exit would ensue, resulting in the same failure as though one was tardy. It meant that Terry and Marty had to be prepared for everything. They both wore watches—Marty an old Timex with a scratched face and Terry a cheap Casio watch that he thought fashionable. They were among the few at the Saint Anthony who had any concept of time beyond eating or drinking.

Like most city fields, there was no dugout or any fancy area for managers to pace nervously and spit. There were two long benches on either side of the field, each behind a twisted chain-link backstop that could use a touch of city capital. Marty and Terry pulled the wagon up near the batter's box and took a seat on one of the green benches. Marty lit a cigarette, and Terry pressed a few tiny buttons on his watch with his sausage-like thumb.

"Figured we'd just do drills—throwing and batting—see where folks are at," Marty puffed, the smoke heading straight up in the windless air. The breeze had vanished.

"Fine by me, that is if anyone shows up," Terry returned, looking as though he was itching for a cold beer and smelling like he already had a case of it.

Marty strained his body 45 degrees to extricate his wallet. The softball-shaped billfold could have been on display in a creepy museum of oddities. Homeless wallets were suitcases carrying life histories. On occasion, a stray dollar could be discovered folded tightly in the morass. On even more rare occasions, thousands of dollars could be tucked within the confusion. Marty knew an old bridge dweller who carried thousands of dollars hidden in folded up newspapers. Sadly, he was a Korean War vet who never made it back from the horrors of war. Everyone loved Zeke, but only Marty knew about the money.

Marty's wallet did not contain a single item of marketable currency. It did, however, contain the team roster.

Jim

Terry

Harry

Johnny Luck

Ray

Wesley

Jerry

Me

Marty stared at the roster, refolded it, leaned 45 degrees, and filed it away in his life history.

As Marty and Terry pondered what a team would look like with no players, they were startled by the thundering sound of clanking metal, gravel, and broken branches. It was not Jim's car.

They stood up from the splintered longboard and watched with admiration and worry as Wesley flew through the bushes alongside the railroad tracks on a beat-up Schwinn Varsity bicycle, its tricked-out fenders clanging against the frame and its general disrepair making a poetic serenade for a noble and joyous entry to the field of play. Wesley had arrived, and he was making it clear.

Pedaling from the residence on a pothole-infested street, alternating between street and sidewalk, Wesley made it through the neighborhood to the rail corridor, which was gravel mixed with varying levels of debris from kids and transients. Miraculously, Wesley made it to the field's edge without a scrape. Marty attributed this to some higher power's desire for a game to be played.

The proud Wesley took it upon himself to plow through center field and travel the bases with his shiny new ride. Marty and Terry stood in silence as the show transpired, not for a second wondering how Wesley had procured the bicycle.

Making the turn around second base, Wesley was losing control. Taking a wide arc to the edge of the base path, he spun his arm like Pete Townsend, waving himself home. Of course, since a speeding bicycle typically requires two hands to comply with the laws of physics, the bike began to gyrate, sending Wesley at full speed toward home plate. By this point, he would have been called out for leaving the base path, but he barreled toward home, tumbling face-first into the wiry backstop.

To the uninitiated, it appeared that Wesley was injured. On the contrary, Saint Anthony residents had become hardened to their fumbling foibles. For insiders, falling face-down was such a common occurrence that witnessing it would elicit either nonchalance or full-blown laughter.

Terry sauntered to the backstop, a smile on his weathered countenance.

"That was quite the show, Mr. Wesley," Terry said, lighting up a cigarette. "Are we OK?"

"All good, coach, all good," Wesley said, snapping to his feet and brushing off his gravel-covered body. The tiny rocks made it under his skin, with specks of alcohol-infused blood dotting his snap-on denim shirt. The fresh scrapes allowed access to the full odor of a chronic alcoholic. He literally smelled like a distillery.

Wesley immediately produced a tattered handkerchief, wiped his face, and readied himself for his next adventure.

"Ready to play ball! Just put me where you need me."

Marty approached home plate, wary to light a cigarette in the vicinity of Wesley's toxic breath.

"Bikes over by the bushes, grab a seat on the bench," Terry motioned, as if he hadn't seen the Ringling Brothers show that just transpired in front of him. Despite the excitement surrounding a divergence from routine, there was one thing Marty and Terry knew from the tipple-soaked get-go. It was beginning to appear like another day at the Saint Anthony.

Wesley obediently took his seat at the end of the bench, imaginary bubbles popping around his head. His face gleamed. Wesley was intoxicated and ready to play ball.

Marty and Terry stood quietly at the rusty backstop, smoking cigarettes. City ballparks do not have ashtrays, so Raymond Field would soon amass a noticeable collection of cigarette butts. Eventually, each base would be accompanied by a small pile of butts.

Another 15 or so minutes passed when, in usual fanfare, Jim's car skidded to a halt against the curb nearest the field, its wide doors quickly screeching open to produce just Jim and Jerry.

Marty and Terry collectively breathed a smoker's sigh of relief. They now had five players on the field, counting Jim.

Jim looked ready to play. He had a baseball mitt, and he was wearing a baseball cap that made him look even more like Freddy Krueger, with stringy hair hanging down from the tiny hat. He was also the only one wearing cleats. That was enough for Marty and Terry.

"OK, coach, let's get this party started," Jim exclaimed with atypical exuberance. He lit up a smoke, towering over the diminutive Wesley to the point that he looked like his dad at Little League.

Just as Jim's still-lit match flew through the air in a daredevil baton twirl, Harry stealthily emerged from the bushes and took his seat on the bench. He was crisply dressed as always—tall-brimmed baseball cap; navy T-shirt tucked into straight, unfaded jeans; and bright-white tennis shoes. Harry's first thought on the bench was his shoes on the dirty gravel. Luckily, he had plenty of liquid polish in his drawer at the residence, unless someone had absconded with it for its ethoxylated alcohol.

"OK boys, ol' Harry is ready to knock one out," he said, welcoming himself to the discussion with unusual positivity.

Surprised that Harry showed up, Jim downplayed his elation with sarcasm.

"Nice work, ol' Harry. Now we got a team," he gruffly said.

They didn't have a full team, but at this point, it didn't matter. They had Marty, Terry, Wesley, Jim, Jerry, and Harry. It was a mark in the win column.

- -

Terry walked in front of the bench with his head down, turned toward the field, and stopped midway through the pitcher's mound and the first base line, his hands clasped together. Marty took a position behind him, just off to the side of the mound, facing the team with his head down and his arms crossed.

They weren't deliberate in their attempt to appear managerial. They just weren't sure what to do next.

Terry slowly turned around.

"Gentlemen, welcome to the Saint Anthony Residence softball club." His voice was higher-pitched than usual.

"On behalf of Mr. Peterson and myself, we are pleased you could join us today. You are here because you want to be here, and not because anyone told you to be here by virtue of a house edict or court of law." He paused. He knew to keep his mindset on the point that just throwing a ball in the general direction of a glove would be an accomplishment.

"You're here, boys, because you want to have a few laughs, maybe take a shot or two at some naysayers, and generally have a good time executing the workings of America's favorite pastime, so let's get started."

"That's right, coach!" Wesley loudly proclaimed in revival fashion, jumping to his feet and running out to the field. Marty and Terry took it as a sign of what to do next.

"OK, team, let's hit the field for some basic drills to get the ball rolling," Terry fired off as though darting to the field was the order he was going to give anyway.

Jim, Jerry, and Harry slowly rose from the bench, discarded their still-lit cigarettes, and creaked their way to the outfield in a collective manner befitting of weathered souls. They were hardly into fitness and, coupled with the usual maladies of alcoholism, their movements were slow. By the time they joined Wesley in the outfield, it was time for another smoke.

They stood side by side in short right-center. None of them had brought a glove. Common elements of survival are often missed by the destitute, and the ballfield was no different.

Terry yelled out with a chuckle, "Gather back in here and grab a glove—you can't play ball without gloves, ya knuckleheads!" He knew right then that Jim was not his ringer, despite the cleats.

Marty handed each of them a mitt.

"Drop them back with me after practice," Marty quietly indicated, knowing full well that if he allowed them to keep the gloves, they would be sold for a swig.

They were now into practice for half an hour and not a single ball had been thrown. They only had another half hour left before the unannounced conclusion.

"Alright, let's take some balls to get warmed up," Terry ordered.

Terry and Marty had not talked about who would lead the practice. Luckily, years of life at the Saint Anthony eradicated pride, making most decisions those of expediency.

Since Marty was holding a bat, Terry rolled him a ball.

Marty tossed the ball into the air on a perfect upward trajectory, took the required step, and with a textbook swing, delivered a clean liner. If not for the effects of industry-leading alcoholism, he could easily have been mistaken for a minor league batting coach. He had it in him, and it felt good.

What transpired as the ball sailed toward the outfield was another story.

Three of the four teammates in the field were already enjoying another round of tobacco, so it was up to Wesley to make the play.

Excited and terrified, he ran toward the ball with both hands outstretched, his eyes wide like an anxious Little Leaguer.

He reached out his oversize glove and yelled, "I got it!"

Coming off Marty's bat, the ball had unusual velocity, nearly screaming through the air. Wesley immediately outstretched his arm farther than when he unsuccessfully challenged his cell-mates to a pull-up contest at the county jail.

With the ball on the rise, it abruptly and loudly met the weathered glove, sending Wesley and his straightened arm careening backward as though struck by a bullet train. Landing flat on his back with his arm still outstretched, he sat up and revealed his yellow and uneven teeth.

"Got it!" He was gleaming with pride.

Jim, Jerry, and Harry were either standing in awe or their dulling senses had simply missed the speed of what transpired before them. They stood motionless as Wesley puffed his chest like a Broadway dancer.

"Nice one, Wes," Jim exclaimed, coughing through smoke.

"Not bad." Terry turned to Marty, "Maybe we have something here."

"Give it time," Marty said, tossing up the ball and delivering a hard grounder right to the middle of his outfield crew. While Wesley was still holding the other ball from his epic stop, the new ball quickly scooted through the other three players, their heads turning too slowly to keep up with the puttering ball. The residence was slo-mo every day, which apparently applied to the ballfield as well.

"Look alive out there, boys," Terry yelled, preoccupied with a desire to have a cigarette. He tossed another ball to Marty.

Jim walked toward the ball that slipped through, his lanky body moving like a Sasquatch. He picked up the ball, turned around, and to the surprise of the others, he made an extraordinarily weak throw toward Terry. The throw was not unusual for brittle bones, but it seemed disappointing that the towering man of the people did not have a howitzer.

Terry moved it along. "Alright, let's stay focused!" Terry threw another ball toward Marty, who had a smoke pinched between his teeth in full concentration as the fungo master.

Over the next 30 minutes, Marty hit liners, grounders, and pop-ups toward the slowly congealing group of misfits. In the beginning, most of the balls scooted through the tight-knit pack, but as the hits kept coming, the group began to gel.

Practice was working. Wesley would get in front of the ball and Harry would get behind it. Jim would field the ball and relay to Jerry, who was only 6 feet away. It was not a well-oiled machine, nor did it seem to be well lubricated in other ways, which in one case was a good thing.

Years of brotherhood under bridges brought them together in one way, but this time it was for another, and it seemed to be working.

Pray to Saint Anthony and you will find it—or field it.

- -

Marty continued to shag liners. In the distance, a Little League team trickled in toward the field. Anxious parents began to gather behind the backstop, with their equally anxious children starting warm-ups behind the visitor bench. The Little League team was the antithesis of the team on the field. They had a lifetime of hope and opportunity in front of them.

They also had a city permit to play at 5:30 p.m. every Monday and Thursday evening for the next 60 days.

The ubiquitous 12U Tigers refocused their pregame ritual to observe the unusual scene before them.

The typical sixth-grade class would not find the Saint Anthony Residence on their list of places to save the world. Their eyes were untrained, and the reaction was fear and mystery. The kids had witnessed homelessness, but not the inner workings of a home for record-setting alcoholics. Except for the Saint Anthony residents themselves, few outsiders had viewed the bottom of this bottle.

What would normally be a wild pack of preteen gamers—throwing balls, carelessly swinging bats, and secretly inhaling sugared treats—quickly became a dazed gallery of onlookers. In front of them were four apparent derelicts in the outfield and two in the infield, seemingly harmless and playing softball.

Oxymoron is one of those complicated words that young people somehow know, and they focused on it. Hobos playing softball. If the scene were downtown or, worse yet, in their neighborhood, fear would be in their young eyes. On Raymond Field, it was wonderment. No one was panhandling and no one was covered in newspaper. Blood alcohol levels were mostly hovering around nonviolent limits, and the lingering booze waft was dampened by the spring air. Bottles of Mad Dog 20/20 were nowhere to be found, in sight or in bags.

A few of the kids wore pro-style eye paint and dual batting gloves. They all stood dumbfounded. Marty continued to fungo sizable drives, Terry looked as though he was managing, and four players were amassing a decent fielding percentage. For the moment, the residents were a softball team, not the dregs of society.

The 12U coaches and parents were unsure how to react. At first glance, the team practicing appeared to be a collection of locals who took over their field and danced around the park, drunk and happy. Upon closer review, they were homeless and threatening. A call to the police would allay the impending danger from "those people."

Before the nervous parents could head for a pay phone, Marty and Terry walked toward them. It was a moment of terror. What do they want? Are they panhandlers? Should we run?

The kids went back to warm-ups. The parents put their car keys between their fingers.

"Field's yours, boys," Terry quipped as he readied the wagon. "Our work is finished here—see y'all next week."

Terry wasn't sure he would see them next week. Any schedule he had over the past decade mostly related to drinking.

The parents stood motionless as the Saint Anthony team packed up and departed.

The only thing that remained were three cigarette-butt anthills dispersed toward the strong side of Marty's bat, in front of the bench, and in right-center. There was a small puddle where Wesley made his first catch. He had vomited.

They may have been grizzled, but the Saint Anthony squad walked off the diamond like an elated Little League team.

Players zigzagged mostly without chemical inducement.

Wesley and Jim gleefully recounted moments of outfield heroism as they bumped into each other in a moment of worker-client solidarity.

"He hit it like a rocket, but I dove for the out," Wesley recounted, walking his bicycle as it rattled against him like a string of tin cans.

"You got that right, Mr. Wes—you were a stud out there," Jim laughed, his cigarette nearly falling out of his mouth.

Terry and Marty insisted on highlighting areas of improvement. "All in all, it was an excellent first practice," Terry proclaimed. "Jim, try to square up on the ball, and Wes, you need to move forward to the ball, not wait for the glory dive."

Marty had a Parliament hanging from his mouth and a glimmer of a smile. He knew Terry had no clue what he was talking about, but it sounded good.

The Little Leaguers and dads observed from a distance, avoiding the field in disbelief, fear, and awe.

Jim, Wesley, Harry, and Jerry approached Jim's car, laughing and telling stories as though their 60-or-so-minute practice was an entire game against the Yankees.

Jim offered an opportunity to skip the rubbing alcohol celebration in the bushes: "Alright, boys, time to hit the road for the Lord's duty. Anyone need a lift home?"

"I'll take a flyer on the ride. Thanks, Jim," Jerry responded.

Public displays of indecision at the Saint Anthony routinely meant that a resident would seek solace in chemicals. Jerry had coins in his pocket that dictated opportunity like a divining rod, the small amount assisting a bulk purchase among friends. He disappeared into the bushes.

Just as Jim was about to get into his car, a police cruiser pulled up behind him. The officer walked toward Jim. The older man was large and heavily equipped with leather holders containing unknown devices.

"You all have a permit for this field?"

"I reckon I don't," Jim responded, angrily.

Harry had quietly walked away, and Terry backed out of

the conversation. It was instinctual. Marty lit up a cigarette, also instinctual.

"Can I see some ID?" The officer looked mad and had his hand on one of the mysterious leather pouches.

The Little Leaguers were staring at the police officer as their nervous dads struggled to hustle them from the impending scene.

"Don't got no ID."

Most of the team was up the tracks by now. They hustled more than they did at practice.

"I don't like your attitude. Up against the car!" The officer moved toward Jim.

"Make me." Jim was inexplicably defiant.

The two men immediately engaged in a multilayered guy-hug, first a midair arm wrestle and then the embrace.

"Mr. Jim B.! How's the skinny, old salty dog?"

"I'm alright, Adam, what brings you to this side of town?"

"Got a call that there were ne'er-do-wells at the park. Didn't figure it would be ol' Jimmy."

One of the dads had made it to a phone.

Two decades prior, Adam had wrestled Jim to the Rice Street pavement in front of Honky Mike's Bar. Jim was a boxer, and Adam was a wrestler. Intoxicated boxers don't land punches against sober wrestlers in uniform. Jim spent the night in the Ramsey County jail on a continuing path downward, and the officer continued his nightly path on Rice Street. It would be years, troubles, and eventual sobriety before their first guy-hug.

"You know, you should probably get a permit for the field or I'm going to get a call every week. It's great to see you, old friend, but I'd rather do it over lunch."

"Maybe you and your boys should get on that," Jim said to Marty.

"Sure, Jim. Good to see you, Adam."

"Absolutely, Marty."

Marty caught up to the retreating Terry and they headed home. They enjoyed an easy walk back to the residence, making it just in time for funeral lasagna left by Cossetta's Ristorante. The cycle of life often ended at Saint Anthony, but on occasion it ended somewhere else, much to the elation of 50-some chronic alcoholics.

The kitchen had cleared out and the sound of a Hobart filled a room of clean plastic tablecloths, a fan blowing in the kitchen, and the general lull of satiated residents. Since most of the drinking was completed during the day, it was strangely calm in the evenings.

Terry lit up a cigarette and offered his non-technical assessment. "I thought we actually looked good out there."

"Not bad," Marty replied, his sauce-soaked fingers lifting a Parliament. The cigarette would be worthless once the burn hit the grease spot he deposited on it.

Marty and Terry completed their discussion of the day's practice, moving to Harry's office, the day's observations, and *Kojak.* The TV illuminated the room.

Eventually, everyone retired to a quiet night at the Saint Anthony. The windows were open for the season, and the residents were asleep, naturally or otherwise.

MARTY INTERLUDES

Untitled

By Marty Peterson, Undated
(Written on DRYCO Stationery)

These are the lonely ones
picking cigarette butts from the street
or out of sand ashtrays
What thoughts invade their
bowed heads
obvious to strangers'
passing eyes
They cast their staring eyes
upon the ground
old clothes and worn shoes
add sadness to the body bent
Other days perhaps
found their head erect
looking skyward

CHAPTER TWENTY-TWO

HOME FIELD

Raymond Field was never officially called Raymond Field. According to city records and the rusty sign covered in buckthorn, the field was Langford Park. It was named after Nathaniel Langford, an early local leader and the eventual first superintendent of Yellowstone Park.

The neighborhood was proud to call it Langford. They cited its namesake whenever possible, thrusting it as a point of pride in conversations throughout the quaint historic neighborhood.

Despite the tenuous link to a national park, the old-timers, the really old-timers, called it Raymond Field. They remembered that, in Saint Paul, neighborhoods are identity. East Side, West Side, North End, Highland, Rondo, and Frogtown defined lives.

Raymond Field was just off Raymond Avenue, one of the central thoroughfares in the Saint Anthony Park neighborhood. Thus, it is Raymond Field. The newcomers never challenged the old-timers, and vice versa.

For Saint Anthony residents, geography ruled over history.

As spring settled in, one thing for certain ruled Raymond Field: baseball. Little League baseball, old-timer baseball, grade school baseball, high school baseball, T-ball, softball, beep ball,

Wiffle ball, coach pitch, fast pitch, and slow pitch—any iteration of ball-to-bat was in the field of play at Raymond Field.

Children wore oversize jerseys as they swung wildly at balls set on tees. Teenagers wore undersize, pressed uniforms and wristbands to be like their MLB heroes. Old-timers wore oversize sweatpants covered with shorts for no reason. Teams were lined up two and three deep, and games were played one after the other.

The day after practice, Marty and Terry emerged from the bushes. They needed a home field.

Entering the field through the back bushes was the preferred route for Saint Anthony residents, as demonstrated by an impressive range of strewn malt liquor bottles and empty canisters of cleaning fluid. Marty and Terry took notice of the small pile of empty Windex bottles next to a 2-liter soda bottle.

Marty and Terry were on a mission to lock down the field, something they realized was escalating in importance with each step toward the warming house. The field was packed.

In Minnesota, park buildings are known as warming houses. Their primary use is as a warm respite for Minnesota's most prolific athletic participants—ice-skaters. Like fine fortified wines, the buildings were aged with the smell of sweaty socks and vintage hockey equipment. Feelings of olfactory nostalgia were certain for anyone who ever wore a pair of skates in Minnesota.

Approaching the warming house in hopes for a conversation with a parks worker, Marty and Terry were worried. Being worried together was an unusual concept at the Saint Anthony. Normally, one party was worried because the other party was confident.

Without dedicated use of Raymond Field, their options for a team would be limited.

There were no other fields within walking distance. Taking the bus would lead to immediate defections, mostly inadvertent.

The percentage of residents who would embark and disembark a bus at a prescribed time and location would be low. Some might never come back to the residence. They would forfeit every game.

Marty and Terry entered the warming house. The cement floor was dotted with chips, and there were wooden benches lining the walls. They approached the solitary metal desk and its teenage occupant.

Terry stood tall and businesslike. "We would like to reserve the south field for a softball team."

"You need a permit," the parks worker responded, disinterested and failing to make eye contact above the tattered paperback in his hands.

"How do we get one?" Terry was concerned that the young gentleman had neither knowledge nor authority.

"Just fill out the form." The worker pulled out a piece of paper from the metal desk and slid it past what was revealed to be *The Official Rules of Baseball.* The worker's notes intimated that he was studying the diminishing art of baseball scoring. Terry started to like him. Marty liked him right away.

Marty and Terry scanned the form. The selection of dates and a payment section stared back in large print over multiple paragraphs of tiny print. The fee was $50. It was the middle of the month. If every single resident at the Saint Anthony emptied their pockets at the same moment, they would be short about $49.25. Add the petty cash drawer and they would be short the same amount.

"Will do. Pencil us in for the next 12 Thursdays from 4 to 5:30 p.m. We'll be back with a check."

"Roger that." The worker surprisingly agreed. The worker liked Terry. He pulled out a schedule book and looked up, "What's the name?"

"Saint Anthony Residence."

Terry and Marty looked at each other. They were officially on the city books.

The youthful apprentice scribbled "Saint Anthony Residence" in his book through the end of July. It was shocking that any field in softball-hungry Saint Paul would be available on prime-time Thursdays in the summertime. A first stroke of luck.

It was even more shocking that the Saint Anthony was the group who reserved it. They would need more luck.

Marty and Terry walked back to the residence, confident that Jim would take care of the fee, a bargain. They were filled with adrenaline. It was natural alchemy.

Neither Marty nor Terry were sullen people. Unlike most Saint Anthony residents, Terry and Marty never felt it was the end of the line or that they had fallen into a life of hopelessness.

While clearly the end of one road for some, Saint Anthony did not mean a total loss of hope for Marty and Terry.

But they knew exactly where they were.

Marty and Terry noticed something peculiar as they stepped over the Windex bottles on their way back to the residence. Normally, those at Saint Anthony were without victories. They had forgotten that brief, particularly satisfying moment after accomplishment. It was the finality of success; a moment of calm reflection and understanding of a job well done.

Walking into the residence, Marty and Terry remembered that feeling, and good decisions had led them there.

They rolled into Harry's office, lit celebratory cigarettes, and contemplated strategy. They handed over the permit information to Harry for Jim's signature and hopeful payment.

"You're going to have to ask Jim to handle this. Above my pay grade," Harry responded.

"Sort of figured as much," Marty responded, unusually sarcastic.

The wheels were in motion. Harry smiled through his well-coiffed Abe Lincoln beard when he saw the permit. An eternal pessimist in a house full of underachievement, Harry also felt a momentary rush at the team's official christening, an unusual emotion that quickly retreated. He knew that he could handle the signature and fee, but he wanted Marty and Terry to lead the process, and the men.

"Hey Harry, someone threw up again in the laundry room," Ray announced, his $2 aviator sunglasses dangling on his nose like Tom Cruise. "We ready to play some ball, boys?"

"Practice is next Thursday at 4 p.m. at Raymond Field. I'll post a notice on the bulletin board. You're the first to know, boss," Terry proclaimed, deliberately not asking Ray why he missed the first practice.

"I'll be there, gents." Ray quickly left the premises on his way to do nothing.

"There you have it. Practice Thursday at 4 p.m. I'll post it on the board." Terry never posted it.

"I thought the boys did well yesterday. Now we just need to get a full team." Marty said, uneasy with another practice of only six players.

Marty knew that the real challenge wasn't a permit. It was a roster. He needed nine players to arrive on time and in a condition well enough to avoid attention. Playing would be secondary.

He also worried about alcohol. Half of America played softball with a cooler of suds on the bench. How could a few 16-ounce cans of malt liquor make a difference at this level? It was not the malt liquor that worried Marty. It was the rubbing alcohol.

Marty knew that his roster would withstand an occasional case of Schlitz. Unfortunately, the end of the month could be an easy out.

Team chemistry, on this team, would be literal.

CHAPTER TWENTY-THREE

FRONT-OFFICE SUPPORT

The next day, Marty, Terry, and Harry gathered over a breakfast of scrambled eggs, some sort of rectangular meat product, and stale toast that refused to be softened by oily margarine. The crumpled foil ball of oleo may have been on the table since the building opened.

Neither Terry nor Marty had seen much of the team since practice. The middle of the month was ending, and alchemy was in the air. Marty and Terry were concerned.

There was a Twins day game with the Yankees at the Metrodome, which would make for an early 12:10 p.m. start. This would cut into *Cannon* reruns for Harry. Harry loved William Conrad's Cannon. He was a tough, sophisticated straight shooter: "The truth is like rain—it doesn't care who gets wet."

The game was a tough go for the Twins against the mighty Bronx Bombers. Maybe it was the world's most powerful metropolis intimidating the down-home charm of Minnesota, but somehow the Yankees always had the Twins' number.

Marty was particularly interested in the game. The Twins' former phenom catcher and all-American boy, Butch Wynegar, was now a Yankee. Fans across America vilify their bright-eyed heroes for defecting to the Mighty Yankees, but Marty liked the kid, looking past the defection and the fact that the "kid" was already into his 30s.

"Wynegar hit a game winner off Catfish Hunter in '76. Rookie. The kid's first home major league home run. Good kid," Marty mumbled as he lit up his fifth Parliament. It was shocking to think that Marty would remember anything at all from 1976, an especially difficult year with his face mostly against the pavement and his brain submerged in Blatz.

From baseball stats to pyramids of empty beer cans, Marty remembered everything. His recall likely had something to do with the fact that, even in his hard-drinking days, he read voraciously—calisthenics for the brain. He watched television sparingly, except for baseball and a few favorite shows. Even in Harry's office with the TV blaring, Marty was thinking and hardly watching, except for baseball.

Bob Kurtz transitioned to a commercial, "And that's the end of the second—no score here at Yankee Stadium. We'll be right back." A spring breeze sifted through the basement-level screens to cleanse the odors with Minnesota-nice and offer a comforting whistle of nature to an otherwise quiet building full of street-level alcoholics.

With the score still tied at zero in the second, the solace of spring was interrupted by the great American sound of gravel being crushed by Detroit-powered Pennsylvania steel. Jim's car buried a shoulder into the world. While his gaunt face hardly lived up to Detroit toughness, he was a giant at the people's helm of Saint Anthony. He still looked like a skinny Sasquatch.

Jim's timing was opportune.

"Jim, just the man I wanted to see," Terry announced as Jim turned the corner into Harry's office.

The conversation lasted 20 cigarettes; at 7 minutes per cigarette, divided by four people, it equaled 35 minutes. It was long enough for the Twins to fall into a hole.

Jim was pulled in a thousand directions. Ordinarily, in social service hierarchies, there was a top-level director who handled all the public politics, there were policy managers, there were site managers, and there were janitors. Jim was all of them, except for the politics. The stress he suffered as a result was giving him insomnia enough that he had to drink coffee and take nutritional supplements just to stay upright.

"OK, if the permit is your main issue, I'd say we're looking good. I would have thought players in detox were the issue." Jim concluded, finishing a hard swig of the vanilla supplement with a long drag from a wet cigarette.

The permit fee was easy, and no one was incarcerated, at least not yet. Fielding a team was the real issue, and at some point, they would also need an opponent.

Later that evening, Jim and the Queen were decompressing at home. Springtime in Minnesota is an odd moment for the social service industry. The change of season brings a new dawn of possibilities, leaving behind the dangers of the cold and bringing with it the promise of opportunity. Without winter bearing down on their mittenless digits, transients could now seek employment, housing, and forward motion. For Jim and the Queen, springtime mobility loosened the focus of their audience. Many would go forward, and many would go backward. This meant busy times.

“We need to get those boys a game,” Jim mumbled, his voice garbled by the permanent mucus of lifetime smoking.

“I’ll figure it out. Leave the business side to me,” the Queen replied.

That was it for the evening’s conversation. Exhaustion ruled the moment, and *Magnum P.I.* closed out the hour like a night-light on their tired faces.

CHAPTER TWENTY-FOUR

SMOKY BACK ROOMS

The Lexington Restaurant on, surprisingly, Lexington Avenue is a storied institution of meat and memories, a locus of deal-making where cherry-wood walls surrounded the inner workings of a community: celebrations, questionable financial arrangements, sordid affairs, and political and corporate stare-downs. The back entryway appeared to be a secret entrance for politicians and ward bosses, its hallway adorned with photos of mayors, executives, and deal-makers.

The Queen loved to be at the Lexington, and she hated to be at the Lexington.

At the Lex, she was among the local power set, only a few conversations away from civic action at her behest. Shelter for the homeless, food for the hungry, or even jobs for the drunks—at the Lex she could point a finger in the face of someone from city hall or the corporate boardroom, and after a gin martini or three, the orders would be written. The Lex was Saint Paul's smoke-filled room. Cartoonishly large slabs of bloody prime rib dipped in creamy horseradish filled the senses, and the room buzzed with deals and purpose—but only at lunchtime. Dinner was reserved for families, the same politicians and corporate behemoths blankly sitting at the end of the table as if exhausted from the lunches, spouses tending to children dressed like show dolls in the finest frilly dresses and crested suits with bow ties.

At lunch, it was blood and guts. The Queen secretly wanted her picture in the back hallway . . . but she didn't want anyone to see it.

As much as she admired the atmosphere, she also hated it. Despite her purpose, The Lexington was inaccessible to those she served and, as such, an object of contempt. Equity was her motivation, and any place where the table did not have a seat for the downtrodden was a place without a chair for the Queen. She never sat comfortably at the Lex, as if she were always ready to leave in a hurry.

Today, the Lex was her corporate boardroom. She was also craving the King's cut of Prime Rib, medium-rare to rare, resplendent with blood and salty au jus.

Mr. Long and Mr. Ryan obliged the Queen's power lunch. Mr. Ryan was the construction-magnate counterpart of Mr. Long. He was Jesus in the shiny new development, and he, too, heard the Queen's siren calls for justice. He had a stand-up desk and didn't wear Cosby sweaters, but the two gentlemen were kindred. They were called to make a difference, and they did.

Mr. Long ate at the Lex regularly and never thought twice about its grandeur or its accessibility. It was a regular stop in business and in life, from meetings with Cadillac executives to First Communion brunches with his children. The martinis were off-limits, but that didn't matter. For Mr. Long, it was about the pot pie, a legendary extravaganza of puff pastry that defied science. Mr. Long also loved the Lex because the Lex loved him. He was a regular; in Saint Paul, becoming a regular was a rite of passage into the foundation of a historic community. Hailing from Chicago, Mr. Long wanted Saint Paul to be his City of Broad Shoulders.

Mr. Ryan wished the Lexington was in downtown Minneapolis, but if the Queen and Mr. Long were involved, he was obliged to make the journey to Saint Paul. He rarely indulged in anything more than a salad, and he spent most of his time at the Lex being approached by people who wanted to sign contracts with him—or by people who wanted to thank him. He was gracious to all.

The empty wrappers from the Lex cracker basket had hardly begun to congregate before the Queen jumped into the task at hand. Typically, as a matter of strategy, her meetings at the Lex did not turn to business until the King's cut had been reduced to at least half of its original size—the Queen's cut. Today, the Queen wanted to cut to the chase before she cut the meat.

"I could use some help with that softball team over at the Saint Anthony," she said. "They need an opponent, and they could probably use some more bats, balls, and gloves, what have you. You know, spiff it up a bit."

The two gentlemen were asked for many things over the course of their charitable lives. They had businesses with their names on the masthead: requests for galas, political fundraisers, free cars for a hole-in-one, or even new construction.

They were different. They enjoyed being asked to help. In fact, they invited it. It was not a philosophy or a business theory. Their success was the community's success. For many, the smile present during a charitable request faded as quickly as the cameras disappeared. Mr. Long's thin, kind smile remained in place all year long. Mr. Ryan's broad smile never left, even when looking the most destitute straight in the eye.

Mr. Long was still waiting for his pot pie to cool down. Mr. Ryan was halfway into a Lex Salad, light dressing on the side.

"How is that team?" Mr. Long started, while Mr. Ryan greeted a local banker graciously and without a banker harrumph. He knew that the bank possessed a sizable checkbook ready for charitable distribution.

"The team is fine, sort of. Like I said, I mean it could all be good if we had a bit of help from the front office—the team owners, if you catch my drift." The Queen gave them the look. She lowered her fork, twisted her head, and stared. She would freeze in position until her intentions were properly acknowledged.

Mr. Long's fork had a steaming chunk of pot pie on it. Mr. Ryan quickly ended his conversation with the banker, who gave a quick nod of charitable compliance. The banker would write the check when asked. In their dealings with the Queen, veiled requests were orders. A direct response was unnecessary, as they understood orders. Major capital gifts, political assistance, meetings with wealthy friends, and even bars of soap all eventually arrived after such subtle responses.

Mr. Long burnt his tongue on the pot pie.

The true charitable mobster evokes a call to action. It was an underlying theme of Saint Paul's charitable giving scene, which in fact made local philanthropy mysterious and attractive. A charitable mobster could swing the pendulum of poverty at will—all while enjoying the King's cut in the corner table at the Lex.

The Queen finished every inch of the slab, clearing her plate of meat and gristle to leave behind only a small pool of room-temperature au jus mixed with blood. Mr. Long cleared out the pot pie, miraculously finding a way to fit the expansive pastry mushroom cloud into his tiny stature. Mr. Ryan easily finished the salad and politely declined the Key lime pie. None of them cared too much about the symbolism of the clean plate club during a conversation about poverty. It was good food, the lengthy consumption of which would extend their conversation, friendship, and ultimate power over the hope of mankind—or at least a few downtrodden chronic inebriates in Saint Paul.

CHAPTER TWENTY-FIVE

ROUTINE

The next day, soon after breakfast, Marty walked down to Harry's office.

Marty sat in the metal chair wearing his usual powder-blue jeans. He was wearing a high-crown baseball cap without a logo and had his legs tightly crossed, enjoying his fourth Parliament. Harry was stoic, appearing to focus diligently on what was in front of him, which was nothing.

The Twins were playing at 1:05 p.m. in Detroit, which would make it 12:05 p.m. in Saint Paul, so that left about three hours of game shows. Momentous happenings were a step away, on TV and in the hallways.

Around 10 a.m., Terry meandered his way to Harry's office. The three of them sat quietly. Many of the residents had already chosen their itineraries for the day, so the facility sat quiet except for the dusty buzz of an old oscillator fan.

"What time are the Twinkies on?" Terry asked over the tricky combination of a dangling cigarette and a yawn.

"Noon," Marty replied. "Against the Tigers."

It was as though one softball practice had earned Marty and Terry the right to do nothing. On the seventh day, they rested. On every day after the seventh day, they rested.

It was also possible that a sense of accomplishment was beginning to set in for Marty and Terry. A sense of moving forward can erase the past, although many chronic inebriates were too pickled to remember the past, which easily resulted in the backward juggernaut firing on all cylinders. No memory, no remorse.

After a lunch of bologna sandwiches and funeral potato salad, the Twins game set in for the afternoon.

Bob Kurtz dominated the conversation, "And that'll do it for the fourth: Tigers 2, Twins nothing." The 12-inch black-and-white faded to a commercial for the new Plymouth Tourismo. Terry wanted one of those.

"You know, they should bat Gaetti at the top of the order," Marty whispered. "He's consistent, and his speed gets him to second. Puckett can take it from there."

"No argument from me," Terry returned.

"None here either," Harry chimed in, not looking up from his mysterious paper. The paper was large enough to have another paper on the inside of it.

As the pitch of the baseball chatter rose from agreement to argument, it was clear that, in one short practice, Saint Anthony now had a team of keen baseball tacticians.

"I still would not have sent him home if I was coaching third," Terry whispered, putting a cigarette out in a nearly full ashtray.

The game waned to another Twins loss.

The softball team took a back seat to routine. Marty and Terry were aware of the upcoming practice, but it seemed anticlimactic after weeks of a so-called draft and a one-practice spring training.

The rest of the team completely forgot about softball and returned to the reason they lived at the Saint Anthony.

With an unusual tinge of leadership, Harry posted the notice of Thursday's practice on the bulletin board in the cafeteria, removing outdated day-labor notices and plasma specials. There was a bonus on blood last week. Harry always wondered why anyone would want plasma from a chronic alcoholic. Perhaps it was reserved for other alcoholics.

The practice announcement stood alone in the center of a now-clean bulletin board.

Marty and Terry failed to accomplish anything significant that week other than staying mostly sober. It had been months since Marty heavily imbibed, but Terry occasionally snuck in a cheap can or 10. This week, he stayed calm, except for one uneventful evening of mild drunkenness down at the Ace Box Bar. Drunk had levels at the Saint Anthony.

Terry's restraint at the Ace was unusual. Sitting at the bar, he waxed about a softball team that had yet to play a game. The story kept him in control.

Back in Harry's office, the old calendar with the metal hoops failed to notice that the days had passed.

Marty was sitting in Harry's office and broke the silence, "I guess we should check in with the team about practice tomorrow." His voice barely rose above the sound of *Barnaby Jones* and the fan oscillator.

"Works for me," Terry quietly responded in between a burp and the snap of his lighter. He wasn't certain as to the origin of the bent Marlboro he pulled from his sport shirt pocket, but he was certain of the origin of the headache that prompted him to light the cigarette in the first place. It was the cyclical force of the Saint Anthony bad-habit machine.

That was the extent of the two-way baseball conversation for the remainder of the day. The odd heat and odor in a home with the world's foremost underachievers can abscond with motivation. Marty knew they needed to get a move on things. Yet he remained in his metal chair, watching Harry go about menial items of the day, alternating between meaningless cordialities and Twins games, despite the Twins' continued slide toward the depths of the American League West cellar.

It reminded Marty of the motivation he had when he slid into the depths of his own cellar, and he felt an unusual wave of guilt pass over his usually emotion-free Norwegian body.

While there are few cathartic moments at the Saint Anthony, at least from the inside looking out, Marty had the realization that he was missing something.

He snuffed out his Parliament short of the butt and made an announcement: "Someone needs to rally this team." No one in Harry's office responded.

Marty walked up and down the hall, looking for Jerry, Ray, Wesley, Johnny Luck, Freddie, and Charlie. Except for Charlie, he had seen everyone over the past few days. He couldn't remember if Charlie was even on the team. Instinctually, Marty was looking for him because he knew Charlie was lost. He forgot about Eric unless he confused Eric with Charlie.

He knocked on each team member's door without a response. He ended his clubhouse tour by stopping in the cafeteria to finish the Parliament and have a cup of stale coffee. He was not dejected.

Marty was starting to nod off when he was tapped on his shoulder. "Hey Marty, you got room on that team?"

"Sure," replied Marty, coming out of a grog.

Standing over Marty, but hardly towering, Jerry Nickerson looked as though it had taken him the better part of a month to gin up the fortitude for his request. It was Jerry's nature to take orders and quietly follow them, but this time, he wanted something, and he had to ask for it.

"Thanks Marty, I'll see you tomorrow." He slowly turned around and walked away. It was another Jerry.

Jerry N., as he was dubbed by Harry, was a stocky fellow who came to the residence a few years ago; he largely kept to himself. Marty was polite with him, but he did not know his background or intentions. Jerry N. never seemed to smell of alcohol or anything else.

Many residents thought Jerry N. couldn't speak English, which was an unfortunate cultural assumption. He also looked like Freddie Mercury to the slight few at the residence who had an affinity for Queen.

Jerry was indeed part Mexican, but not only did he speak English, he had taught English.

Jerry N. arrived at the Saint Anthony with a résumé that boasted more than a dozen stints in treatment. As with many residents, just beyond the treatment history lurked a record of accomplishment.

Jerry N. spent over a decade teaching English at a local community college. In those times, he was a respected and gifted educator.

Other than the drinking part, the staff did not know what brought Jerry N. to the Saint Anthony, but they imagined the usual causes—relationships, tragedies, and mental health all wrapped into one. It could also have been the constant search for self-meaning evident in the literary works of his obsession.

For the residents, it didn't matter, as he was a chronic alcoholic like everyone else. He was just another Jerry.

Marty was unfamiliar with this Jerry's ability to transcend the halls of Saint Anthony for the woods of Walden. Had he known, they could have spent hours discussing literature, although Marty looked at literature as entertainment, while Jerry N. focused on inner meanings and life messages.

They could have also talked about baseball.

Jerry N.'s physical build intimated the possibility of athletic prowess and that intrigued Marty. He was stocky, barrel-chested, and he wore gym shorts and over-the-calf tube socks.

Given a daily regimen of over-starched, fatty foods and beer, it was a miracle anyone could stay in shape at the Saint Anthony. Excessive walking, foraging, and a tendency for compulsiveness apparently made the difference, as Jerry N. looked ready.

Marty failed to mention Jerry N. to Terry or Harry. There were just too many Jerrys.

It was Thursday. Practice day.

The sticky heat had transitioned to a welcome cool breeze at the residence, leading to anticipation and a positive atmosphere.

Harry wanted to get out of the sublevel office. "I'm going to fire up those damned dehumidifiers. Watch the office." Marty and Terry were lounging over lukewarm coffee and cigarettes.

Marty and Terry spent the better part of the day in Harry's office, not really talking about the team or anything else. Not a word was uttered about Terry's recent head-butt with barley.

"'Bout that time. Let's head to the ballfield," Marty whispered, slowly pulling up from the metal chair, creaking his way to the back of Harry's office to grab the equipment.

Marty and Terry loaded up their gear in the wagon and, without too much conversation, started their journey to the field. Harry had yet to return from his date with the dehumidifiers, and the gravel hadn't been thrown by the whitewalls of Jim's car.

They had not seen a single player.

The Little Leaguers were surprisingly on the field for an early practice. Marty and Terry would never have known it was a half-day in the Saint Paul schools.

The Tigers did not have a permit for the early field time. Terry wanted to call the police, something he had never done in his life.

The Little Leaguers were still clueless as to the Saint Anthony team's origins or intentions, but at least they could see that the wagon was used to haul baseball gear. Pleasantries were on the horizon, but for now, it was still awe, wonderment, and lingering trepidation. The fear was reserved mostly for the parents.

The Little Leaguers wrapped up scrimmage and bent their necks as they departed. One of the parents approached Marty and Terry.

"I'd like to ask what you guys are doing here, but I sort of don't want to know." He was young. He wore slacks, a white T-shirt, and hard-soled black shoes. His Twins hat had lost its crown.

"Just playing ball like you all, with a permit, of course," Terry responded, irritated. The dad looked nervous.

"You all playing 12U?" Marty asked. It was an instinctive response. The kids were not wearing uniforms, and nothing indicated their age.

"Yes, we are."

"The kid with the red hat with the 'S' on it has a hot bat. He should square up in the box." Marty had only seen the boy from a distance.

"Maybe so, we'll have to take a look at it." The parent was taken aback. He quickly turned and caught up to six kids who were piling into a wood-paneled Chevy Caprice wagon.

"Jackass," Terry whispered.

Marty and Terry waited for the group to depart before they raised their respective torches for ignition. To the social service professional, this was progress. To Marty and Terry, it was professional courtesy.

At the halfway mark on their cigarettes, with stealthy intentions, Jerry N. simultaneously patted each of them on the back.

"Ready to play, guys," Jerry N. said as he grinned. His white T-shirt was tucked neatly into gym shorts, his white tube socks perfectly aligned up his tan calves. He was wearing a high-crowned, nondescript black baseball cap. He looked like a cross between a private security guard and a grade school gym teacher.

Mysteriously, he had a baseball glove in hand. He was ready.

"Jerry!" Marty exclaimed with surprise, pleased that Jerry N. showed up and that he at least looked like a softball player.

Before Terry could express surprise or disappointment in the fact that he was left in the dark, Jim's General Motors mound of steel plunged into the curb, kicking up a cloud of dust and an oversize helping of anticipation.

Harry emerged from the passenger side; Wesley and the other Jerry poured out of the back seat. Wesley and Jerry stumbled from the low-riding vehicle. They didn't smell of alchemy, but their blood alcohol was registering toward the top of allowable limits, whatever that might have been in the 1980s.

Now on the field for the Saint Anthony Residence—Marty, Terry, Jim, Harry, Jerry, Wesley, and Jerry N.

Seven ball players do not make a team, but they make a practice. Johnny Luck was a no-show. Marty was still not sure he was actually on the team.

Terry and Marty assembled the group around home plate and gave them their assignments—fielding drills and a round of batting practice. No calisthenics.

Starting with the usual drills, the players took to the field with enthusiasm, running out to deep shortstop, each anticipating a handful of ground balls and an occasional liner. They were still short one glove, but they were in line and ready—Wesley, Jerry N., Harry, Jerry, and Jim—in that order. Jim lit up a cigarette, thinking that it would take 2 minutes to get organized and 2 minutes per player of fielding, instruction, and fetching errant balls. He finished with a minute to spare.

"Nice work, gents, let's bring it in," Terry called out after about 20 minutes of fielding drills. Terry and Marty were impressed with the marked improvement just one practice brought to the team of gentle ruffians. It was scientifically possible that they just needed to dust off a few dormant motor skills and work off a snifter or two of blood alcohol. Fielding was crisp and footwork was not lightning, but it was better than walking a line. They looked like a team.

And then there was Jerry N. Smiling the entire practice, Jerry N. seemed to transcend years of drinking Olde English and reading Old English all the way back to a time before heartache and his own search for meaning—a time when all that mattered was baseball, cold beer, and girls.

Jerry N. was a baseball player in high school—a great player on a not-so-great team. He knew how to play, and he loved the game. His analytics of the human struggle between pitcher and batter arrived in grade school. Now, so many years later, he always played the game with a smile.

Marty and Terry conducted the practice as methodically as they could. Fielding drills and some hot pepper, sandwiched between intermittent coughing attacks.

Terry and Marty were unsure how a practice should end or how long the squad would maintain their apparent enthusiasm, but the team stayed on an upward trajectory for what seemed to be well over an hour. On the cigarette clock, Jim had inhaled no less than six heaters, which is the equivalent of 42 minutes. Adding non-smoking time, it was reasonable to suggest that the practice was approaching 90 minutes—a milestone for an organized non-drinking social activity at Saint Anthony.

As if to solve the conundrum of when to end the practice, a clean, gray Chevy Suburban pulled up to the curb with their decision.

Several 40-something men emerged from the vehicle, bones creaking and pear shapes rolling out of the car like fruit falling in the grocery aisle.

Men's softball season had begun.

Marty and Terry took a break from practice to observe America unfurling before their eyes. It was a parallel universe—an assortment of slovenly men dressed in attire ranging from obligatory shorts over sweatpants to matching Rocky Balboa sweat suits and terry-cloth headbands. At least half of the new arrivals appeared intoxicated, and virtually all of them were consuming some form of tobacco product, largely chew.

Despite their vastly different backgrounds, the two teams looked the same.

The apparent leader of the team approached the third-base

bench where Marty and Terry were standing. Despite the balmy weather, he was wearing a full gray sweat suit and a black baseball cap with a plain white font inscription: "The Nickel Joint." He was portly and smoking a cigar. He appeared to be chewing tobacco at the same time. Even Terry was taken aback by his tobacco use. The leader clearly had begun the afternoon with more than a few beers.

He spoke to Marty and Terry. "Field's ours, boys. We just need to warm up our drinking arms and we'll be ready. Feel free to take a few more cuts on your way out."

It was an attempt at "guy humor" that flew over Marty and Terry's heads like a Puckett line drive. They knew what he meant, but it wasn't funny. Years ago, they may have laughed.

"No problem, we'll be out in a jiffy," Marty quietly replied.

Terry was less than impressed by the display of manliness and took the leader's attempt at humor in an alternatively negative fashion.

"Who do you all play for, Sweat Suit?"

"The Nickel Joint down in Frogtown. What about you all? You in the City League?"

"We play for the Saint Anthony Residence." Terry was proud.

"What the hell is that?" Sweat Suit was visibly angling toward a position of dislike for Terry.

"We're part of Catholic Charities."

"Ah, social workers and do-gooders."

"You might say that," Terry quickly responded, not certain what to say. He knew what he wouldn't say: *We're a group of residents from a drunk house.*

"Let's mix it up out here one of these days. We play in two leagues, so we'll be here all summer," Sweat Suit returned, as he walked back toward his now fully assembled team.

"Works for me. Tell Jimmy at the Nickel Joint that Terry T. sends his regards."

"Will do. Now get your tired and your poor asses off my ballfield."

Sweat Suit angered Marty. Sweat Suit was the drinking side of the Nickel Joint. Marty was the baseball side, even though he also passed out on the same bar as his heroes. He was disappointed that the namesake bar of the 1944 AA Men's Amateur baseball runner-ups had devolved into a group of rude old men playing softball.

The thought made him competitive. Marty's eyes followed Sweat Suit as the oafish man took the field. Sweat Suit took a nervous look back at Marty and knew that he had made a mistake. Marty wouldn't ever start a physical fight, but his time would come, and it was always on the diamond.

Marty initiated the slow process of moving the Saint Anthony team off the field. Some of them walked down the street, Jim slinked to his car, and a handful more disappeared into the bushes next to the railroad tracks.

Marty and Terry loaded up the wagon and headed home. They might not play the Nickel Joint for months, but it was on.

CHAPTER TWENTY-SIX

SCHEDULE RELEASE, NOT SCHEDULED RELEASE

Two practices did not sober up the masses. Marty and Terry could not prohibit drinking, but they were hoping that the ballplayers would manage themselves in a somewhat loose professional fashion. Terry had his own moments astray, and he expected that others would have theirs.

Jerry N. swaggered in the entryway to Harry's office. "Yo' boys, that was a heckuva practice today, ya think?"

It was only a few hours after practice, and he had clearly been celebrating, or perhaps wallowing, as his normally measured gait had been consumed by a topside wave of inebriation. Whatever it was, he achieved his desired result.

Harry was long gone for the evening, and the night manager, Bill, was hardly good at anything except turning the channel on the TV. Marty and Terry never asked or were interested in his last name. The night manager was a solitary figure at the Saint Anthony. Most activity happened in the daytime, and Bill never did rounds, which often infuriated a surprised Harry.

Bill was quiet as Jerry N. bounced against the doorway.

"You bet, Jerry. Stay tuned for an update on the bulletin

board," Terry responded, feeling apprehensive about Jerry N.'s uneasy state while, at the same time, nostalgic and even jealous.

"Roger that, Terry. Great game," he finished, using the wall as a guide and eventually falling through his door to the bed, leaving the door open for no one to care, except Marty.

"I'll check on him, then I am turning in," Marty whispered.

He walked down the hall, peered into Jerry N.'s room, then retired to his own room to read. Practice had worn Marty out. Lying on his bed, his mind drifted from the discarded library book he found on the bus stop—a tattered copy of *The World According to Garp*. Something was happening, and Marty knew it. He dozed off quickly, dropping the book on the floor and onto a cold cup of coffee, the coffee seeping under the closed door and into the hallway.

After breakfast, Marty and Terry assembled in their usual positions, with Harry's brow furrowed deeper than usual.

"Those pancakes were incredible," Terry proclaimed as Marty nodded, firing up a cigarette. It was Friday.

"Some kid dropped off a whole garbage bag full of them last night," Harry muttered.

With the residence now entering the end of the month, the facility moved toward solitude and despondence. Alchemy was everywhere.

Marty and Terry went through several Parliaments before a single resident walked by. After lunch and a few TV game shows, notably an impressive streak on *Tic-Tac-Dough,* they were still in Harry's office.

"The Queen left a message during lunch, by the way," Harry surprisingly whispered. "She's coming by around 2:30."

It was now clear why Harry's brow had been furrowed below its normal end-of-the-month position. It wasn't the vomit that Bill forgot about in the bathroom. Fear the Queen.

- -

The end of the month had little bearing on Jim and the Queen. Their lives were intertwined with payroll, broken toilets, hiring and firing, and a community and its underlying secrets. At the end of the month, the work was just a little more demanding and possibly slightly belligerent.

Jim and the Queen's house had become decidedly more upbeat in the past weeks. All households in Minnesota experience a resurgence when spring arrives, but the Queen's uptick rose above the average. Windows would be open, and fresh air would extricate the stale winter. The Queen left her windows open day and night, which was risky in her neighborhood. The Queen trusted the community.

"I heard from Harry the other day that the team has been practicing. He actually sounded positive for the first time in God-knows-how-long," the Queen said to Jim over a mouthful of stale glazed doughnut. Jim wondered why the Queen didn't know he was at the practice.

"They need a game to keep things moving," Jim responded, gulping a chocolate Ensure to wash down the dry pastry.

"It's what they needed over there. The place was getting stagnant. I'll try some of the other places in town to see if they have clubs, although I suspect that Saint Anthony may be the only team of drunks in the state," she said, smiling and eating at the same time.

"No argument here," Jim burped through a drag of his smoke.

Later that afternoon, the Queen did what the Queen did best: She picked up the phone and berated the community. She decided to wait on Mr. Long and Mr. Ryan for the corporate teams and instead focused on other social service agencies. This would be a start. While her heart wanted to let it ride and set up the first game with one of the thousands of men's corporate softball teams in the Twin Cities, she knew the risks of failure, settling on the thought that a team from another social service agency might be a better match. They might at least go a bit soft on them. They would even understand when someone vomits on the way from first to second base.

The Queen did not have to spin the Rolodex too far to find the right fit for what was to be an inaugural game. No one could refuse the Queen for most things, but this was different. It was an opportunity not seen in the hallways of social service professionals and self-described social engineers.

It was a softball game with the downtrodden.

Midafternoon, Harry was in a quivering sweat. He had known and seen the *delirium tremens,* and he was thankful that he could differentiate. This type of sweat he could handle. He was too old to worry about his boss's predilections for confrontation.

Everything seemed to be in order. No one was incarcerated, the facility was in relatively decent shape, and the residents appeared to be under control. Harry did not have time for 12-step programs or counseling. Was the Queen coming by to berate him for not pulling enough people out of the depths of addiction?

At 2:45 p.m., the gravel crunched above Harry's window. Marty and Terry were in the office inhaling tobacco.

Jim's car slid loudly into the parking lot. Both Jim and the Queen exited the car, their bodies struggling to extricate themselves from the low-riding vehicle.

"The Queen is here," Marty continued.

"I see that," Harry angrily responded, rising from his freshly dusted desk and heading to the doorway. Harry did not mind that Marty and Terry were in the office. It made him look like he was working on something, maybe counseling the two old men.

The Queen lumbered down the ramp and toward the office, Jim trailing several feet behind, lighting up a cigarette and dropping his keys. Jim's movement to retrieve the keys transpired in slow motion.

"Harry," the Queen motioned in the doorway.

"Hello," Harry responded, as though her greeting was to a friend.

"What's going on in here? Anyone working today?" she quipped.

"Every day of the week," Harry responded.

The Queen barreled into the office and immediately sat down in Harry's chair. Jim stood in the doorway, winded, while Harry stood near the corner of the office.

The Queen greeted Marty and Terry with affection. She was eager to make an announcement.

"Hello, boys."

They responded in unison, "Hello, Queen."

The Queen took her usual deep breath. "I hear from my

various sources that you have actually made progress on our little softball team. Mercy in heaven! Well, it's time to make this thing real, so I thought I would stop by to let you know personally that I scheduled a game for you this Monday against the staff at the Windward Foundation. They were ecstatic at the prospect of playing you ruffians."

The room was silent for several moments. Jim was smiling in the doorway, and Harry now believed that the game announcement was the Queen's reason for the visit. His sweat dissipated, slightly. He wasn't sure if he was happy.

Marty and Terry reacted as baseball managers react. Terry led off, "We'll be ready. Where is the game?"

"Over at Raymond. Isn't that where you practice?"

"You bet. It's our home field, which I guess is to our advantage, if any advantage at all is possible with our group." Terry was self-deprecating, his humor covering his guilt. He was excited. The plan had come together, and it validated him. It made him feel like a proper conniver.

Marty had lost track of what it meant to be excited. The thought of a game reminded him of earlier days, playing ball with friends and feeling like he was part of something. He focused on the long way back to the diamond of his youth. Sitting in a residence for chronic alcoholics, he wanted to be Roy Campanella.

Later that evening, long after Jim's car spun doughnuts in the parking lot, Bob Kurtz closed out the Twins broadcast with, "And that'll wrap it up, another rough go in Baltimore and a sweep for the Orioles. We'll start anew on Thursday night when the

Twins take on the Brewers, live from County Stadium on KMSP Channel 9." He elevated his voice as the sentence expired to at least build a modicum of excitement for the lowly ball club.

Bill turned off the TV. Marty and Terry slowly stood up, their bodies unfolding like aluminum foil.

"We should try to get a few backups. At the very least, I want to have enough players," Terry whispered.

"Right," Marty whispered in return.

Not a single person in the day-long discussion realized or acknowledged that Monday was the first of the month.

Out of sight, out of mind. Perhaps literally.

MARTY INTERLUDES

Early summer, 1990

Marty felt out of place in a car.

Marty's case manager drove the two of them to K-Mart in a $250 Mazda. He'd gotten the car and a girlfriend from the same friend of his brother's. Neither of them lasted, to his dismay.

Marty sat low in the passenger seat. In their conversations, the stories of baseball at the University of Minnesota and overnights at the post office quickly disappeared, and all the case manager could think about was a thin old man whose body had been ravaged. Marty rarely left Saint Paul. At the Saint Anthony, the farthest he traveled was to the softball field. And his job at the mission only took him across the parking lot.

It was possible he hadn't been in a car since his life stopped moving forward. Marty looked out the window, "This neighborhood was my whole world."

They were driving down University Avenue to the Midway area so the case manager could purchase a pair of khakis and a blue Oxford for Marty. It was the standard job interview outfit for clients. The city grant covered everything except the Blue Light Special bologna hoagies.

"Terry Schreiber's dad had a barber shop right there, and Lexington Park was over there." Marty's eyes looked sad through his thick, smudged glasses. "We loved baseball. We loved watching the Saints."

His nostalgia for the neighborhood was a surprise. They had only been in the car for 10 minutes. Saint Paul was a small community, with short bus rides covering most of the city. On a summer day, he could have easily walked from the mission to the White Castle at Lexington and University. From the Saint Anthony Residence, it was longer but still doable. One would have thought that Marty often made it to the old neighborhood, if only for the Blue Light Special.

"I rarely come back here," Marty said. "My old stomping grounds are in between my old place and the mission, and I never make it back."

The White Castle sat directly on what would have been the left foul pole for Lexington Park. What was now the kitchen of the fast-food joint had once been the spot where Marty and his friends looked through the fence to witness countless legends step into the batter's box, then jack it to Coliseum Pavilion past the wall. Today, their stories are buried underneath a griddle of steamed double cheeseburgers.

"We would play baseball all day. Wherever we could get a game. When the Saints played, we were there. Maybe not inside the stadium, but we could hear it. Those were great days."

Marty's life to that point had consisted of three stages: an emergence, a retreat, and a meditation.

Marty's emergence began on ballfields and street corners with Ron, Terry, Jim, and the boys. Playing ball or just standing on the corner—the neighborhood was all he wanted to know, and it was wonderful. At home, it was alcohol, and he wanted to forget it.

Marty's retreat was into addiction. He had a government job. He loved his family, and his family loved him. He wasn't a criminal. But after the joyful life of the neighborhood, he could not relate to a life that wasn't youthful and carefree, and he retreated.

Marty continued his stories of the neighborhood as they drove back to the mission from K-Mart. They took Thomas Avenue, which runs parallel to University Avenue and directly through the south end of his old neighborhood.

His meditation was not a lamentation. It was reflection on the joys and promise of youth against the powers of addiction. In those moments, he knew himself.

Marty stared straight ahead, "What else do you want to know about the Saint Anthony team?"

"I love the old stories." For the next 20 minutes, the case manager took a series of wrong turns to extend their journey back to the mission. The case manager might have been driving the car, but it was the team that brought Marty home.

CHAPTER TWENTY-SEVEN

ROSTER DEADLINE

Marty and Terry posted the game announcement on the cafeteria bulletin board to little reaction, which was expected but also worrisome. It was the end of the month.

Marty looked at the piece of paper sitting on Harry's desk. It was dog-eared from his back pocket, but it was neatly folded and legible.

"OK, here is what we have." He read the roster to Terry. Harry was reading the newspaper, not paying attention to the paper or the conversation.

Jim

Terry

Harry

Johnny Luck

Ray

Wesley

Jerry

Me

Marty scribbled Jerry N. in at the bottom, giving the appearance of nine players on the team, which was true only if they believed that Johnny Luck would make it to the diamond. He still lived in the residence, and he had been sighted, which was a start. He looked like Jim, with long hair, sallow cheekbones, and his Yeti-like elusiveness.

Terry was enjoying a morning cigar. "We need at least one more player, and we also need Johnny Luck and Jerry," Terry proclaimed, "I haven't seen Jerry since practice, and God knows where Johnny Luck has been."

On a weekend before the end of the month, the mood was as low as it could go. Day labor was infrequent, the recycling center was closed on Sunday, and the alchemists were in force. Residents teetered toward irritability and belligerence even when they weren't intoxicated, and those who were under the influence were often in hiding, dangerously satiated.

Terry and Marty fanned out over the residence.

"I'll take the right hallway, and you take the left." Terry commanded his plan.

"Got it. We'll meet back in Harry's office."

Marty discovered Jerry locked in his room, sobering up. Repeated attempts to procure others were fruitless.

It didn't take long to end up back in Harry's office. Terry and Marty resigned themselves to the possibility that they might be short on game day.

"Do you think there are forfeits in this league?" Marty asked.

"I'm not sure it's a league, so who knows? We'll figure it out." Terry said, always confident.

The alchemists had taken over.

It was game day.

The morning of the first of the month was a new dawn. Breakfast was crowded and chatty, and it was as though 50-plus men were about to embark on an expedition, even though the anticipation was a check for $47. Marty and Terry saw it as an opportunity to fortify the team and maybe recruit a few new participants. They arrived in the cafeteria early and planned an organized and aggressive effort.

As the men devoured heaping plates of scrambled eggs and a semisolid cheese substance, Marty and Terry extinguished their cigarettes and walked to the front of the room. Terry stood in front, squarely in his element.

He stood on top of a chair and heaved to the room, "Gentlemen, may I have your attention, please?"

"No," roared an unidentified feaster in the rear of the room.

Terry smiled and quickly returned, "Two seconds is all I need, sir, so let's have it! The food is already expired, so a few more seconds won't hurt." He got a few mild laughs, which only happened around the first part of the month.

"As you know, we now have a softball team here. After careful planning and practice, tonight is our first game. If you're on the team, be at Raymond field at 3 p.m. for warm-ups. If you'd like to be on the team, be at Raymond at 3 p.m., but check with Marty and me first."

Terry unwittingly assumed that everyone knew Marty, owing to a touch of delusion as to the camaraderie of the facility. He had at least gesticulated in the right direction.

"If you want to watch the team, be at Raymond at 4 p.m. I can't guarantee beer, hot dogs, and girls, but one never knows."

Jim appeared in the doorway during Terry's speech. He was already a quiet man, but he was speechless. Folks seemed to listen to Terry, which was no small feat in itself.

Terry and Marty walked toward Jim. Terry looked at him with a smile, "Ready for a rouser tonight, good sir?"

"Jim is always ready," he returned in the third person. "I have something for you boys. C'mon down to the office."

In Harry's office, they found Harry standing over a large cardboard box. Inside the box was an array of black T-shirts, a row of black baseball caps, a box of new softballs, and a smattering of mitts.

Harry was smiling and holding a T-shirt that was way too big for him. "How about that, boys? Uniforms!"

The T-shirt had the words "The Saint Anthony Residence" on the front in white block letters. "Long Cadillac" appeared underneath in small letters.

"Your benefactor, Mr. Long, felt that it was important for you all to be properly outfitted," Jim smiled through his cigarette. "There is plenty to go around, hopefully enough for any extra players you discover on the tracks. The resale value is zero."

"They look great," Marty smiled, avoiding the thought of his depleted roster.

Looking at each other in a brief silence with their high-crowned caps on, they knew that it was real. It felt good, maybe even better than good.

At the Saint Anthony, hope was a commodity, and it was sparse. It had all but left the building.

The Queen and Jim knew this. This would not be an experiment. It would be a bona fide attempt to play ball. They would not interfere with the team, as much as they wanted to, and they would see to it that Marty and Terry had everything they needed to get the job done. Forfeit was not an option, even though no one had a backup plan.

The team would be called "The Saint Anthony Residence." The patron saint was particularly important to the Queen, Jim, and anyone else at Catholic Charities who was once lost. They wanted everyone to see what they were up against: This is who we are, so we tell them.

There would be hope, but no justice—unless the other team knew they were just clobbered by a bunch of drunks.

PART FOUR

PLAY BALL, NO KIDDING

CHAPTER TWENTY-EIGHT

GAME DAY

Monday, June 2, 1986 (the first business day of the month)

Except for the spring morning when the residence's rusty doors first opened and 50 chronic alcoholics went from the streets to a bed with three squares, it was possibly the most unusual day in Saint Anthony history.

For most of the day, there was little to do other than watch TV, smoke, and hope the team showed up on time and in shape, relatively speaking. But it was payday, and Marty and Terry worried about The Cromwell Bar.

Situated at the gateway to the University of Minnesota, The Cromwell anchored a border of Saint Paul. Inside, factory workers, day laborers, and Saint Anthony residents would head to the back corner and cash their checks at the tiny window with the brass bars.

At the wooden bar, lines were two-deep by noon, with the full range of the western hemisphere celebrating the American dream through the exchange of money for revelry. In this neighborhood, payday was New Year's Eve and Saint Patrick's Day all rolled into one.

Terry and Marty hoped that any softball teammates at the check-cashing cage would enjoy a mere touch of revelry and leave it at that. Sitting in Harry's office in the solitude of an empty residence, wearing a fresh uniform, Terry was uneasy about not being at The Cromwell spinning yarns, but he was squarely and unusually proud.

Game time approached, so Terry and Marty packed the wagon and began the trek to Raymond Field. Unsurprisingly, only a handful of residents had bothered to stop by and pick up their jerseys, so Terry and Marty toted the large cardboard box on top of the wagon as though it was filled with their life's possessions.

Marty and Terry approached the field 15 minutes before warm-ups. They were delighted and surprised to find Wesley and Jerry N. eagerly seated on the bench and ready to play ball. The thought of at least Wesley being on time was new to them. More surprising was that neither of them was even remotely intoxicated.

"Thought practice was at 2, coach," said Wesley, not telegraphing who he thought was the coach.

"You're here now, and that's what matters," Terry responded. "Now let's just hope the others thought like you."

Terry hardly finished his sentence when Jim's car rolled into the curb, the engine chortling the announcement of his arrival. Jim, Harry, and Jerry exited the low-riding vehicle like the *A-Team* walking slowly in front of an explosion.

Jerry stumbled as he got out of the car. He quickly straightened up and walked tiny zigzags to the field. He was still short of annihilation. It was apparent that he left The Cromwell before it was too late.

They were now at seven players, including the two player-managers.

As the arrivals removed their shirts to don the new jerseys,

Terry and Marty watched with grins as neighbors in their yards dropped garden tools and stared. A couple walking toward them quickly diverted in the opposite direction.

"Maybe we should skip the uniforms and just go shirts-skins?" Terry chuckled to Marty.

"Might be an advantage for us," Marty said, his eyes peering over his glasses at a kaleidoscope of jailhouse tattoos, sagging bellies, and scars.

Once the team struggled into their jerseys and covered their weathered bodies, they resembled a company softball team like any other, and the neighbors went back to their hydrangeas. The couple continued walking in the other direction but slowed down to eliminate the appearance of fear.

Terry and Marty immediately called for warm-ups, but Marty was fixated on the roster count. The rules of forfeiture were unclear, with Marty and Terry concerned less about the "experiment" as a failure than about losing the game.

They wanted to win, and a forfeit was the worst kind of defeat. They had been forfeiting all their lives. It was time to win one, or lose one, square.

Marty was hitting pop flies. "I hope we get a team out here."

Terry was tossing the balls and smoking a cigarette. "We better get a team out here, or I am going to thump someone."

About halfway into the warm-ups and all the way through a collective pack of cigarettes, a 15-passenger van slowly pulled in behind Jim's car, nearly bumping into it.

Terry stopped and looked at the van. He knew what was coming. Marty kept hitting flies.

One by one, crisp, muscled ballplayers with clean, professional uniforms emerged from the shining van. Tall crown caps, wristbands, and eye paint were the norm as they efficiently and effortlessly gathered near the bench. Without announcement, they began a show-like warm-up session, throwing the ball in crisscrosses, taking batting practice to the depths of the outfield, and sprinting like soldiers in basic training.

Marty stopped hitting flies.

Marty and Terry stood like children watching the circus.

The apparent Windward manager shouted through a large clump of chewing tobacco, "Who's the leader of this posse? You, Jack?"

Was this really a team from the Windward Foundation or were they guns for hire?

Windward is one of the largest nonprofit foundations in Minnesota. With hundreds of employees, odds would have it that they had burly softball players in the ranks.

If Monday-night softball in America was a circle of men in mismatched sweat suits guzzling beer and cramming hot dogs, this was not it. This team was ready to play.

Terry was annoyed. "We are, and it's Terry. This here is Marty."

"The name is James. I'm in accounting. You boys ready to mix it up?"

"You bet. Give us another few minutes to rally the squad and we'll be ready."

Terry was intimidated by the sight of the opposing team, but his expectations remained squarely in line with the nature of Saint Anthony Residence: Expect nothing, so even the smallest victory warrants the largest celebration.

Most companies and organizations in Minnesota had an official softball team and a series of unofficial teams. Official teams played for keeps, corporate legends on the diamond that filled watercooler conversations with exaggerated heroics. Unofficial teams told stories of what happened after the games. This team was Windward's official squad.

The Queen was unaware that even social service organizations sometimes had excellent teams. Not every social worker or accountant buried themselves in books and numbers and politics in high school. Some excelled in Strat-o-matic baseball; many excelled in actual athletics.

Democrats can play sports. Really, they can.

Except for Terry and Marty, the other Saint Anthony team members were not intimidated. The rest of the Saint Anthony players barely knew what was happening. They were simply happy to do something different from the normal routine.

It felt different to be on a ballfield wearing the same shirts, although they had worn matching shirts in the past, notably those emblazoned with *Minnesota Vikings, Super Bowl XI Champions.* A fourth Super Bowl loss affected fans universally, albeit a bit differently at the Saint Anthony: Free T-shirts.

James shouted across the field, "You boys ready?"

"About a minute, sir," Terry returned, pretending to be cordial, but stalling for time.

Terry and Marty were certain that James noticed their incomplete roster. James seemed like a nice-enough character, but he was clearly a competitor, and he was an accountant. Marty and Terry hoped they could delay the game long enough so that a few more players would arrive. Maybe James would let them play shorthanded.

After a few more minutes, but still before the prescribed starting time, the bushes by the train tracks began to rustle, and it was not the wind of a passing train. It was Ray, and he was drunk.

Stumbling up to the Saint Anthony bench, he addressed the group, "Ready to get it on, boys? The ringer has arrived."

Like admonishments, accusations at the Saint Anthony were not prohibited, but they never happened. Taking it all in stride was a mantra, and it applied here on the diamond. Technically, he was not late for the game.

"Pick out a jersey and try to warm up," Marty directed, aware of the predicament and resigned to make the best of it.

"Walk it off" had an entirely different meaning for this squad.

It was nearly game time, and they had eight ball players, one of them a bit tipsy, another heavily intoxicated.

Moments before the first pitch, a car skidded against the curb behind the Windward van, and out poured the Queen, Mr. Long, and the final player on the team—Johnny Luck.

The Queen yelled out of the car. "Look who I dragged out of the gutter!"

Johnny Luck made his way to the bench, grabbed a shirt, sat down, and lit up a cigarette. He wore a high-end baseball glove, although Marty was the only one to discern its quality.

Johnny Luck was intoxicated. Johnny's eyes always looked sad and lost, even more so when he was intoxicated. His body and his eyes were visions of a lost life.

Johnny looked up to Marty and Terry and quietly said, "Let's play some ball."

The game was on.

Marty knew that he would eventually be a player-manager, so this was his time.

He cleared his mind to the game in front of him. It was just a black T-shirt and a plain cap with block letters, but Marty felt the power of a uniform.

Marty had given real thought to the lineup and to positioning, and he walked slowly along the bench as he announced the lineup, positions, and baseball nicknames:

Wesley—left field for Smiley

Terry—pitcher for the Manager

Jerry N.—catcher for the Other Jerry

Me—first base

Jerry—third base for Jerry One

Johnny Luck—center field for New Guy

Jim—shortstop for the Boss

Harry—second base for the Other Boss

Ray—right field for the Mechanic

The nicknames poured out effortlessly. Luckily, they weren't the ones he was thinking.

Johnny Luck could only conjure an image of despair.

Nicknames were temporary at the Saint Anthony and typically generated from drinking events. They would quickly be replaced with new nicknames from new drinking events. It was Marty's baseball obligation to assign them, but they were forgotten immediately.

With Ray's obvious intoxication, Marty moved him off second base to right field, putting Harry in an uncomfortable leadership position at second. Marty did not notice any apparent left-handers on the Windward squad, and his experience told him that few righty softball hitters could purposely hit to right field. Marty hoped Ray would at least sway back and forth, appearing to stand ready for action . . . but really, he was just drunk.

A coin flip would determine the home team. Terry and Marty approached home plate.

James was already there. As Marty fished in his pocket for a coin that was not there, James flipped up a shiny 50¢ piece and yelled out, depositing specs of tobacco spit on Marty's brand-new jersey, "Call it!"

Terry reacted quickly, "Heads!"

James looked disappointed, "Heads it is."

Terry did not hesitate to announce his preference. "This is our home, so we'll take home."

Slowly and confusedly, the Saint Anthony squad took to the field, each player choosing a field location in an acceptable range of their assigned position. They were methodical and quiet as they assembled. Jim lit up a cigarette at short.

Terry and Marty never had a conversation about their own positions, but it was obvious that Terry would be the pitcher. Along with the catcher, it was the most physically demanding and it required focus, a lack of alcohol, and the desire to win. Terry was close enough.

Marty took first.

Terry looked good on the mound. He was tan and imposing, his high-brimmed, solid-black cap fiercely staring at all comers.

The Windward team formed a circle, engaged a war chant, and lined up on the bench. Perhaps doing good all day made them into warriors by night. They were motivated to win, potentially at all costs.

The Windward team failed to notice who they were playing. It was unclear if the Queen's contact at Windward mentioned it to them. It was more likely that the Queen failed to mention it in the first place. The Queen was also motivated, but in a different way. Watercooler braggadocio didn't interest her.

Batter up for Windward.

The leadoff batter was sizable and out of shape. It appeared that he had tattoos underneath his red, white, and blue sweatbands. He spit something large onto the gravel and a piece of it stuck to his goatee. He moved into the box.

Terry took a moment. He crouched forward with his head toward the plate, moved the ball back, and released the first pitch. The windmill windup was not in his arsenal. It would have separated his shoulder.

The batter took the pitch. A relaxed Jerry N. at catcher caught the ball squarely in his fielder's glove. The glove was too small for his large hands, but Terry's pitch was so slow that he barely felt it hit the glove.

Jerry N. took the liberty, "Strike one!"

"Whatever, dude." The batter was irritated with Jerry N.

Balls and called strikes often were not official in some rec softball leagues. The games would last forever, and arguments would overtake America's summer ritual. It didn't matter to Jerry N. He wanted to let everyone know that Saint Anthony was in the house, even if it was just one lobber down the pipe.

Fake count at 0-1.

Terry nodded to Marty, and then to Jerry N. as though he was taking a sign. He was in the game. With one softball pitch from a portly, chronic alcoholic, the entire Saint Anthony team was in the game.

He wound up and lobbed another gimme right over the plate. It was the only pitch he had, and it would have to work. He was just happy that he was getting it over the plate.

The Windward batter went full Bo Jackson into the pitch,

swinging for the tracks in the hopes of sending a message. He missed it by a mile.

Actual strike one.

Gaining confidence, Terry sped up the pitches, throwing wide and high each time.

Quickly recognizing his own ability, he lobbed another gimme over the plate.

The batter chose a more calculated swing. Liner to short. Jim stopped it with his body, clumsily fumbled it, and threw to first, his long arm reverberating from his fingertips through to his body like a Halloween skeleton. Marty easily scooped the one-hopper.

Safe.

Although Jim was fiercely coughing and the batter was safe, they had executed a play, smoothly and efficiently. Their preparation had paid off in some tiny way.

Marty and Terry were pleased.

Behind the backstop, the Queen was in shock.

James stepped into the box. Terry wanted more than anything to send a message to James that Saint Anthony meant business. He slowly leaned forward again, wound his arm back, and threw awkwardly toward the plate, exerting obvious forward effort to accelerate the pitch beyond his capability. He stumbled forward and fell flat on his face, the pitch sailing over James's head and into the top half of the rusty backstop.

Terry picked himself up with an air of confidence as if the entire sequence had occurred as purposeful intimidation. He looked at Marty with a "should I have said DiMaggio?" smirk.

No one else saw it that way, including James, who cracked a competitive smile. "Nice one, dude."

"Save it, dude." Terry said, believing the accountant-man was cartoonish in his surfer-boy language.

Terry returned to previous form and hurled a gimme across the plate. James took a full swing, lining hard to third. Jerry was paying attention, his buzz beginning to take a backseat to the game. He only needed to stand upright and take one small step toward short, where the ball sailed into his glove and remained.

Out!

The reaction on the field was like any team in America. Each of the men lobbed praise toward their teammate in a moment of real brotherhood.

Even Ray managed a few words, although barely coherent. It was only one out, and they may have looked like grizzled old miners hee-hawing at one another, but it didn't matter.

James trotted back to the bench, frustrated. One less chance for a story at the watercooler.

With one down and one on, Windward's largest player approached the plate. He was strategically placed in the lineup to advance the runner through power and intimidation.

He immediately swung at Terry's invitation, lining a base hit over Terry's head and into left-center, where Wesley ran like mad to deliver the ball to third base.

One out, and base runners on first and second, luckily.

The batters were beginning to look similar, each of them with apparent physical ability to heave a ball deep into the outfield.

Physicality did not intimidate Terry. Each ball he tossed was one that was in play. Let the boys do their job.

Terry lobbed the ball toward the next batter. The wild-eyed player took a full swing at air. Strike one.

Another pitch. Strike two. Another. Strike three.

Swings and misses count. The dude was out.

Maybe the head-banded guys were not that talented after all. It was hardly possible that the Saint Anthony team was better than imagined, so the other team had to be worse.

Two outs, ducks on first and second.

Terry found a groove in the strike zone. His pitches were so slow that it was a mystery each stayed in the air, but they made it across the plate. He also looked good. His cap stood tall, and he was confident. Any appearance of sweat was hidden in his greased hair.

After a lob from Terry, the next Windward player took another swing for the fences, producing only a short hopper to second. Harry charged the ball like an excited grade schooler, scooped it up with his borrowed glove, and tossed it awkwardly to Marty at first.

Out!

For a moment, it was like the end of the World Series. Saint Anthony players hooted, hollered, and patted each other on the back, all while actually running back to the bench. Ray stood in right field until Terry yelled his name to awaken him from a standing slumber.

Almost everyone lit up cigarettes. It was better than Champagne.

Terry addressed the team, "How about *that,* boys?! For a bunch of drunks, you all looked pretty good out there."

He whispered to Marty, "Really, how about *that?*"

"They looked pretty good, although we're still in the first." Marty responded.

Marty was not sure how to react. He was filling with excitement. Anything could happen, but whatever did would not cheapen what he had just felt.

Terry's comment about the drunks irritated him, which was unusual for Marty. Marty still had to manage the game, so he addressed the team.

"Nice work out there. Time to put some runs on the scoreboard. Here's the order. Make sure you know who is in front of you."

Wesley
Terry
Jerry N.
Me
Jerry
Johnny Luck
Jim
Harry
Ray

Marty spent real time on the order, hoping to scrounge up a few base runners and possibly a rip or two to advance them. There were no game tapes or instructional videos. He knew what he was doing, and yet he did not know what he was doing.

He definitely knew to move Ray from the middle of the order to the bottom. Any extra time in the sobering process was a bonus. By the bottom of the order, he might be cognizant enough to swing the bat after the pitch.

He also knew to put staff toward the bottom. The search for hope and redemption needed to go first.

Wesley looked at Marty, "Who's in front of me?"

"No one is in front of you, Wes. You're up!"

Wesley stepped to the plate. Saint Anthony only had one wooden bat. The Windward pitcher was in full form, or at least he looked that way. He crouched forward with his tall-crowned cap, staring at Wesley. He wound up, hurling the ball in a roundhouse motion. The ball went no faster than Terry's.

Wesley took the first pitch with a grin. He was not paying attention. The Queen yelled from the two-person gallery, "Knock it out, Wes!"

The Queen liked Wesley. He was simple in his thoughts and courteous in his manner, welling up empathy in the Queen that she typically could not afford. The Queen cared mightily, but in her mind, emotion is an obstacle to justice. She never saw him when he was drunk.

By the second pitch, it was clear that Wesley had sized up the delivery.

In an instant, Wesley took the ball hard over the shortstop and into left field for a base hit. Jerry N. yelled at the top of his voice, "Get after it, baby. Run, Wesley, run!"

Johnny Luck lurched up to cheer and fell flat on his face. Marty turned to Terry, "Well, now that's a bit of a shocker."

He struggled to first, rounded the bag, and stepped back on top of first base with two feet, his smile ear to ear. Amid the sparks of flying cigarettes, the bench went wild. Even Jim creaked upward and cheered.

Terry stepped into the box. His nerves were gone, but he desperately wanted to continue the rally.

He squared into the now-unmarked batter's box, raising his bat high above his back. As the pitch arrived, he gave it everything. Strike one. The next pitch, he flatly missed by a mile. Strike two.

Now he was nervous.

The pitcher wound up for the third pitch.

Terry stepped into the pitch and swung, barely nicking the ball toward the pitcher's mound. He ran to first as fast as he could, his thick Norwegian frame lumbering with effort, but no motor. He didn't make it halfway.

Out!

Terry was disappointed in his first at-bat, but he was determined to maintain composure and leadership. One at-bat was hardly failure.

"OK, boys, don't follow my lead—let's get Wesley home," he proclaimed upon his return, lighting up a cigarette. His hands were shaking, and it wasn't the DTs. Wesley was standing on second.

Jerry N. took to the plate. He was wearing his standard shorts and clean tube socks, looking like a jock who came ready to play.

He took the first two pitches. He wanted to be sure. On the third pitch from an increasingly frustrated pitcher, he hit the ball hard and fast to third, carrying the bat with him as he ran. The third baseman stopped the ball cleanly, and after a quick look at Wesley at second, he launched it to first where an outstretched James made the play.

Out!

The order rounded to Marty, and he took a moment.

He was standing in the box for Wilson High School. Anything external to the pitcher and batter was set aside. It was between the two men. One would emerge elated, and one angry and frustrated.

Marty kicked the dust.

Seeing the playing field from the vantage point of the batter's box is the greatest moment in sports, and Marty was right back in it. It hardly mattered that they were two softball teams in a meaningless game on a meaningless field. The feeling itself was meaningful.

The game of baseball is filled with metaphors, and some of them are even true. All players are equal when they step onto a diamond, but not so equal once the game is played. And then it starts over.

Standing at bat in a real game, Marty was starting over.

For almost four decades, Marty took the first pitch. It was partly to size up the pitcher and partly to get relaxed in the box. He thought about it again.

Marty's body and positioning took the pitcher's notice. To the pitcher, Marty looked too old and too frail to be a factor. This would be too easy.

With a smile, the pitcher threw as though he was playing with his 8-year-old child, leaning forward with a soft underhand.

Marty's old frame swung with grace and determination, sending the softball on a seemingly endless upward trajectory, carrying it deep into left center, where it arrived on the grass and rolled toward the bushes. Forty years prior, it would have been a clear triple or an inside-the-park home run. Marty dashed toward first and Wesley took off running for third. Marty could hardly breathe as he ran. Wesley was already home by the time Marty rounded first base.

He slowed toward second and trotted to the top of the base. Marty had been there before, and he was delighted to be there again.

Saint Anthony Residence 1, Windward 0.

After a quick grounder from a weakly sobering Jerry to end the inning, Terry walked out to second base, handing Marty his glove.

"That was quite the rip. If we were in a stadium, the joint would have erupted. Instead, Ray threw up."

"Oh gosh," Marty said, smiling.

The game continued. Marty was the ringer on the Saint Anthony squad, but he was backed by a surprisingly capable defense and a decent cache of contact hitters. Even Ray was starting to pay attention. To the outsider, a bunch of drunks were playing an over-equipped team of middle-aged men. To the insider, the game was a rumble.

By the top of the seventh inning, the score was tied 3-3. Another squad was assembling its coolers for the next game while watching the spectacle before them. It didn't look like a regular softball game. It was a real struggle.

"Last inning, gents," Terry announced to the team after emerging from a summit of junkyard softball leadership. "Let's see if we can pull this one out."

He wanted a victory beer so bad he could feel the cold dribble down his chin. Actually, he wanted a whole case of victory beer, and maybe an extra case to spray on his teammates in celebration. Then again, he could also drink the extra case.

He refocused. It wasn't about the beer.

The team took the field like Little Leaguers dreaming of a trophy. They were unconcerned about contracts or free agency. Suddenly, with a term used loosely at the Saint Anthony, they belonged.

Terry tossed the first pitch of the final inning.

The brawny social worker toward the bottom of the order took Terry's pitch deep into the right field corner. Who knew a right-handed social worker could hit an opposite-field softball that far?

Ray, still on the St. Anthony disabled list, somehow managed to weave his way to the ball, throwing cut-off to Marty at first instead of Harry at second, allowing the lumbering base runner to round second and stand in at third.

Harry surprisingly yelled in multiple directions to cries of acknowledgment, "No worries, boys, just three more outs!"

When the Queen first thought about the team, she worried that a loss or an individual player mishap could lead to feelings of dejection.

Hearing the rally cry from Harry after Ray's only mildly errant throw, she thought differently.

OK, let's see what this team can do, Terry whispered to himself, knowing that he was going to use the same pitch. Luckily, he knew that in recreational softball, no one could blame the pitcher for serving up a meatball. The pitches were supposed to be meatballs. The unlikelihood of his service as a defensive scapegoat was pleasing to him.

Another lob down the pipe. Liner to first.

The game had come back to Marty. He snapped his glove around the liner, touching the base and checking the runner on third. He looked like a skeleton in powder-blue jeans, completing a textbook play at first and a heads-up check to the runner.

One down. Runner on third.

It was the top of the order for the increasingly lethargic Windward team. Much like golf should be 14 holes for the casual player-drinker, softball played past the fifth inning could drag on for those envisioning a cooler of ice-cold beers and embellished conversation.

It was the opposite for Saint Anthony. Embellished conversation was standard language and coolers were ubiquitous.

It was still one out, man on third. Thirsty man on third.

The tattooed accountant at the top of the order was the most competitive player on the Windward team. He wanted to end the game and head to the cooler to tell stories of his own heroics. He was a fine gentleman, but he wanted to win.

Terry lobbed a fat, juicy meatball.

The batter took another monster swing and missed the oversize ball by a ledger page. Strike one.

The ball back in his hand, Terry turned toward the outfield as though mentally preparing to hurl a heater. It was a scheme.

He lobbed another tasty meatball.

This time, the bulky competitor shot the ball upward into left field, where Wesley cleanly fielded it on the bounce and threw to second base. Runner scored.

Windward 4, Saint Anthony 3. One down. Man on first.

Terry worried that the game was getting away from them. He wondered if these guys were told to go soft on the drunks. Maybe this is what competition feels like.

James was in the box. He relished competition.

Terry lobbed a pitch that sailed right over the plate.

James laced it, and it took a hard one-hop to short, leaping onto Jim and sliding off to a complete stop in front of him. He picked it up with his lengthy arm and tossed it to Harry at second base. Harry then threw it to first, where Marty almost split his no-name jeans to stab the ball on its way past him.

The runner was out at second and James was barely halfway down the first-base line when Marty had the ball in his glove. Double play.

Wanting again to "act like they have been there before," the team unleashed only a few outbursts before hustling back to the bench and rallying around Terry and Marty. They envisioned a celebration, preferably one with beer. But the celebration would have to wait.

Terry started the rally cry.

"OK, gents, one more at-bat. Let's show these guys what

we're made of!" He could see the Windward team rallying, and it was now obvious that both teams desperately wanted to win.

Marty took command, "Harry, you're in the box."

Harry stepped up to the plate with an assertiveness he could not recall. He had been sober now for exactly five years and 87 days. Standing at the plate, he recalled a time when his decisions were tentative and his life seemed out of his control. For so long, something had been missing, and it took spirals and treatment and finally sobriety for him to identify it.

It was confidence, and he lacked it.

At the plate, he was aware of his struggle.

The slow pitch arrived, offering him plenty of time to avoid a decision. As the ball approached, Harry grimaced as he swung, his neatly bearded face turning demonic. He high-stepped into his swing and lined one of the cleanest shots of the game, firing a dart into left center. The sight of Harry running, seen in public only a handful of times, was shocking to the Queen.

Man on first.

The two-person crowd of the Queen and Mr. Long erupted. It seemed so out of place for Harry even to play softball, let alone knock a key single, that anything other than elation and celebration would also have been entirely out of place.

The Queen shouted, "Way to kick ass, Harry!"

The entire Saint Anthony team turned around and roared with approval. Harry stood on the base and shined a half-toothed grin that no one had ever seen before. It was both startling and beautiful.

Unfortunately, the next batter was Ray, and he was near pickled. Without a pinch hitter within miles, it was time for Ray.

Ray weaved up to the batter's box, appearing to have found a way to enjoy a beverage or two during the game. He could hardly stand. He struck out in cartoonish fashion on three pitches.

One out. Man on first.

As Ray struggled to secure himself to the bench after sauntering back, Wesley stepped to the plate with an ear-to-ear grin. Wesley never felt pressure. He was part of a team, and it made him smile.

Wesley saw five pitches, two of them strikes—his smile never departing—before he made contact, resulting in a roller to second. The second baseman turned for the force at two, but the shortstop was dreaming about the cooler too much to bother for the textbook 4-6-3. With no one covering second, the second baseman turned a 180 and side-armed it to first.

Two outs. Harry on second.

Terry stepped up to the plate and experienced an almost out-of-body experience. And he was sober. He wanted to get a hit, but he wasn't desperate. He was relaxed, devoid of schemes, and simply happy to be in the situation. If it all ended with this at-bat and the entire team retreated to the Ace Box, never to step foot on the diamond again, his effort would have been complete. Standing in the box, Terry knew he was in the right place.

He straightened up and took his stance.

Foul ball.

Foul ball.

Stepping out of the box, he nodded to James across the field. As softball players, they were now brothers.

The pitch came in a touch high and right over the plate. Terry stepped and swung hard, sending the ball flying over the right fielder's head and down the line, coming to a complete stop in the overgrown crabgrass. Terry flung his bat and sailed off to first, pulling up his jeans in preparation for the sprint. The ball landed just left of the line. Fair.

Terry rounded first base, puffing through an easy double. Unfortunately, Wesley failed to pay attention to the game and was still standing on second base.

"Go to third, third!" Terry implored Wesley, trying not to erupt in laughter right in the middle of the game.

Wesley turned at Terry and was immediately bounced out of the daydream he was enjoying and jolted back into the game. His smile widened and he executed. The ball was still resting comfortably in the crabgrass.

Man on second and third.

Jerry N. was having a blast. He was with friends. He also assumed that cold beer would be a part of the picture, and he could envision girls. It was Jerry N. in the game, and he remembered it well.

By this time, the city league teams were loosely warming up while craning their necks toward the spectacle before them. Something about the game was different. A sharp-looking group of professionals versus a team of oddities—men in black shirts, jeans, and white shoes. Cigarette smoke was everywhere. They had little choice but to root for the obvious underdogs.

As he stepped into the box, Jerry N.'s strategy was simple. Swing hard. His instinct would guide the rest.

He took the first pitch. He was not sure why. This was not a time to be choosy. Stay in the moment.

He sent the second pitch deep along the left field line. An incredible shot almost to the bushes. Foul. The pitcher shook his head, and Jerry N. smiled.

Roundhouse windup. The pitches were getting faster.

On the third pitch, Jerry N. roped it again, this time straight to center. For all parties involved, this game needed to end.

Jerry N. took off for first. Wesley heard the crowd and took off for home. Terry took a moment. He followed the ball over his head. Terry had a plan—not a scheme, but a plan.

With Wesley nearly at home and Jerry N. safely heading toward first, Terry took off from second. It was preposterous to think he would make it home, but in his mind the game simply had to end, and it had to end in glory—for everyone. Marty would probably knock them both home on the next at-bat, but the game needed a moment, and this was it. Marty knew it, and he was smiling.

Wesley had already crossed home plate when Terry made it to third and began rounding the base toward home. The Queen was bellowing to Terry.

"Bring it home, bring it home!"

The center fielder made a textbook throw, falling flat on his face to send a one-hopper bouncing on the mound and right into the catcher's glove. It was lucky and it was perfect. Terry was barely two-thirds down the line and the catcher was standing at the plate with the ball.

It was time for a scheme.

Stopping in his tracks, Terry feigned to turn around and head back to third, which was ridiculous in its own right, but still a scheme.

The catcher, thinking it was ridiculous that Terry would head home, threw back to third, creating a fresh path for Terry back to home.

Terry turned back toward home and sprinted, which he hadn't done since a pool game gone awry years ago in Duluth.

With the ball sailing over his head, he lunged to home, stretching out his left arm to reach for the plate.

Safe!

Saint Anthony Residence 5, Windward 4. Ballgame.

An extended roar heaved from a crowd of strangers and the Saint Anthony team, who leapt in the air like Little Leaguers. Terry picked himself up from the dirt, replaced his hat, and cracked a full-toothed smile toward Marty.

- -

The city league teams tried to take the field amid the mayhem of the Saint Anthony win.

Standard pleasantries were exchanged between the Saint Anthony squad and Windward, with James and Terry earnestly shaking.

They were men, though, and James was angry. Even as a do-gooder, he hated to lose. He thought for a moment about how he would feel if the team that just thumped him was full of bulky ringers from a bank. Somehow, he felt better about losing to the Saint Anthony.

The Windward team surrounded their coolers.

Gathering around the cars, and fully aware it was the first of the month, the Saint Anthony team swapped stories of the game. Credit was distributed fairly, even to Ray, who deserved no other credit than for his hard work to show up and not pass out. Johnny Luck was solid as well. No hits, no runs, but he was present.

Terry, of course, needed to offer a small managerial statement.

"Bring it in! Hey, I think it goes without saying that this team here should be proud of what happened on that field. No one gave us a chance, but we got it done! Hands in!" The entire team rallied in a circle with their orangish, frail hands in the middle. Every single one of them was smiling. In total, there were five full sets of teeth.

Even the gardener across the street stopped and smiled. She didn't recognize Jerry N. She called the police on him a year ago for being passed out in the middle of her cucumber patch.

She dropped off cucumbers at the residence a week after calling the police.

Terry's speech was manager-talk from any post-game rally in America, and that was his point. It was all quite standard.

The team dispersed to celebrate the victory and, unfortunately for some, the first of the month. Terry and Marty gathered up the equipment, loaded the wagon, and stopped to talk with Mr. Long, the Queen, Harry, and Jim.

"Heckuva game, boys!" the Queen exulted. She was glowing. She knew it was more than a game.

Harry and Jim lit each other's cigarettes. Mr. Long just smiled.

"Thanks," Terry replied. "Maybe a celebration is in order?"

"Maybe," she smiled.

"How about after the next game?" Terry was sort of thinking ice cream, sort of not.

Terry turned to Marty, and the two of them walked down the street with the wagon.

Silence can be blank at the Saint Anthony, or it can be reflective of lives turned backward. Today it was neither.

Marty and Terry walked with the wagon, neither saying a word.

MARTY INTERLUDES

"Broken Sky Tonight"

By Marty Peterson, 1984

Vision of a broken mirror
scattered clouds jagged edges
of soft whipped cream intrusion
hide the evening stars
in the distance the moon appears
then disappears
behind the cloud cover
lights of the night
the moon and stars
cast gleams to the water bright
then skip away
hall light and dark
my mind reacts tonight
much like the moon and stars
truly moon beams skip tonight
big lake echoes of your voice
between the movement of space
and broken succession of thought
finally, all these years
big lake the moon and stars
an image of the face I sought

CHAPTER TWENTY-NINE

LOCKER ROOM BUFFET

Back at the residence, it remained the first of the month.

Most of the team disappeared to neighborhood watering holes. Any thought of backslapping around a charcoal grill full of cheeseburgers was quickly lost. They each had $47 in their pockets, and it was time to roll, literally for some. The stories on the bar rail would be new, but the result would be the same.

Ray spent most of his money before the game and quickly passed out after. Johnny Luck disappeared for the evening. The rest of the team hit the town.

Marty and Terry skipped the monthly festivities and returned to their positions in Harry's office. Harry was long gone, riding the bus with a rare smile, and Bill was nervously expecting to make decisions regarding the consequences of first-of-the-month transgressions. He always smoked an extra pack on the first of the month. Those early days of the month were often messy, but peaceful. Belligerence arrived with lack of funds and alchemy. All Bill really needed was a mop and a telephone, or earplugs and a nose clip.

A cold-cut tray from a funeral had arrived earlier in the day, offering late-night eaters an attractive assemblage, enough for a celebratory hoagie. The fare reminded Marty of his old neighborhood. After games at Wilson High School, the boys would ride their bikes to Stasny's Market on Thomas Avenue for a soda and a beef stick. The butcher would give the boys thick slices of fresh salami. If they won the game, he might throw in the soda, no charge. The warm salami was magical; the company of his teammates even better.

Sitting in Harry's office enjoying the sandwich, Marty recalled his days at Wilson. He was open and detailed.

"You know, I remember when we won games at Wilson, we would ride over to that meat market on Thomas for salami and beef sticks. I never needed to oil my glove. The meat did it for me. We won most of our games."

"Anything is better than that lutefisk you Norwegians eat. What do they make it with, lye?" Terry said.

"My mother hated it, which was lucky for us all." Marty knew that Terry was also a Norwegian.

The Twins were on TV in their downward spiral, exuding the haplessness expected from a team of recent minor leaguers hovering near the bottom of an expanding MLB pay scale.

"That Puckett is something. He's a fireplug," Terry mused.

"They're definitely a team of scrappers—sort of like us," Marty said.

"Yeah, like us." Terry's voice was trailing as he dragged a cigarette through a tiny smile.

The evening never erupted as Bill feared. The Twins lost handily. Marty and Terry sat quietly until the game finally ended. They retired to their rooms, not a drop of distilled or malt product in either of them.

- -

The Queen and Jim retired at the same moment, boxes of celebratory lo mein and egg foo young consumed, then left on the coffee table next to heaps of cigarette butts. They had laughed, they had reflected, and they had sat quietly, wondering what happened that day and if they had found something truly special in a home for the drunkest people in America.

CHAPTER THIRTY

ALL-STAR BREAK

The next morning, Marty got in line for a plate of eggs, oddly symmetrical bacon, and toast with margarine. Terry trailed in after Marty and piled on an exact replica.

Marty turned to his co-manager, "Seen any of the team?"

"Not a one."

"Wesley's door was open, and it looked like his bed was still made," Marty whispered with worry.

"I suspect the boys hit up a celebration. I hope Wes found himself a bed with sheets," Terry laughed, knowing that it was commonplace for a few residents to "find themselves" in ditches and alleys on the second day of the month. It was always in the industrial neighborhood, just short of the residence.

Despite the unproductive camaraderie of alcoholics, concern was fleeting at the Saint Anthony. They were either too drunk or too tired for that.

By dinnertime, Marty was worried. He spent the day in Harry's office watching TV and engaging in occasional conversations with returning residents. No one from the team was among them.

"Doesn't it strike you as odd that we haven't seen anyone from the team?" Marty asked Harry.

Harry snapped, "What do you want me to do about it?" He had noticed and he was also worried.

"Nothing, I was just noting it," Marty whispered through a fresh Parliament, suddenly irritated at Harry.

After dinner, Marty still had not seen any of the team. He hoped that most of them were in their rooms, passed out.

Marty was worried for the first time since he walked down the Saint Anthony ramp.

Worried, maybe, for the first time in his life.

"Hey Marty, when's the first ball game? I'm ready for some action!" Freddie proclaimed, only his head visible through the kitchen doorway.

"It's coming up, Freddie! I'll find you. Good to have you on board, my friend." Marty returned, kindly.

He was still worried, but his worry was leapfrogged with guilt for forgetting to tell Freddie about the first game. They might have won the game, but he could have used Freddie in right field.

The third day of the month was a fork in the road. At the watering holes, many of the more flamboyant residents told their last story and bought their last round. They dove into the depths of their pockets to find cigarette remnants and possibly a phone number from the happy-hour patron who believed they could be a savior.

"I can take you away from all of this."

Only once in the history of Saint Anthony did a resident actually find and keep a job derived from the empty promise of a tipsy businessperson at happy hour. No one got sober.

With pockets suddenly devoid of currency, residents would eventually work their way back to the ranch and sink into the normalcy and boredom. They would seek funds for refreshment through conventional means, and they would find their way back to their barstools for at least a few more rounds, after which the cycle would reignite.

The more reserved residents would stretch their funds a little longer, typically utilizing the bargain liquor store. They were not thinkers or strategists: they just wanted to be drunk as long as possible. A case of Milwaukee's Best beer for $6.99 and a liter of plastic-bottle vodka at $4.99 would suffice. Later, factions would formulate to pool funds.

As for the softball team, they were split down the middle, with Jerry and Ray telling stories from a barstool, Jerry N. telling his stories in an alley, and Wesley strolling the neighborhood with a smile. Johnny Luck was nowhere to be found.

Marty remained on post in Harry's office. He had not seen Terry since breakfast a day ago, and he still had not seen any of the team, except Freddie. He kept thinking about Freddie.

It was almost time for the Twins day game against the Brewers.

Marty's irritation toward Harry was on an upward slope. Only a few days prior, Harry had smiled in the sunshine of a seventh inning. By the third of the month, his smile, and the shining sun, had disappeared.

The Twins game reached the second inning before any real activity at Saint Anthony's. There had been a few doors opened and closed and the sound of the occasional toilet flushing, but up until a Twin's line drive, the residence was dead silent.

"Nice rip for the local boy," Wesley slurred.

Wesley had been standing in the doorway since the top of

the second. Harry noticed him right away, which was his job, but he failed to mention it to Marty, which was not his job.

Marty quickly turned around. "Wes! Where have you been?"

"Really nowhere, sir. Just out and about in the neighborhood. Any food back there?"

"There's cold cuts in the fridge and bread in the usual place," Harry responded.

Wesley took his smile and his smell and stumbled down the hall to the kitchen. He downed several sandwiches, including one without meat, before falling asleep at the table, eventually being carried to his room by the next residents who were there to do the same thing.

Marty's smile slowly retreated as he returned to what had become a decent ball game. All it took was one arrival and Marty knew that normalcy had found its course and that his brief stint of worry was partially allayed.

Terry was on Marty's mind. Marty knew that, despite Terry's recent leadership, a conman, storyteller, and all-around dreamer lay in waiting. Terry had an innate desire to be in the middle of the room. It fueled him. His alcoholism was partly borne from those moments where his own depleted confidence forbade him from being the nexus of attention. He drank to get back in the center. At the top of the roller coaster, he was a leader of men. At the bottom, he was a loud drunk.

Marty was never the life of the party, which is exactly how he wanted it.

Marty was comfortable with Terry's patterns. They were predictable. The roller coaster would go back up, and then down, and then back up again. But like most roller coasters, it would never fall off the track. Almost never. He was a Saint Anthony resident, after all.

Marty settled into the final innings of the Twins game, knowing that the Twins would likely lose. He was hopeful. He saw that young talent in the likes of Puckett and Hrbek offered hope for a team that hadn't been in the playoffs since the early days of the Nixon Administration. Marty crossed his legs and lit up a fresh Parliament, finding unusual comfort in his extended stay.

Terry would be OK, for now.

In Marty's eyes, it was not a regular week. The team changed the paradigm. They were managers of a ball club. Marty was not sure if they were going to have another game, which would determine whether or not they were actually a team. In his mind, the ball was rolling, so they may as well see where it could go. Marty worried that, without Terry, everything would stop, and they would once again just be residents in a home for chronic alcoholics.

Marty wanted the team to keep playing.

Leaving his chair in Harry's office, Marty became a one-man search party.

Disappearances were commonplace at the residence, with searching usually left for police and fire personnel. On some occasions, residents would end up deceased, with the other residents never knowing what happened to the disappeared. The Queen would eventually be notified, but word would only spread quietly among the residents, if it did at all. Marty knew that he would search alone, and he accepted it.

"I'm going to see if I can find Terry," Marty told Harry, hoping that Harry already knew something but had failed, though not deliberately, to share it with interested parties.

"OK," Harry returned, uninterested in anything but avoiding controversy and watching reruns.

Marty had a few leads in his search for Terry. He was certain that Terry was not hidden away in the residence or in the wrong room. Residents and staff knew the facility, and it was too busy to make hiding in a basement or a crawlspace possible.

Marty narrowed his search to the neighborhood: a few old-favorite taverns, the county jail, and the detox center. Detox was an unlikely option, as most police officers in the area knew the residents and knew to take them home. Officer Adam was a regular in that effort.

Terry could have left town, but he usually announced his every move. A planned move would have to be glorious, even if it wasn't really. The taverns were the best bet.

As a well-known storyteller and all-around reveler, Terry's gravity came from a bar. Whether it was a lone bartender in the morning, a group of weathered regulars in the afternoon, or college boys in the evening, the bar was Terry's stage. Any number of exuberant subjects may have offered him a bed or a place to crash. It was possible that Terry was simply on a roll. He may have also been face down in the alley from too many shots.

Marty's first stop was the Ace Box. There, visitors could find an audience from morning until morning again.

Marty knew he was taking a risk by walking into the Ace. He knew that he felt better when he was not drinking, but he figured that he could swig an occasional ale or three without ending up in the gutter. Today, he had money in his pocket, and he was thirsty, so he sat at the bar and summoned his trusted server.

"I'll take an RC Cola, Derek."

"Right on, Mr. Marty," Derek responded while filling a pint glass with the extra-sweet and slightly flat Coca-Cola alternative. They didn't tell anyone at the Ace that the Coca-Cola was RC. Marty preferred the latter.

"Thank you, o' kind one," Marty returned, downing half the glass, "You haven't by chance seen Terry in here lately, have you?"

"Mr. Terry was in the neighborhood a day or so ago, but I haven't heard from him since. He was on a roll."

Marty made his way out the door for the next stop. He was thankful for Derek. He stared up into the bright sunlight. Over the next several hours, Marty visited four bars and had at least five RC Colas, but the whereabouts of his co-manager remained unknown.

Back at the residence, after dinner and several incursions from residents on the early transition from money to alchemy, Marty laid in bed. On a usual night, Marty would be enjoying the comforts of a book.

Tonight, he watched a rerun.

Why is it that whenever one seeks comfort in the whimsical humors of a television sitcom, the unfortunately placed "serious" episode mysteriously appears?

Marty wanted to escape, to be lost. Tonight, he was sadly just alone.

MARTY INTERLUDES

Midsummer, 1990

The case manager squared the video camera on Marty and flipped a few switches until a red light turned on.

"OK, Marty, here we go."

Marty was sitting in the basement conference room at Mary Hall Shelter. The case manager's office was down the hall.

The case manager had arranged for mock job interviews for his clients. He would tape the interview, and then watch it with his client, going through dos and don'ts. Then they would do it again. Snacks would be provided. The case manager told his roommates how innovative he was, including the snack part, but they didn't care.

Marty was wearing the K-Mart outfit the case manager purchased—button-down, long-sleeve blue Oxford; khaki pants; and deck shoes. He was also wearing a blue windbreaker that was not approved for job interviews by the case manager's refined, post-college senses. The case manager let him keep it on, with a warning that wasn't an actual warning.

The case manager purposely penciled in Marty right after the lunch hour so that they could grab something to eat beforehand. They sat in a booth at Mickey's Diner, an old railcar diner in downtown Saint Paul. Half the patrons were there to spend the change they scrounged up in the morning, the other half in suits. The case manager chose the locale for the baked beans and conversation. They talked about baseball. The case manager would later write in his case notes, "Had lunch and talked about life."

Back at Mary Hall after the beans, Marty sat quietly at the conference table. The camera was rolling.

"So, tell me about yourself."

He didn't say anything. The last interview Marty did was with the case manager for his intake into the program. He answered all the questions, and the case manager checked all the necessary boxes.

All his other interviews over the past 30 years were for treatment, transitional housing, or the Saint Anthony.

"You have to say something. Tell me about why you want this job." Marty smiled. When he was lost, he smiled.

"OK, let's try this again. Tell me about your last job."

"I worked at the post office."

"And?"

"I sorted mail."

The case manager spent the next 30 minutes going through questions and short answers. At the end of the interview, the case manager realized that no one, other than his kids, had ever asked Marty to tell his story, or worse, no one had ever asked how he was doing.

After the interview, the case manager gave him a bus token and watched as he slowly walked to the corner. It was the first time that the case manager's job had made him sad.

The next appointment arrived right on time, forcing a hard refocus on the next interview.

The interviewee was wearing a button-down, short-sleeved blue Oxford; khaki pants; and deck shoes. He was over 6 feet tall, with long black hair and a beard. The camera quickly picked up a four-letter jailhouse tattoo the full length of his forearm.

He should have gone with the sleeves.

CHAPTER THIRTY-ONE

THE SHOW MUST GO ON

Summer had arrived, and the windows were open.

Marty finished his breakfast and returned to his room to read. It was a biography of Winston Churchill that Jim gave him many months before. It was difficult reading at times, but Marty enjoyed World War II history and delved into as much as he could to gain at least some understanding of the irrevocable sacrifices others had made.

Part of it was also guilt.

Marty served in the military and was stationed in Germany not long after leaving the baseball team at the U of M. His service was short and uneventful, and he regularly drank boots full of lukewarm German beer. He thought he did his part, but he never liked it. There was always a touch of guilt in him for never crawling on his belly under fire. The only roaring fire for Marty in Germany was in the hearth of the local Ratskeller. Marty never asked for danger, and he never wanted it, but a small part of him needed it.

Deep into the book, Marty was brought to attention by the sinister appearance of a shadowed Harry in the doorway.

"Just got a call. The Queen is stopping by this afternoon."

As quickly as he appeared, Harry disappeared. It was apparent that he was seeking solidarity for the upcoming visit, but Harry would never ask for help, certainly not from a resident.

Harry wondered what had happened to the softball team and its moment of brotherhood. His office was empty, and he needed it to be full.

After a short walk to the Corner Market for Parliaments, Marty made his way to Harry's office. He took a moment at the store to ask about Terry, but the clerk denied any knowledge of his whereabouts. Marty hoped that the store clerk would have been chattier, but the clerk looked down on his indigent customers, who didn't have much of a choice. That would require a paid bus fare, and the bus service didn't allow either smoking or an open beer.

The Corner Market had cornered the market.

Back at Harry's office, the silence was ominous and uncomfortable. Harry had made all his preparations for the Queen's visit: air freshener, mopping, and a few loose ends of paperwork. But it was incomplete without Terry, which confused Harry.

Terry was just another resident. He flew hard off the wagon on occasion, he told a few stories, and he had a red nose. It was standard stuff. Yet his absence was obvious in the silence.

It was even more obvious because Harry now felt that the team was part of his job description. It didn't matter that Harry was only a minor role player and, in his mind, hardly a contributor. The Queen wanted the team, and Harry worked at the residence; therefore, the team was his job.

Harry loved the old joke he'd heard from Terry—and a hundred other people:

God is love.

Love is blind.

Ray Charles is blind.

Ray Charles is God.

Like many things at the Saint Anthony, it sort of made sense.

The day moved slower than normal, and despite the cool breeze, Harry was starting to sweat at the edge of his receding hairline. Marty hardly noticed it.

With the Twins playing a night game in Detroit, the afternoon silence was broken by the usual slate of game shows. This time it was *Joker's Wild,* the ticks of spinning wheels clicking like an old clock in a quiet room until they hit pay dirt.

"Joker, joker, JOKER!!!"

Luckily, the alarms of a few jackpots kept Marty awake.

Harry left for the evening without a visit from the Queen. As he rode the bus through the city, he was relieved and hopeful. His mind drifted.

Marty resigned himself to a quiet evening in the office with Bill and the Twins game. He knew that the Churchill book would lead to instant slumber, whereas the Twins game would lead to instant gratification, even if they lost. He would at least remain alert and entertained by the game despite its outcome. There were far worse things he could do than immerse himself in the frivolity of a sporting contest.

He was thinking too much.

"And that'll do it for the third," Bob Kurtz proclaimed.

After staring blankly at the television through another few innings, Marty was interrupted by the sound of gravel in the parking lot, which was unusual in the evening at Saint Anthony unless accompanied by flashing lights.

None of it fazed Bill. He was engrossed in the combination of a *Richie Rich* comic book and the Twins game. Marty turned toward the window.

"It looks like The Queen is here," Marty casually said.

Bill kept his head in the comic book, "Really?"

The Queen walked in and pleasantly took a seat in Terry's chair without Harry's usual fanfare.

"Hello, boys," she smiled and sighed, appearing to have found what she had been seeking after a long day of serving the disadvantaged and dismantled.

Marty responded, "Hello."

Bill looked up, "Hi." He was not worried.

The Queen turned to Marty. She wanted to get to the point.

"Just thought I would check in on the team. I have another game lined up for your team next week. You play Commercial Savings Bank on Thursday. They're in the city league, and they're serious. Where's Terry?"

Bill was clueless as to the whereabouts of any resident, so the conversation was all Marty's.

"Not sure. I haven't seen him."

"Not seen him? What does *that* mean?"

Marty lit up a cigarette, "He hasn't been around for a few days." Marty tried to appear nonchalant, but his worry was obvious. Marty was a terrible card player. He had the numbers part but not the demeanor. Even in baseball, he was inept at faking.

"So, are you saying he is missing?"

"I guess so. We have Freddie, though."

"Alright then," the Queen responded, retreating to silence for several minutes as they watched the Twins game to its end.

The Queen avoided further details on the Commercial Savings team. She had worked through Mr. Ryan to set up the game. Along the way, she heard stories of their prowess on the softball diamond. They were well funded and they meant business, just like their actual business. It wasn't meant to be a test for the Saint Anthony team, it just happened that way. It could be a bloodbath, or it could be a moment for the ages. It could also be a forfeit.

"We'll see you tomorrow from the Metrodome on KMSP 9. I'm Bob Kurtz, and with Harmon Killebrew, we bid you good night!"

"OK, I am headed home. If you find Terry, tell him we have a game scheduled for Thursday at 4 p.m. Hopefully, you'll be ready," the Queen bellowed. Her car backed hard out of the lot, skidding sideways down the driveway.

Marty went through two cigarettes as Bill spent the next 15 minutes rotating through the channels, arriving at Ted Koppel and *Nightline.*

MARTY INTERLUDES

"To the Chemical Dependent"

By Marty Peterson, 1984

What curious people are these
who always perch on the thin edge
balance, seeking strength
hold tight, with knuckles white, the narrow ledge.
Eyes forever between wet and running
minds and face reflect an instant gladness
warm, humanities children of the night and day
sitting on the edge, other half eternal sadness.

Cold rain makes the edge grow slippery
sunlight gives warming to decrease the fright
and dries the tears in hopes of love
while drying precarious ledge, sends hope in flight.
But you, dear child of the night and day
what gives you right to balance on the edge in vain
when love was all I had to give to clear the way
come quick to me, to ease the fear, and
soothe the burning pain.
Hurry, hurry fast, your body leans too near the edge
that swiftly carries you down the darkness of the
night and plunges all that is left of you to silent
death, then burns me out and deadens all my
loving light.
Descending, I too late to help you in your grief
the edge has claimed you, and I in disbelief
cast my hopeless body into shame
too late to help, and helpless, share the blame.
Farewell, dear child of the night and day
the edge is dim now, as you fall in sad decay
spring has gone, since we met in glowing May
I, too, have left with you, and time became
an endless day.

CHAPTER THIRTY-TWO

INTERIM LEADER

Without Terry, Marty had to step in as player-manager-GM. It was more leadership than he wanted.

Marty was not Billy Martin. He could manage a game, but he needed to elevate his motivational senses to avoid a forfeit and an almost-certain team collapse. Harry could have been a choice from the front office, but his rallying skills were lost on a playground some 40 years before, never to return.

Causalities.

Marty needed to keep the team together for one more trip to the diamond. He loosely defined a season as a winning percentage based on more than one game. Two games would be a season.

As to Terry, management gave lost residents about a month. For the storied ones, the favorite sons, they might give two. Staff had leeway. Roster checks by the county were nonexistent. It was up to Harry to send notice up top. But since beds were coveted, an ethical clock was ticking, and it conflicted with hope and compassion for the missing.

Terry was a favorite son. Harry would keep his room ready. The waiting list was as transient as those on the list itself, and an empty bed for a few months would hardly cause a run on detox. Harry would take the bet of Terry returning just to avoid the labor and risks of a new neighbor. Change is bad for those who live on convention. Harry survived on convention.

The team didn't have two months to wait for Terry or a new neighbor. The Saint Anthony softball team would be a memory in a week if Marty didn't take his seat in the skipper's chair.

Marty was aware of the predicament. If the team disbanded, it should be a setback, not a failure. What is failure in a house full of failures? Who would notice? The *Pioneer Press* sports page would remain focused on the Twins and handwringing about the Vikings. Chit-chat around watercoolers across the city would be focused on the lovable Mr. Puckett.

Marty knew that no one on the outside would care if the team went away. But he knew that Wesley would care. He knew that Jerry N. would care. He was certain that the rest of them would care, even Ray. He knew that he would care. Johnny Luck might not have thought about it, but Marty cared about Johnny Luck.

He puffed through a cigarette, sitting upright in Harry's office, "Harry, do you have some scratch paper?"

Marty pulled his chair up to Harry's desk, grabbed a pen from the cup, and slowly wrote.

Softball Practice, Monday, 2 p.m., Raymond Field. See Marty for questions.

His handwriting was ghoulish in its scribble. The message, however, was clear.

Marty walked down to the cafeteria and placed the notice over an expired announcement for a prayer meeting. No one ever showed up for the prayer meetings. No one even knew who posted the messages.

Marty was the manager. Practice would be another story.

CHAPTER THIRTY-THREE

HOT DOG!

Over the next few days, residents drifted back to their rooms. Many prepared for the next phase of imbibement. Moods were relatively high. The cafeteria was full again and chatter was robust with embellishments. A few residents were still unaccounted for, including Terry. The pleasant weather in Saint Paul lifted the senses and brought a new hope to the Saint Anthony.

Most of the team was in-house. Most residents were in between intoxication with money and on the hunt for intoxication without money. They were jittery but ready to play.

Monday's wind blew in with a chill, but by afternoon it was a warm spring day. This was the true Midwest, where the seasons can change in the course of a morning.

Marty planned the practice for early afternoon, hoping that the field would be open and that Harry would get a sub for desk duty and join him. That didn't happen, which left Marty alone with the supply wagon.

Dragging the wagon out of Harry's office in frustrated silence, Marty hoped to run into his teammates. That also didn't happen, leaving Marty to wheel a loaded wagon several blocks to the diamond.

By the time Marty arrived, Wesley and Jerry N. were on the field and in the moment.

"And Wesley makes it across the plate for an inside-the-park home run," Wesley yelled while Jerry N. provided makeshift crowd noises, wheezing a bit in the process.

"There you are, Mr. Marty. Now we can play with gloves and balls," Jerry N. said, grabbing two gloves and tossing one to Wesley.

It was Terry's idea to collect the gloves at the end of every practice. It was a good idea in the beginning, and even better toward the middle and end of the month, when gloves would become tradeable commodities in a street-level exchange.

Marty organized a standard softball practice, running simple drills first for the amenable Wesley and Jerry N., and then for the remaining players who showed up—Jerry and Ray. Jim never made it, Terry was missing, and Harry was working. Marty was certain that Johnny Luck was drunk somewhere, as he saw him stumble out of the residence around lunchtime, likely with remnants from the previous evening's alchemy. Alchemy started early for Johnny Luck.

No matter how one would look at the Saint Anthony team, it was a skeleton squad.

The practice progressed nicely, the players hustling and following the current skipper's lead.

Despite the lingering smell of whiskey on the spring breeze, none of the players appeared to be overly intoxicated. A couple of them even broke a sweat.

No one said a word about Terry. As the Queen often reminded her staff, the choice of "Out of sight, out of mind" or "Absence makes the heart grow fonder" was clear. The line of the needy was too long to dwell.

Except for Marty.

After practice, a tired Marty packed up the wagon with a little help from Wesley and made his way back to the residence. He was confident that he could manage the team, but he missed his partner. Marty might have been the brains of the ball club, and the soul, but Terry was the motivational speaker.

He realized that he forgot to let Freddie know about the practice.

- -

The lines were long at dinner. In Harry's office later that evening, Marty thought about Terry.

Marty turned to Bill, his quiet office companion, "Do you have a piece of paper?"

Bill handed a piece of paper to Marty, who scribbled on it quickly and then walked to the cafeteria. It was snack time and the bill of fare for the evening was ham sandwiches and pasta salad. The pasta salad was brought in that afternoon from a funeral luncheon. No one in the room was able to spear a forkful, and the spoons were useless. Marty didn't have a will, but if he did, the only thing it would have said is, "No pasta salad at my funeral."

Marty tacked the piece of paper over the practice notice:

Softball game THIS Thursday at 4 p.m. Raymond Field. All welcome.

He stopped to make a sandwich and then sat down next to Donald, who wore thick glasses and crisp blue jeans and spoke in Southern cowboy slang:

"Don't let your yearnings get ahead of your earnings. . . . Always drink upstream from the herd."

Terry disliked Donald immensely. Marty liked everyone.

In the 1930s, the name "Donald" was the seventh-most popular boy's name in the United States. By the 1980s, it was 66th. Donald was old-school.

No one knew where he picked up the Southern accent. The only drawl usually heard in Saint Paul was at the State Fair for two weeks.

"You boys still taking players for that-there softball team? I used to play in the military," Donald said to Marty, clearly intoxicated and with several dollops of mustard deposited on his snap-up plaid shirt. Donald apparently did many things in the military, and he regularly indicated his prowess at complex tasks.

"Sure thing, Don," Marty said, "Just be at the field on Thursday, and stop into Harry's office to grab a T-shirt."

Marty did not want Donald changing shirts at the field. Marty was a manager in many respects, not just softball.

"Hot dog! I'm on the team," he repeatedly pounded on the table, splashing Marty's coffee onto his tray while displaying a mouthful of decaying teeth.

Marty was exuberant, as well, unveiling a wide smile for the first time since Terry was officially declared "possibly missing." Celebratory convulsing was not his thing, but he was both humored and happy at the spectacle. Donald's contribution to the success of the club would likely be minimal, but he was a ringer against a forfeit, and he would most certainly be entertaining, depending on who was asking.

If Marty reminded Freddie, all could be well.

MARTY INTERLUDES

Payday, 1990

"Freddie and I went way back. Pretty sure he was from the neighborhood, but I met him at Saint Anthony. He was a gentle guy," Marty said, leaning back in his chair and staring toward the ceiling. "He came by the store once. I don't think he knew I was working here."

The case manager stopped at the mission thrift store to deliver Marty his paycheck; he was paid $4.10 per hour, provided by the city grant. The case manager never understood it, but it was tax-free.

Some of the guys in the program would promptly spend the money; some, like Marty, put it toward the future, whatever future $328 every two weeks could provide.

The store was empty until a mail carrier dropped off the mail. The case manager wondered why the store would receive any mail at all. Of course, the mail carrier knew Marty. They talked briefly.

"You know I worked at the post office? Not as a mailman, but in the plant or whatever they called it."

The case manager knew that Marty had worked for the post office because he filled it out on his intake form when he entered the program.

"We had a party in the parking lot after one of the softball games. Mr. Long brought in burgers and hot dogs, and I think someone had a keg hidden behind the building. I thought that was odd," Marty said, "We did that once at the U, and Coach Siebert almost kicked us all off the team. I found a way to keep the party going, and look where it got me."

Marty was partially joking, but not about the keg. He knew that alcohol was his destructive force, but he never wallowed in misery. He might have been nostalgic about the good times, but he also knew that the good times only happened at the Saint Anthony because he was at the Saint Anthony. And he was at the Saint Anthony because his life fell apart.

Marty was not going backward. He had been sober now for many months, and he knew it was better than the alternative. At some unknown turning point, Marty had looked within himself.

As they sat quietly in the store, the case manager thought about Marty's alcoholism. It was his job to think about it. He wasn't totally sure how many times Marty had been to treatment, but it was more than three. He wrote five on the intake. Who knew about detox? A hundred times?

Marty lived at the Saint Anthony for five or so years until he made it to the Christ Center.

Watching him fumble around the store cataloging books and hanging clothes, it looked like he was focused. But the case manager couldn't figure out what brought Marty to focus. He had been lost for over 30 years. He didn't just press a button and end up a model citizen. Was it treatment? The Saint Anthony? The Christ Center?

The case manager was certain it wasn't Marty's realization that he was at the end of the road. Marty was cerebral. He had known the bottom since his face first hit the pavement. Living at the Saint Anthony was the end, but Marty knew that before he arrived. Alcohol did not warm

Marty's reality. He knew it was destructive, and yet he proceeded.

Something along the way made him feel like he mattered. The case manager was coming to believe it was the softball team.

It was the case manager's job to talk with Marty about his life, and the case manager wanted to talk about all of it—the good, the not-so-good, and everything in between.

"I had an early edition of *Ulysses* that I found at a garage sale," Marty said after several laborious drags of a Parliament. He was sorting books by author. There were no Js for James Joyce in this load. It was mostly Cs for Jackie Collins, and they sold quickly.

"Not sure what happened to that one."

The case manager and Marty sat in the thrift store for the rest of the afternoon. By the time Marty opened the envelope with his check in it, the only liquor store in the neighborhood was closed.

CHAPTER THIRTY-FOUR

ROSTER CHECK, AGAIN

Game Day. Bill inadvertently left the windows open overnight . . . which was a good thing. Damp, fresh air permeated most corners of the residence.

Bill pulled double shifts. He worked for eight hours, and then he would sleep off and on for another eight with the door open in an empty room near Harry's office. He had an apartment on Rice Street, but he slept at the Saint Anthony. He was a former client of another Catholic Charities program, which made the unusual arrangement less than unusual.

He wasn't supposed to leave anything unlocked, but he fell asleep to a Natalie Wood movie. He woke up only moments before Harry arrived.

Unattended and unlocked openings were an evening no-no at the residence. Residents had 24-hour access, but it had to be residents and staff only at night. Chronic drinking attracts enemies and newfound friends. Open windows and doors are invitations to trouble. Not everyone was welcome at the Saint Anthony. This time, luckily, the door stayed closed.

At breakfast, Marty enjoyed an unusually fresh doughnut, coffee, and a sizable round of Parliaments. It was a quiet morning in the cafeteria.

Marty continued his routine in Harry's office. A few residents stumbled in from evening festivities. Harry had a few issues with residents to attend to, but the day was normal, except for one incident particularly irritating to Harry and the staff. Thankfully, the fresh air had immediately washed the odor of what was an extraordinary accident in the bathroom. It was not all about vomit at the Saint Anthony.

Just as Marty and Harry were about to drift deep into *Tic-Tac-Dough,* a shiny Cadillac crept into the parking lot, the slightest dust swirling around its white-walled tires and only a single piece of gravel thrown to the side in its wake. That single piece of gravel gave way to an avalanche when the Queen kicked out her leg from the passenger side of the vehicle.

Marty and Harry took immediate notice.

Harry nervously turned to Marty. "Aw, jeez, I didn't know she was coming today. It smells like crap in here."

"Not at all," Marty returned, staring up to the window but still paying attention to Jim Caldwell hosting the game show. Marty missed Wink Martindale. He vaguely remembered when Wink interviewed Elvis on TV. It was 1956 and the Peterson family was gathered around the fuzzy television for Elvis's first live interview. He mostly recalled that his mom and dad were drunk.

As Harry quickly shuffled magazines into his desk drawer, Marty's mind drifted.

The Queen stopped at the front of the car and waited as the driver door slowly opened.

Mr. Long emerged with a smile. The gentleman kicked up no gravel.

She pointed to the mess of gravel, "Like I said, we could use a new parking lot!"

"You could use a whole new building," he returned, closing the sizable door. The driver-side window was still open.

After an introspective, they turned the corner and sauntered down the ramp toward Harry's office.

"Harry, are we ready for the game this afternoon?" The Queen asked as she charged into the office, her shadow eclipsing the diminutive automobile executive.

"I didn't know you were coming today. Yes, yes, we'll be ready," Harry responded.

She turned to Marty, "Well?"

"We'll be ready." Marty smiled confidently. He was not confident without Terry.

The Queen sat next to Marty, emitting a long sigh as she lowered herself to the metal chair.

"I sure hope so, because I've been talking quite a bit about our little ragtag team. Those suits over at Commercial Savings think they're going to thump you."

"Anyone can talk. Let's see what they do on the field," Marty replied with an unusually competitive tone, his lips pursed and a wisp of smoke trickling from his nose.

"I did a little checking and have not been able to find your boy Terry, by the way." What the Queen meant by "a little checking" was that she put out a Saint Anthony–style APB. She sent a phalanx of aides to every bar, drop-in center, detox facility, and morgue in the seven-county area. Because it was Terry and because it was the team, she even made a few calls on her own to high-ranking county officials. No sign of Terry.

"I did find Eric in a morgue over in Wright County, though, so you know."

Harry stopped pretending to do paperwork and looked up

at the Queen. He had experienced many deaths, and he had even seen a few, but it had been awhile and he was rusty.

Marty stopped mid-cigarette and stared blankly through Harry. He only faintly knew Eric, but he knew where downward spirals ended, and it brought him sadness.

"How did he die?" Marty asked, resuming a full drag on the cigarette.

"Some sort of alcohol poisoning and likely a blow to the head, the usual toxic cocktail. They found him in a ditch behind a bar." Death by anything other than alcohol was unusual for residents.

Mr. Long stood in the doorway and knew that he was in the right place. The Queen had already told him about Eric. He knew that death was expected in life, but he also hoped that the Saint Anthony had brought Eric at least some life before death. No one had other expectations of the residents, even those writing the checks for dignity in despair.

The moment of silence abruptly concluded when Donald immersed his sizable head through the door, immediately shifting the mood.

"What y'all talkin' about in here? We ready to play some ball today?"

His tongued snapped through the large space in his front teeth, sending a fire hose of saliva over Marty and the Queen. Marty was oblivious, and the Queen pretended to be oblivious.

"That's right, Mr. Don, let's play some ball," the Queen proclaimed, rising out of the chair. "I'm going to grab a cup of coffee in that sty of a cafeteria. Harry, c'mon down and kill some time with Mr. Long and me."

It was still a few hours before *reveille* for the drunks on the diamond, but the conversation had successfully shifted from

Eric, and that was a good thing. Luckily for Harry, the conversation was about what items he could envision on a wish list. He wanted to ask for a new TV for his office.

Marty donned a fresh T-shirt and baseball cap, and he sat square at the tiny desk in his room. He wrote out the batting order and then stared blankly at it. He wanted the order on paper and to provide a hint of confidence that he could field a full team. Attendance alone was a feat. Roster check was imperative.

Leaving his room, he turned in the opposite direction of Harry's office and poked his head in at the cafeteria to say, "I'm headed down to the field in case anyone asks." The Queen, Mr. Long, and Harry were gathered near the rear of the dining hall.

"Knock 'em dead," Mr. Long yelled out as Marty exited the cafeteria.

"Really dead," the Queen added.

Marty walked away from the kitchen and into the storage room, where he collected the gear, loaded the wagon, and headed to the diamond. He was already sweating.

- -

Marty didn't see any of the team on his way out and he didn't see anyone on the way to the park, either walking straight or stumbling against cars and trees like a pachinko ball.

He wasn't concerned about the stumbling part. Roster check didn't ask questions.

It was 3:15 p.m. and Marty was at the park. He hoped the players noticed his small print on the announcement: *Warm-ups at 3:30 p.m.* And he prayed that they saw the large print: *Game at 4 p.m.*

Marty believed the Saint Anthony team, if they showed up, had a chance against the more experienced squad of country clubbers and Wall Street wannabes. Marty had disdain for no one, but he wanted to win.

His positive outlook took over, despite his lifetime of disappointments and failures. It was his time.

As he approached the field, Marty's cigarette slipped out of his mouth through his unexpectedly widening grin.

"We ready to play some ball?" Terry grinned, his ballcap standing tall against the backdrop of a nearly full team slowly moving toward the field.

Marty's smile quickly turned to a chuckle as he grabbed his glove and walked onto the diamond. "Let's do it," he replied in the most competitive tone he had ever used.

Marty wasn't going to ask Terry where he had been for the past two weeks. At the Saint Anthony, whereabouts rarely mattered.

But this time, Marty really wanted to ask.

Terry would tell a version of the story, true or not, when he was ready. Today, it was time to play ball.

The end of a heart-wrenching disappearance. This was the Saint Anthony. It was how they arrived at the Saint Anthony, how they stayed, and how they left. The end does not rationalize. Life was so abnormal that normal itself changed. Ray Charles is God.

Marty was aware of his reality at the Saint Anthony, but Terry's disappearance reminded him of the desperation of the residence and the 55 people there, including himself. He found hope in the team, and he almost lost it when Terry went missing.

With the team, he was out of place, and it was the best place he had been in years.

The game would have gone on without Terry, but as he stood there with a smile, Marty knew they were going to win, even if they didn't score a run.

The Saint Anthony softball team hit the field, thankfully not literally. They snapped into warm-ups like a disciplined high school team. Balls popped into gloves, throws defied the absence of muscle mass, and there was even a chant.

"Chili dog, chili dog, can o' corn!" It was the only chant they could remember.

They were ready. An old-school bus pulled up to the curb and deposited a Major League franchise masquerading as a rec softball team.

"Look at 'em, they're huge," Ray whispered.

"I thought they were bankers," Terry chimed.

"They have a bus? Why can't we have a bus?" Wesley asked.

"That's a nice bus," Freddie smiled.

As the team emerged, it was apparent that they were one of two things.

On one hand, they could be that group of guys who insists on the finest equipment, right down to the matching cleats, eye paint, and newest bats. This same group of men in tight uniforms would talk about the team all year long at the office, yet when the time came to take the diamond, they would perform well below the standards that their appearance and demeanor would indicate. They were also golfers.

On the other hand, they could be that fierce group of corporate warriors that takes a low-level corporate softball game too seriously, living up to all performance expectations while vanquishing opponents and marking corporate territory. It was not just a game; it was part of their job.

Marty and Terry watched their synchronized warm-ups. These guys were the real deal.

As the team began assembling on the bench, their apparent leader approached the Saint Anthony bench.

"Who's the leader of this posse?" The Leader inquired. He had tape on his wrists and multiple sweatbands on his arms. There was something written on the tape. Marty wondered why anyone would tape their wrist. In high school, his team had one roll of tape for the entire season.

Marty and Terry looked at each other, as to admit mistakes had been made. Poor decisions were not new to them. They should have practiced more.

Marty smiled and pointed his bony finger at Terry, "He is."

Terry was emotional. He took a deep breath to hold it back, and said, "Right here, sir. The name is Terry. We ready to play some ball?"

"You bet, Terry, let's get it on, I guess," the Leader returned, his face scanning the field with an air of disbelief.

Terry was also in disbelief, but he was proud. The Leader saw a collection of misfits and oddities who would be easily conquered. Terry saw a collection of the forgotten, their appearance on the field an unheralded success in a much larger ballgame. They were his brothers.

Pray to Saint Anthony and you will find it.

But first, a smoke.

Terry looked at Marty, "Should we do another chant or something?"

"How about '99 Bottles of Beer'?"

Terry put his hand on Marty's shoulder and they both smiled. It was time to play ball. The Leader yelled across to Terry and Marty, "Let's get it on, boys!"

Terry, Marty, the Leader, and his apparent sidekick walked to home plate for the unannounced coin tossing. Despite the Saint Anthony's obvious familiarity with Raymond Field and its surrounding bushes, ditches, and hovels, a home field had not been declared, thus warranting the coin toss. Terry could easily have argued for home field, but by that point they were on home plate.

All Terry had in his pocket was an Alcoholics Anonymous coin, which he promptly removed from his pocket. It was a One Year coin that Terry earned many years before, after his second or third run at treatment. He carried it with him every day as a reminder of something. He pretended that the reminder was frivolous and the coin just a conversation piece. It was neither.

He held the coin tightly in his hand and a wave of emotion ran through his body.

"I said, let's get it on," the Leader frowned, using the stock phrase for his third sentence in a row. He looked down at the coin with his thick black eye paint and was moved to silence.

Terry hurled the coin to an unusual height, "To Thine Own Self is heads. Call it."

"Tails!"

"Tails it is."

After an inexplicable conference with his sidekick, the Leader indicated that he would accept home field advantage and take the field.

Terry and Marty gathered the team around the bench.

Terry rallied the team. Marty stood behind him with his arms folded.

"OK, boys, let's show them all what the bottom of the barrel can do. Nice bus, nice uniforms, but no heart. Let's give 'em some Saint Anthony heart and ram it up their asses!"

Cursing was unusual at the Saint Anthony. Profanity was reserved for the street and the unpolished and angry-at-the-world.

It was a short speech. Since most of the residents failed to notice Terry's absence, he was under no obligation to apologize or explain his mysterious foray. His acknowledgment of their position on the so-called social ladder, however, was an unusual indication of their underdog status. Not only were they underdogs in the game, but their odds were also long in the world.

Vegas would agree.

The Saint Anthony players looked intently at Terry and Marty. On that field in Saint Paul, they knew for once they had a chance.

It was time to get it on.

As the Commercial Savings and Loan team took the field, Marty pulled the batting order out of his back pocket. He stared at it, and he looked at the bench. And then he did it again.

"Uh, Terry, I think we have a problem."

CHAPTER THIRTY-FIVE

PICKLED BALL

Terry and Marty looked at the bench and then looked at each other. They were short a player. Jerry N., Johnny Luck, and Donald were missing, which made for a roster of eight.

Maybe if the team had a bus, they would have made it.

Terry stared at the team, scanning the field in the hopes that two men would somehow appear. One would suffice.

“Well now, this is a bit of a predicament. There’s no way we’re going to forfeit this game.”

The Leader walked toward the Saint Anthony bench.

“You boys bringing a full team? I’d hate to load the bus with an easy win, if you catch my drift.”

It was ridiculous to think he was going to demand a forfeit from a team of chronic alcoholics, but that was the case in friendly Saint Paul that day.

Neighborhood sportsmanship had given way to an affected manliness to conquer man. It was a class war come alive. The bankers could not lose to the disheveled alcoholics.

A victory by forfeit against a team of chronic inebriates is not manly by any lift, but those at the watercooler wouldn’t care. His coworkers wouldn’t read the true story, and his teammates wouldn’t tell.

"According to the books, we have 30 minutes to cancel, so hold your horses, Jack," Terry proclaimed, pulling a rule rabbit of his hat. He wasn't sure a rule book existed.

The Leader conferred briefly with his cabinet, not admitting knowledge of the rule but not denying it.

"Right. We'll start the clock in a few minutes," the Leader returned, extending a courtesy to a team he believed he would vanquish, one way or another.

Terry, Marty, Jim, and Harry huddled around the Saint Anthony bench and didn't say a word. Marty and Jim lit cigarettes. There had to be a positive somewhere. Some predicaments can be good. The agony of defeat could be a positive, as it would at least be an emotion. Jim wanted to talk about life lessons, but he kept his mouth shut.

They were rationalizing. No one likes to lose. In particular, no one likes to lose without even playing.

"Let's try and wait it out. I talked with them last night, and they knew we had a game," Marty said, knowing that Terry had been absent and was likely taking responsibility. Marty couldn't remember if he had actually spoken with them.

The Commercial Savings squad fidgeted, alternating between playing quick games of pepper, and criticizing the Leader for choosing the unusual opponent.

For the Saint Anthony squad, the concept of waiting was not new. Between a host of cigarettes and the usual stories and embellishments, the Saint Anthony squad appeared to have as much fun sitting around as they would playing the softball game.

The clock ticked, and Marty and Terry grew worried.

It did not help when the Queen arrived with Mr. Long. They pulled in with unintended stealth in Mr. Long's new Cadillac, which rolled up quietly. No high hums or revving cylinders, just the smooth churn of a brand-new Motor City piston.

Ray was the only one who noticed the sound of the car's engine. "Damn."

The Queen and Mr. Long were merely spectators, and to the trained Saint Anthony eye, all appeared as normal as the situation would allow.

Almost 20 minutes had elapsed, and the scene was becoming uncomfortable. The Leader started to sweat, and he was saving the beers for a celebratory finale. The wait angered him.

Just as though someone had prayed to Saint Anthony, the bushes in right field began to rustle. Everyone noticed it, but only the Saint Anthony players knew what it was.

Marty immediately recognized the stumbling figure in the distance, simultaneously igniting relief and fear.

"I think that's Jerry N. walking toward us," he whispered to Terry. "He doesn't look good."

Jerry N. luckily did not drive a car. The State of Minnesota made sure of that. If he had a car today, he would have drilled it into a tree. The man was drunk, and the only way he could possibly travel was with public transit. No one would willingly give him a ride. Even then, he was lucky to make it on the bus. How he made it from the bus stop to the tracks was another unknown.

Walking to the ballfield in a perfect zigzag, Jerry N. approached the team with a beaming white-tooth smile and an odor of vintage Johnson & Johnson.

"Hello, boys, we ready to play some ball?" He yelled to the team standing right next him.

In unison, they stepped back against the power of his breath.

He was sputtering, "Terry, how ya doin', old pal? Where ya been?"

"Better, Jerry, better," Terry responded, suddenly feeling good about himself.

It was clear to Terry and Marty that Jerry N. was too drunk to play ball. They had no choice.

Jerry N. was intoxicated in totality. Because of his incredible ability to absorb alcohol, there was almost a point of no return on the physical sobering process. Whatever he ingested that day was the result of alchemy, and it put him in another world of the drunk, blotto, blitzed. He was functional and nonfunctional at the same time.

The Leader was unaware of the true nature of a Saint Anthony alcoholic. He was a banker, and he was confused.

As to playing ball, Terry and Marty knew they could pull it off. They were veterans at managing drunken behavior. Marty thought about what legendary Minnesota Vikings coach Bud Grant said about the end zone, and it applied today at Raymond Field.

"Act like you've been there before."

Terry turned to Marty, "Alright then, I guess we've got us a team."

And then he turned to the Leader, "Sorry, buddy, no forfeit today. Let's get it on."

A backup would have been nice, and Johnny Luck was still a no-show.

Marty put Jerry N. at the bottom of the order, which would presumably allow him at least half an inning to sober up without notice, if at all possible. He would then put him in right field, where, if he could stand still and avoid liners to his cranium, he might just make it through the game.

Right field had become the most important position on the team.

The Saint Anthony squad was disadvantaged from the start, but with one of their best players nearly incapacitated and still in the game, and another player missing, they had arrived at an unusual rock-bottom. This was, in itself, hard to believe.

Five miles away, Donald was sitting by himself on the bench at Dunning Field. He had his own glove, and he was wearing cleats.

Five miles in the other direction, Jack was alone on another park bench.

They both saw the notice on the board while they were both sober, but neither of them could read anything beyond, "Game this Thursday." Harry knew most of their alcohol histories in the residence, but he never asked if everyone could read. He just assumed they could read the label on the contents of a bottle, so he left it at that.

CHAPTER THIRTY-SIX

RALLY CAPS

Today, baseball is full of observations, theories, and analysis. Sabermetrics, Cluster Luck, and Moneyball are ubiquitous. In the dugout, clipboards, chalk, and gut feelings have been replaced by physiological assessments, warlike strategy discussions, and boardroom decisions involving hundreds of millions of dollars.

At Raymond Field, despite a collective blood-alcohol level above any safe limits, the game was played in an unusually pure form. No bragging rights, no money, no pressure. A few of them could *walk* a line, but there was nothing actually *on* the line. A million-dollar assessment of Jerry N. from a team of highly paid medical professionals would reveal super-human abilities to consume alcohol, but it would fail to reveal the obvious—that he had *heart*.

Teetering at the end of the bench, Jerry N. wanted to get in the game. Unfortunately, his legs were shaking. Just as Jim stepped into the box to start the order, a listing Jerry N. fell off the bench and rolled several feet, stopping on his back, laughing uproariously. It was now apparent to anyone even near the field that Jerry N. was drunk.

Marty looked at Terry. "I think we need to do something about ol' Jerry."

"I would hate to interrupt his happiness, but I think you are correct, sir," Terry returned. The Queen was keenly aware of Jerry N. Her brow was furrowed, and she was head-motioning to Jim. Jim head-motioned back to her, and they agreed. This was Terry and Marty's team. It was difficult to believe in learning moments at the Saint Anthony, but if there was one, this was it.

Terry conjured up a plan.

"Hey Jerry N., since you're bringing up the rear of the order, and you were late anyway, how about a couple of laps around the field to warm up? The rest of us did it, so how about you get your butt out there?" The plan did not have a hint of addiction-and-recovery theory but rather a strategic urgency to sober him. Terry had lied about the team laps.

"Roger that, Terry!"

Jerry N. bounded up from his now-comfortable position on the ground and sprinted outside the third-base line. His pants were soaking wet.

The Leader was too shocked to do much. He just wanted to get the game over with.

"There we go," Terry turned to Marty, surprised that Jerry N. responded without protest.

Jerry N. was already long gone down the field when the first pitch crossed the plate in front of Jim. It was an easy out for the bank. Jim was experiencing heavy abdominal pain, his years of excess catching up to his ability to live outside the slow-moving confines to which he had become accustomed. A few cups of Ensure and a pack of cigarettes, although not prescribed by anyone other than himself, were all that was keeping him upright.

One down.

Marty lined his third pitch down the right field line for a clean double. It was shocking that a man of Marty's frail build and years of booze could rip a heavy softball down the opposite line. Only a perfect swing could make that connection. Many things had left Marty, but not his swing. If he had any wheels at all, it would have been a stand-up triple. It was a miracle that he made it to second without breaking a bone. Sliding was never an option.

Batting third, Ray stepped to the plate dressed in full black, his team T-shirt and hat plus matching black leather pants he had procured from a catchall bin at Goodwill. A gearhead at heart and an alcoholic by trade, Ray was never one for the sporting life. Since early grade school, he had found his place among the oil-soaked garages in his working-class neighborhood. In the beginning, his older brothers thought it was fun to hand little brother an ice-cold ale in the garage. What started as a rite of passage became a problem. He learned how to fix cars, but he also was on his path to Saint Anthony. He finally thought it was time to give sports a try.

At the plate, Ray stood tall and straight, as though he was a child at his first Little League at-bat. He held the bat high in the air and intently stared down the pitcher.

As the slow, arcing pitch approached the plate, Ray, seemingly intoxicated, awkwardly stepped into the ball long before its arrival, twisting his body and hitting the dirt as the ball slowly traveled over the plate. The bat flew into the air, landing just short of the visiting bench.

The bankers were too confused to flinch, and Ray was too pickled to be embarrassed, but he was so annoyed with the tiny scuff on his new pants that he threw his hat to the ground in a flurry of expletives.

Baseball purists often invoke the study of physics to describe the movement of bats and balls. The *American Journal of Physics* outlines the swing in detail:

The force acting on the bat is determined from the velocity of the center of mass, and the angular velocity of the bat provides additional information on the couple exerted by the two hands. . . . It was found that a couple is needed to start the swing, and a large opposing couple is required near the end of the swing to prevent the bat from rotating through an excessive angle before it impacts with the ball.

Ray missed that lesson in high school. Actually, he missed most of high school.

Ray stared down the pitcher as though he was angry at the pitch and not his intoxication or general lack of coordination. He took an actual baseball stance and swung hard into the meat of the next pitch.

Hard single to left!

Rounding first while the throw went home to stop the slow-moving Marty, Ray thought about taking second but stopped after realizing he'd have to slide.

Solid single, clean pants.

Jerry N. was now on his second pass around the field, with the game at one out, man on first and third. Top of the first.

Wesley stood at the plate, chewing what seemed to be an entire pack of bubble gum. He assumed a crouched position in the box and swung his bat windmill style in an attempt to loosen up like the big leaguers. In a waterfall of pink gum and saliva, his gargantuan sugar chaw fell out of his mouth and the bat slid through his hands, continuing to twist in midair as it round-housed toward the mound. The pitcher dove headfirst toward first base while the bat sailed over him, landing directly on second.

The Leader had enough and erupted. "What the hell was that all about?" He looked to Terry in a move to protect his men.

"Take a break, Jack. It just slipped out of his hand," Terry fired back.

"Maybe you all need to take a break," the Leader returned, growing angrier. He started walking toward Terry.

Wesley was squarely focused on his bubble gum. With a confrontation in front of him, Wesley fumbled around the plate to reclaim his lost gum. Luckily, it fell directly on home plate, and he re-inserted the still-dusty wad back into his mouth.

The Leader stopped. He turned around at the sight of Wesley and walked back to first base.

Terry stared at the Leader and yelled, "Batter up!"

Wesley settled into the batter's box, and the pitcher shook his head and wound up. Wesley furrowed his brow, stepped into the pitch, and took a monster swing. He struck the ball on the lower half of the bat, and it took a hard hop in front of the plate and skipped high like a stone skimming on a lake.

The Queen shouted from behind the backstop as the small crowd cheered, "Run, Wesley, run!!"

Wesley sprinted toward first while the shortstop charged the ball. Wesley's body may have been ravaged by alcohol and a variety of other chemicals, but the man had enough heart to sprint. He raced toward first, his bowlegs churning wildly, and dove straight into the base as the throw from short came in behind him.

Safe!

It was a whirlwind play that set the unusual game in motion. Marty made it home, Ray could only make it to second in his leather pants, and Wesley somehow managed to hang on to his bubble gum, with the entire team and fan gallery grinning.

Saint Anthony 1, Commercial Savings and Loan 0.

The gardener across the street had been watching from the first pitch.

Freddie was up next. Freddie knew what he was doing. He was younger than Marty, but if their years had converged, they would have been on the same diamond—Marty at Wilson with a perfect swing and Freddie at Central High School as a reliable, occasionally spectacular switch-hitting third baseman.

Alcohol and time have their ways. Until today, Freddie and Marty had never met on the diamond.

Stepping to the plate, Freddie had his life back. Pray to Saint Anthony and you will find it.

He took the first pitch. He took the second pitch. The Leader was irritated.

At the third pitch, which was not as good as the first two, Freddie took an extra-wide step forward and golfed the low ball with a hard liner to center!

Freddie took off, his center of gravity unusually balanced as he rose up and stood on first. Ray had made it home, and Wesley was on third, panting. Freddie was smiling ear to ear. He was in familiar territory. He just needed a reminder.

The moment was real. They were beating down the bankers, and the bankers were not pleased.

Saint Anthony 2, Commercial Savings and Loan 0.

The bottom of the first inning through the sixth was a softball game like any other rec league in town. Solid hits, deep bombs, a touch of hijinks, and some minor verbal and physical scrapes.

Standing in the crowd, the Queen beamed with amazement and pride.

"Boy, these kids can play," she proclaimed to Mr. Long as she looked out on the field.

Marty and Freddie went "round the horn" after two quick outs led off the bottom of the sixth. They forgot to do it after the first out.

Mr. Long was not surprised. A full life of alcohol had led Mr. Long to despair and separation from his family, but it was the support of his family that brought him back. In time, he realized that he was human like everyone else: He could fall again, or he could achieve whatever his own humanity allowed, which was *anything.* Eventually, Mr. Long was held in high esteem for his deeds, which made him uncomfortable, for in the end, he was just a man.

The ballplayers were also men. And the men could play ball.

Top of the seventh: Saint Anthony 2, Commercial Savings and Loan 1.

By this point, it was an actual contest. Marty and Terry were barking strategic orders with cigarettes dangling from their chapped mouths, the Leader was getting frustrated, and everyone was drenched in perspiration, some of it with distinguishable blood-alcohol content.

Jerry N. stepped to the plate, and he was dry as a bone, on the outside.

The Leader had figured everything out and was infuriated. He looked to Terry. "Really?"

Terry was ready for the scuffle. "Yes, Jack, really. Not sure there is anything you can do about it. Am I right?"

"If that's how you lowlifes want to play it, then fine by me."

Only Terry and Marty heard the Leader. They knew what

was happening. They were winning. They looked at each other, smiled, and then looked back at the Leader and smiled again.

Jerry N. was in the box.

He took his time in the box, lifted the bat high in the air behind him, and grinned the width of his face. His breath traveled to the pitcher's mound.

The Leader was on the mound. He moved off first base in the fifth to take control of the game. He was irritated and his MBA wasn't helping.

He leaned off the rubber toward home plate, stood straight up, leaned again, and wound the ball with the force of a Dust Bowl gust, heaving it toward the smiling batter. The ball failed to arc and instead took a cannon shot toward Jerry N.'s head. Jerry N. dumped to the ground with the speed of a retreating gopher, avoiding what most certainly would have been a permanent hangover. There was only silence—even the wind and the birds took a moment.

Other than an audible cigarette puff from the Saint Anthony bench, the first sound was the dirt underneath Jerry N. as he rose, brushed himself off, and stepped back into the box. He had not stopped smiling.

Terry decided to let Jerry N.'s bat do the talking.

The Leader was fuming, even though he had just thrown the ball at Jerry N.'s head. He pursed his lower lip and tilted his head. Just as he was moving his brow in the direction of an apology, he wound up again like an air-raid siren and delivered another heater down the pipe.

He was trying to strike him out, but he wanted to knock him out.

Continuing to smile, Jerry N. delivered a picture-perfect swing that launched the softball directly to the heavens. The ball sailed and sailed, its trajectory never changing. Before anyone could react, the ball had flown over the bushes, across the tracks, and into the depths of the rail yard in the distance.

Jerry N. had literally gone yard.

Upright and smiling, Jerry N. rounded the bases, leaning in toward the mound as he swiftly made his way home to greet the open arms of his teammates. If only the rest of Saint Paul—or the rest of the world—could see this one moment on this little ballfield in Minnesota.

Behind the backstop, the Queen should have been exhilarated. But she was the Queen, and what transpired was what she already knew. Her heart was racing, her eyelids were half-closed, and she had a tiny sliver of a smile. In the end, she wasn't surprised that they were winning the game—she had long believed they had what it took to succeed.

The team also knew it. At the dawn of their lives, they were no different than anyone else, and at the dusk of their lives, they would be no different than anyone else. The in-between was the murky part that was quickly clearing.

The team celebrated Jerry N.'s dinger in usual softball fashion, jumping together as they embraced the temporary home run king. Half the team ignited celebratory cigarettes.

With just one inning remaining, it was not the end of the contest. The outcome was clear, however, and both teams knew it.

The Leader was frustrated and dejected. But he was also calm. Not once did he ease up on his downtrodden opponent, and not once did he feel bad for them. He knew he was bested. But he now understood the nature of what was before him, and it put him at ease. They were equals as men, but on the ballfield, the team of chronic alcoholics was better.

The remainder of the game followed the trajectory of Jerry N.'s home run. The Saint Anthony squad pounded the proud-but-lowly group of bankers. Marty anchored the team with textbook play, and every player contributed. Even the other Jerry managed to snag a deep fly ball without losing his filtered Swisher Sweet. The bank put up another run, but the game was clearly over on the flight of Jerry N.'s trip to the yard.

Johnny Luck had mysteriously appeared on the bench. After a round of high-fives, he thought he had played in the game.

At the final pitch, Terry lobbed a slow ball that was grounded to Jim at second, who threw crisply to Marty at first. Marty clapped the ball hard in his glove. Jim slowly walked toward Terry on the mound. Marty was on his way.

Marty reached the mound and looked to Terry and Jim. With a grin as wide as it had been since high school, he lifted his voice for the first time in more than 30 years, "Now how about *that?!*"

Saint Anthony 8, Commercial Savings and Loan 2. The Saint Anthony Residence was undefeated.

CHAPTER THIRTY-SEVEN

GOGGLES NOT REQUIRED

The "season" had just begun, but an unlikely camaraderie permeated the rusty backstop and crabgrass of Raymond Field. Amid bankers, Little Leaguers and their watchful parents, curious neighbors, and a softball team from the Patron Saint of Lost Items, a celebration ensued without Champagne or rubbing alcohol. Wesley laughed with the wide-eyed 12U club, Freddie chatted it up with their apprehensive parents, Jerry N. stumbled through a conversation with a neighbor, Harry bantered with Jim, and Terry chatted with just about everyone, a wet cigar hanging from his mouth. It had been in his pocket the entire game.

Marty stood in the middle of it all. He knew it was only the beginning, but the streak of two seemed to span a lifetime.

The Leader ordered his team to put the cooler onto their *Partridge Family* bus. He had transitioned from teammate to Vice President, Banking Team Lead, an unfortunate reminder to his team that he was the actual boss. As he stepped onto the bus, he turned around and looked at Marty.

He gave the brother-nod. Marty wasn't one for the nod, so his thin smile answered. They were brothers. The Leader wouldn't give Terry the pleasure.

As the bus pulled away, Marty, the Queen, and Mr. Long rallied around a crumpled metal garbage can. Garbage cans were natural rally points for the Saint Anthony, even for staff and wealthy benefactors.

The Queen was grinning, and her eyes were wide. "That was quite the ball game, I gotta tell ya."

"Yup," Marty returned, looking out to the field as the celebration began to dissipate toward the bushes and the Little Leaguers started their warm-ups.

"You know, Marty, I always knew you could do it."

Marty was puffing on a fresh Parliament. The feeling of a positive outcome was a moment that he had forgotten. There had been small victories, but this was different. They beat a real-deal team. There was no chance that the bankers had let up on them. Marty puffed his cigarette over the conversation and remembered how good it felt to be accepted.

"Tell your boys to come back to the residence. I want to have a chat with them before they do whatever it *is* they do," the Queen politely commanded.

The Queen hopped in the Cadillac with Mr. Long, Harry took flight with Jim, and the rest of the squad gathered *en masse* for the short walk back to the residence. They arrived at the ballpark from a variety of directions and capacities, but they left as one.

Mr. Long had been mostly quiet during the game, but he was proud. He had lunch plans with The Padre the next week at the Lex, and he was giddy at the opportunity to spin ballfield yarns with the increasingly ornery leader.

The Padre was nowhere to be found on the diamond. He took his pleasure in the stories reported back by his minions, preferably over plates of rare meat, mint jelly, and afternoon scotch.

Marty and Terry brought up the rear with the wagon. The team had stopped on the tracks, without a full bottle in sight.

"That was quite the game," Terry said, looking forward. "Thanks for keeping it all together."

"My pleasure, and thank *you,* sir."

They walked in silence behind the celebratory mob of athletic heroes, each player sharing stories of the day's conquest. Even with full witness to the occasion, embellishments of athletic prowess were ubiquitous.

The team approached the residence and was greeted by the wafting aroma of charcoaled meats. Grills were smoking, music was playing through the office window, and what looked like actual chefs were lording over racks of ribs and perfectly charred halves of chicken. Mr. Long was uncertain what the ultimate result of the game would be, but he knew that a celebration was in order.

A celebration was exactly what happened on top of the crumbling parking lot in the industrial, almost-forgotten neighborhood. They enjoyed ribs, chicken, and a keg of root beer in celebration of a 2-0 record. The smell of charcoal in the neighborhood was usually reserved for Friday-afternoon office parties, but today it was the Saint Anthony Residence, and Marty, Terry, and the boys enjoyed every sauce-soaked minute of it. They had played America's pastime and embraced it as Americans, covered in barbecue sauce, all created equal.

Marty sat down next to Jim and Johnny Luck. The plastic tablecloth was neatly clipped onto the long table. Johnny Luck had barbecue sauce all over his face and hands. He couldn't remember the last time he sat outside to eat, at a table.

Marty was kind. "Good job out there, Johnny. We needed every live body to get it done. Stay with us, friend."

"Thanks, Marty." It was the first thing he'd said all day.

It was the day after the game with the bankers, and the residence returned to its cycle. The middle of the month had passed, and the end of the month was approaching.

Marty and Terry returned to Harry's office and assumed their posts, enjoying conversation, cigarettes, and an acceptable range of the kitchen menu. A Twins day game was on in the background.

Bob Kurtz had hope in his voice, "And the Twins take the lead in the fourth behind another blast from Puckett."

Like a Twins lead in 1986, the day was different.

To the outside world, the Saint Anthony Residence was a cauldron of the stereotypical. Drunkards bouncing off walls, wild stories from grizzled drunks, and overall desperation.

Today, the difference was the silence.

Where silence had once brought self-awareness, today it brought reflection.

Harry looked up from the blank paper he was pretending to read. "The Queen called this morning. She has a game set up for next week with those Nickel Joint guys. I heard they're killers."

Marty and Terry both had wisps of smiles. It was not the joy of victory. It was the joy of equality. They knew they could win.

Marty looked up, his eyes wide open through his thick glasses and his brushed yellow teeth shining in the sunlit basement.

"I can't wait."

CHAPTER THIRTY-EIGHT

TED WILLIAMS AND MARTY PETERSON

On September 28, 1941, Ted Williams woke up with a .39955 average. The second-place Boston Red Sox were 17½ games behind the Yankees and facing the lowly Philadelphia Athletics in a doubleheader for the final two games of the season.

Ted Williams was offered an opportunity. Sit out.

Statistically, official baseball annals would round .39955 up to the elusive .400, and *official* history would judge him accordingly.

But Ted Williams would not round up, nor would the baseball public. He wanted to finish with a legitimate .400 average.

In his first at-bat of the doubleheader, Ted lined a single. In his second at-bat, he hit his 37th home run of the season. By the end of the first game, he had gone 4 for 5. Even if he remained hitless in the second game, his average would have been .400—no rounding necessary.

Dick Siebert played first base for the last-place Athletics in 1941. He would leave the team shortly before the end of the season to assume teaching duties in Minnesota, eventually coaching Herb Brooks and Marty Peterson. Dick Siebert was not at Shibe Park when Ted Williams clinched the last .400 season of the 20th Century. Bob Johnson, a left fielder, was filling in for Dick at first base.

Ted's first single was between first and second. The right-handed Johnson had his glove on the left side. The left-handed Siebert, a seasoned first baseman, had his glove on the side of the liner. History can judge if he would have made the play and impeded Williams's momentum.

For the doubleheader, Ted Williams eventually went 6 for 8, ending the season with an average of .40570, rounded up to .406.

Marty Peterson was not Ted Williams. Through Dick Siebert, he was less than six degrees of separation from Ted—maybe two degrees. Marty could have avoided the Saint Anthony softball team. They all could have avoided it. The only rules at the residence were no drinking on premises and no fighting. No one was required to play. No one was required to do anything at all.

Ted Williams wanted history to judge him accordingly. Saint Anthony residents were not in the history books, but they were being judged. They knew where they were, and they knew why they were there. But they were still men, and they were home.

This was one game they would not sit out.

DIAMOND CONCLUSION

FIELD OF DR(E)AMS

Late summer, 1986 (final game of the season)
Bottom of the last inning, game tied,
now two outs, two strikes, bases empty

Jerry N. was sleeping it off on the grass behind the bench, but the game was on. An undefeated season was on the line. They won pride after the first game against the foundation, confidence after defeating the bankers, and bragging rights with a no-nonsense victory over the Nickel Joint. All of the other in-between victories were gravy. This, the last inning of the final game of the season, was validation.

Freddie was on the bench after a fresh round of backslapping, with the team turning its attention to a chance at ultimate victory. Everyone on the bench was smoking except for Freddie. Freddie didn't smoke. Ray had just started, again.

Marty was in the box.

The small gallery was fixated on the game. The Queen, Mr. Long, and The Padre—who decided to attend a game for the first time—were behind the bench near the curb. Mr. Long and The Padre were on bent lawn chairs, but the Queen stood. It was The Padre's first game, and he was sweating in his all-black priest outfit. The Little League team was on the grass down the third base line. One of the coach-dads secretly bummed a cigarette from Jim and was standing behind Mr. Long's Cadillac. A group of neighbors assembled across the street.

Jim and Harry knew they were there to maintain order. That was the easy part. They were experts at managing difficult moments. If the Saint Anthony had operated like a prison, everyone would escape. Dignity was in the origin of the facility itself. The team was no different.

Jim and Harry were also in the game. Two old recovering drunks had bought into the elixir of America's pastime. They were in the moment. They wanted to be a part of the team, and they wanted to perform on the field. The latter was the hard part.

"You know, Jim, I thought I was going to spend the summer secretly whisking the guys away for throwing up or taking swings at neighbors. I was wrong," Harry whispered.

"The boys definitely have it in 'em. We've always known it, and here we are."

"Got that right, sir, got that right." In three months, Harry had traveled from annoyance to respect. Now, it wasn't a job; it was a mission.

Marty repositioned himself. On the field, it was quiet.

The pitcher wanted to do something to help Saint Anthony. He didn't know who Saint Anthony was and he wasn't used to lost causes. But he thought the captain had somehow tipped the scales, and he wanted to make it right without losing his future. He took his time on the mound. It looked like he was trying to ice his own team. He just couldn't figure out how to cut Marty a break. He dried the ball on his shirt and went into a slow half windup.

Marty was in his stance, his creaky knees bent and his bat loosely hanging parallel to his head. He had been doing his best to avoid controversy for his entire life. Usually, controversy led to rejection, and rejection led to beer. Sometimes it was planned, and other times it just happened. It always led to beer.

Today, there wouldn't be any beer. "Time!"

The pitcher spun his arm around without releasing the ball.

Anyone even close to the field loosened their clench and thought the same thing. "What now?"

Terry put his head in his hands.

The parks worker was at a crossroads between his excitement for the game and his need to move it along for the next team. He borrowed a smoke from the parent who borrowed from Jim. The parent had borrowed a few extra cigarettes for covertly smoking later in the garage. Jim was pleased to support the cover-up.

The captain kept his mouth shut.

Johnny Luck had called time. It was unclear whether he was authorized to pause the game, but his sheer volume caused the entire field to take notice. Johnny Luck stood up from the bench and walked over to Marty. He was the tallest player on the field and the skinniest. His XL uniform was too short, but it hung loosely on his body like a crop top. His cap looked out of place atop his stringy mop of hair.

Johnny Luck did not understand rules. Any rules.

The Little Leaguers couldn't understand someone like Johnny Luck, but they were not afraid as he slowly shuffled in the dirt toward Marty.

No one knew what to make of him, but it was clear to all at Raymond Field that Johnny Luck was a tired soul, as though life had been slowly poured out of him.

At rock bottom mentally and physically, Johnny Luck had not experienced joy or outward emotion that anyone could remember, even himself. This was his moment.

He walked up to Marty. Marty was not surprised as he turned around, leaned on his bat, and offered a thin smile from a friend.

"I just wanted to thank you for letting me on the team." His speech was quiet and broken. "Knock one out for the boys."

"My pleasure, Johnny. I'll give it my best, which is all I got."

He slowly shuffled back to the bench, his head down. All eyes were on Johnny Luck.

Marty turned back into the batter's box. The pitcher's head followed Johnny Luck all the way back to the bench, then turned back to Marty for the windup.

Jim put his arm around his friend.

Marty and the intern-pitcher turned to face each other once more, perhaps finally.

The meatball floated evenly past Marty's knees. Marty knew he didn't have enough power to lift a softball deep. He needed a lobber to drop down into the strike zone. In college, trajectory did not matter. He could hit fireballs long before he drank Fireball.

Marty let the ball pass.

The Saint Anthony bench was restless and focused on Marty.

Behind the bench, past Jerry N., the powerful Queen was a wreck. On the outside, she remained in control, a Virginia Slim 100 dangling from her mouth and her eyes fixed on anyone who might seek to upend the moment. She stared down the captain.

Terry felt like he had the DTs. Twenty years ago, he would medicate his nerves at the Joker's Wild Bar in Superior, Wisconsin. Today, he wanted to be nervous.

He yelled from behind the bench, "C'mon Marty, one time for the boys!"

Marty was pressureless. In the bottom of the seventh with two outs and two strikes, his mechanics were the same as if it were the top of the first. Much like his life, he didn't think about it.

Terry was loud enough for Marty to turn his head. Marty looked at Terry with a long, thin smile and slowly nodded.

The young pitcher was also in the moment, but not for the drywall team. He was out of ideas on how to make it better for Marty, so he decided to get on with it, old-school. He pulled his arm back and sprung it forward in a full roundhouse. He had intended to hurl a straight fastball down the pipe in the hopes that the old man could at least send it to the short outfield and feel good about making contact.

The ball stayed in his hand too long. He knew he missed the release. Instead of stopping or swinging around again, he consciously let go of the ball. His work was finished, and in an instant, he was relieved.

The softball ascended, and to everyone watching it looked like a trick pitch. The captain was proud of his young sidekick. The Queen knew that the youngster had never heard of the old softball barnstormers who played down the road at Midway Stadium. She knew he was innocent.

The Queen regularly blurted out inspirational sayings—some she made up, some she just thought were her own. Sometimes they crossed over.

"No one is in the way. They are the way."

Marty saw an entire life in one pitch. He saw Terry, Johnny Luck, Wesley, and Freddie.

He saw his mother, he saw his old teammates, and then he saw himself.

The slow ball reached the top of the arc and appeared to stop.

- -

Across the street, the gardener was talking to a young couple in front of her house. They were walking a pair of English Labradors. She was wearing a pair of Wellington boots. The dogs were busy sniffing the garden for intruders. The gardener was not young, but her arms were tan and sinewy.

"Just wanted to make sure you're alright. We're new in the neighborhood," the man said.

"I'm fine, thank you."

The gardener had lived across the street from Raymond Field for over 50 years. Her husband had passed, and the three kids were long out of the nest. One was in the military, one was a professor in Colorado, and one was a nurse in Florida. They had many great schisms in their family, but the park bound them. The memories of softball, hockey, and just running around transcended the differences they had about the world.

Half the family called it Raymond Field, and the other half called it Langford Park.

"Well, you call us if you ever need anything. We bought the Haggenmiller house down the block." She knew where the new neighbors lived.

The gardener was apprehensive about nothing. She was often confused but never afraid, and certainly never angry. She knew that, in 50 years, the young couple might know the park as she did.

The gardener knew about chronic alcoholism. She called the police on Saint Anthony residents by the train tracks but only because she knew the train would be coming. She never dialed 911. She called the officer she knew. She contacted Harry once, but he just called the same officer.

She had seen just about everything on the field—occasional

kerfuffles and a host of minor criminal acts that largely involved kids of neighbors.

Watching the first game three months ago, the gardener processed the scene along with her tomatoes. It did not take long for the savvy neighbor to see what was happening between the smokers in jeans and the shiny professionals.

The park invited them to forget their differences.

Over the course of the spring and summer, she recognized a handful of the professionals as sons of friends and neighbors. She also recognized the Saint Anthony players from the tracks. She was pleased that the train schedule didn't matter. She could almost smell the Queen's perfume from the garden, and she knew immediately that the games were more than just softball.

The gardener did not call the police officer that summer, but she asked the council member to put an ashtray by the backstop, which never happened. The gardener decided not to bother Harry and quietly picked up the butts with her hands after every game.

The pitch to Marty was just above her eye level and starting to head down. "Excuse me for a second. I want to watch the end of this game," she told the couple.

The Queen started to perspire. She followed the softball's extraordinary arc as though it was her life.

The Padre and Mr. Long were smiling, confused by the brouhaha. The Padre wished the council member from the ward was at the game so he could see that it wasn't always clients causing the problems. Mr. Long brought a cooler of club sodas, and The Padre had a flask of scotch. At Christmas, The Padre always received at least two monogrammed flasks. Nobody even thought of stepping into his house without a bottle of scotch, and The Padre didn't like the cheap stuff.

The Padre couldn't wait to tell Mr. Ryan about the game. The ball was still in the air, but he could see the olives in his dirty martini at The Lexington. Mr. Ryan knew the drywall team, but The Padre wouldn't tell him about the captain. He would instead tell him about the structural failings of the Saint Anthony Residence building. Mr. Ryan would not just donate a few air-conditioners. He would tear down and reconstruct the entire building.

If Marty won the game, The Padre could tell stories that would open pocketbooks across the city. In so many ways, it was about justice.

The Queen had a different view of the softball's arc.

If Marty laced it, the Queen wouldn't seek accolades for a successful experiment. It wasn't an experiment, and its people weren't subjects.

As the ball reached the top of the arc, everything seemed completely normal.

The Queen was never on a designated path to nonprofit greatness. She didn't eye the corner office, and she didn't think about her paycheck. The money paid for her car, her house, and the egg foo young.

Still, the softball meant something as it hung in the air like a Ray Guy punt. Time had stopped and the Queen looked around. Jim and Johnny Luck were arm in arm, Marty's glasses were off-kilter, Wesley was stomping his foot, and Freddie was smiling.

The Queen's rage at injustice was mixed with humor. She was never too serious, even though her passion meant life or death. Her life had turned in many directions, and much of it was difficult. Her spirit guided her to the moment, and she knew it. As Marty tightened in the box to meet the pitch, the Queen saw it on his face. Anticipation is opportunity. Fun is joy. The softball team was an embodiment of the Queen herself for, in the end, justice is really all about opportunity, including the chance to have fun.

The Queen said it herself, and perhaps even made it up. "Worry, fear, and distrust have the heart and turn the spirit back to dust. There is in every human heart the lure of wonder and an unfailing childlike appetite of what's next and the joy of the game."

She still wanted to pound the captain's skull. More, she wanted Marty to pound the softball.

As the ball started its descent from its apex, the Queen shouted, "Crush that goddamn ball, Peterson!"

She knew Marty had crushed it already.

Marty watched the softball approaching, his skinny legs moving into position and his sinewy, yellow hands tightening his light clench on the bat.

It was his pitch.

The drywall team was in position, about half of them eyeing the cooler and the other half wanting to win the game. The captain did not want the ball to come to him. He was done. On any given summer Wednesday, his hand would be first in the cooler.

The Saint Anthony team wanted to be there. They wanted to tell stories of softball heroics. They wanted to take a team picture with no one missing. They wanted to say that they beat everyone.

Everyone on the field knew that the game would end on this pitch.

Thirty years of alcoholism brought Marty to this point. His life was filled with so much loss. As the ball came toward him, he was standing where he started. He was with Ron, Terry, and Jim at Wilson High School. He was with Dick Siebert. He didn't know Herb Brooks, but he was with him. He was with Terry, Freddie, and Johnny Luck. He was Roy Campanella.

Marty never swung for the fences in anything. He leaned back slightly to meet the ball and took a short step. The swing was magical. In a perfect marriage of bat and ball, Marty took a cut for the ages.

The ball sailed off the old wood bat deep into right field, an opposite field blast.

Marty slowly looked up as the ball hit its apex over the right fielder's head. The drywall fielder was playing in the short outfield. There was no way he would have played deep for a right-handed batter, especially one from this team.

Marty dropped the bat and went for it. He rarely stretched anything in life, let alone an extra base. Time was on Marty's side, but the right fielder had him by 20 years and 10,000 fewer beers.

The Saint Anthony bench erupted. Except for Jerry N., the entire team leapt off the bench and lined up along the third-base line.

Jerry N. rolled over on his side and mumbled, "Go Marty, Marty. Marty, go." No one heard him.

Johnny Luck and Jim were arm in arm, leaning as they shouted. Johnny Luck was cheering toward Jim, "He's gonna do it. C'mon, Marty, you can do it!"

Marty took off for first as fast as he could, his gray hair flowing behind him for the first time in decades. Marty huffed his way to first base, rounding the bag in life-imposed slow motion.

Even at 20, he wasn't exactly speedy. Dick Siebert wanted his bat in the cleanup position, not his wheels. At 50-something, Marty was hardly moving.

The captain had turned toward right field and hardly noticed Marty rounding the corner. The right fielder was young and in shape, but he had a long way to go. The ball tumbled into the bushes by the train tracks. Not only did Marty wallop the ball, but he got a nice roll. The right fielder went through the thicket and found the ball lying next to a 40-ounce bottle of Olde English 800. By the time he found the ball, Marty was rounding second base and losing what little steam he had.

The right fielder picked up the ball and stepped out of the bushes to hit the cut-off man at second. It was a perfect throw right into his glove. In the unfolding moment, both teams took notice of the extraordinary toss. The Saint Anthony squad was for a moment dejected in the thought that Marty would easily be thrown out at third. Then everyone turned on the juice.

"C'mon, Marty, dig it. Dig, dig!"

"You got it, brother!"

As Marty headed toward third, the cut-off man fired off a cannon shot for the third baseman. It was a standard amateur softball throw that bounced hard at short and went wide of the bag past the third-base line. The third baseman made the stab.

Marty was heading for home.

The third baseman turned to make the throw.

Marty sprinted and dove for home. He hesitated for a moment on which position to slide, but he knew he had to do something strategic for the win and something dramatic for the team. He slid on his back, his hand easily touching the side of the plate as he glided across the dirt. He was safe.

Marty jumped up and turned to his teammates. It felt like he was in high school. He was mobbed at home. To anyone who was driving by, the sight was inexplicable. To everyone at Raymond Field, including the gardener, the parks worker, and the captain, the players on the Saint Anthony Residence softball team were champions.

The team stayed in the mob for what seemed like hours. The Queen stood behind the backstop and watched. The smiles were like nothing she had ever seen at any Catholic Charities facility or program. The Queen's smiles were usually sarcastic, but today it was pure joy.

The team eventually made their way back to the residence, where they were greeted with another celebratory meal. This time, there was no dinner in the cafeteria. All were invited to cheer the victorious Saint Anthony Residence softball team, and almost all of them made it. Root beer was the only ale that flowed, and it poured out of the tap like gold.

Terry was telling stories about the season, embellishing a game that was only an hour old. Harry laughed with the Queen. Players told stories to other residents.

Marty didn't drink all summer. He looked around the parking lot at one of the only parties he had ever been to without alcohol. His mom and dad even drank during his birthday parties.

He took a sip of cold root beer and sighed. He thought of the morning he walked into the residence for the first time. Sitting in Harry's office, he wasn't looking for something else in his life. He was too lost.

Pray to Saint Anthony and you will find it.

Marty wasn't praying to Saint Anthony that summer, but the saint was praying for him, and he found his way.

TENTH INNING

There is no trophy case at the Saint Anthony. There was no trophy for the season, no medals. Just the realization that they could beat anybody because they were somebody. And, in fact, they did go undefeated. They beat everybody.

That summer, the Queen set up nine games for the Saint Anthony squad.

They annihilated the Nickel Joint with textbook fielding and pure contact hitting. It was an amicable game of bar regulars. No one drank ahead of time. Terry led the team in hitting, almost going for the cycle. He was adamant that he could have stretched his second double into a triple if he wasn't wearing jeans.

Freddie pitched the entire game. He was laser-focused and proud. After a shaky first inning in the spotlight, he settled into a groove of perfect strikes. Johnny Luck ripped one deep but only made it to first.

Some of the players knew about the history of the Nickel Joint, but Marty was the only one who felt it. He knew that he was playing in a rec-league game of barflies, but it seemed special to him. He went 4 for 4, all clean singles.

After the game, the Nickel Joint team invited everyone back to the bar for expected revelry. The Saint Anthony team was quickly reminded that it was nearing the end of the month, and they were all short. Harry would give them bus tokens to head across town, but they would be on their own for drinks. They knew for once it would be unwise to sell the token home. Marty took a pass on the revelry, even though he still had enough money. Terry was the only one who made it, and he drank for free all night.

They squeaked by against an internal Catholic Charities team. It was not a friendly game. Most of the players were from the business office, including two youthful interns and a Jesuit Volunteer Corps worker. One of the interns was an obvious ringer. He was 6'4", his name was Todd, and he played baseball at D-III St. Thomas College in Saint Paul. He wore a visor and seemed affable. It was clear to the Saint Anthony team that the game would not be a backslapping affair of players with storied backgrounds from the streets. The Catholic Charities team heard about the Saint Anthony squad around the water-cooler and, apparently, their manhood was on the line. Todd just wanted to win and go back to his college house to chug beers from a rubber chicken. The Jesuit worker was hoping there would be a free cookout.

The Catholic Charities game was midseason and midmonth. The Saint Anthony team had finally begun to gel effortlessly, but, unfortunately, a few of the players chose alchemy. The game was back and forth all the way. In the gallery, it was the Queen growing progressively angrier at the employees. On the field, it was Marty in a match of wits, this time with ringer Todd. In another perfect swing, Marty ripped a professional-level heater into the gap. Wesley and Jerry N. both scored, and the game was over.

The Catholic Charities employees were visibly upset. The request for a new toilet at the Saint Anthony never made it out of purchasing.

They solidly beat a team of actuaries from the Saint Paul Companies. Marty threw them off by changing pitchers every other inning. They played a few more construction companies and squeaked by them all.

Each time, the first pitch was delivered through a haze of cigarette smoke and the enduring odor of active inebriation. Each time, the last pitch was delivered to an elated group of failures. They were told they were at the bottom, but they made it to the top.

On the field, the crowds grew. The Little Leaguers and parents came early and stayed late. The gardener brought homemade lemonade in actual glasses. More gardeners joined. The council member drove by, slowly.

After every game, there were celebrations that developed into the usual camaraderie, some of it unfortunate. The barbecues were the longest celebrations. There were no bragging rights because they were isolated by design. They couldn't brag at work because none of them had jobs, and the bar regulars at The Cromwell weren't interested. They could only brag among themselves.

The hallways and cafeteria were buzzing that summer with conversation, even if some of the players themselves were buzzed. Harry's office had visitors all day long, and none of them annoyed Harry, not even Donald.

Jim eventually put a color TV in the cafeteria to handle an influx of new Twins fans. He didn't go through purchasing.

Many of the residents had been fans, but they had forgotten all allegiances, including sports. The players would gather to watch the games and tell stories of the softball diamond. Other residents joined, and it became one of the few social norms that didn't involve a plastic bottle of gin.

The Twins would hover near the cellar in 1986, one year before their first World Series Championship.

In Saint Paul, however, there was a champion.

If this were a movie, there'd be happy endings, but life stories are not that neat.

Johnny Luck died at the facility not long after the softball season. He was a gentle, desperate soul, and alcohol and depression gripped him to his end. Jim watched the covered stretcher leave the building.

Ray eventually left the facility. He wasn't kicked out, but he didn't leave sober. Exiting the facility usually happened in one of three ways: death, violence, or sobriety. Sometimes, folks would simply leave. Rumor had it that Ray eventually shared a crowded apartment with no furniture and a well-constructed mechanism to distill corn vodka.

Wesley never left, enjoying the roof over his head and the predictable fare he inhaled three times a day. He occasionally drank to intoxication and often remained sober for weeks at a time. He would frequently wake up in the middle of the night trembling from nightmares of being escorted out. He was happy to be there, and the bosses were happy to have him.

Freddie also never left. He found his home and had no reason to leave. His family eventually located him, but instead of prying him away, they treated the Saint Anthony as his home. It was what Freddie wanted. He told them about the team. On his dresser, he had a framed picture of his high school baseball team and one of the Saint Anthony softball team. His sister framed them both.

Jerry and Jerry N. departed the Saint Anthony several months apart. They walked out the door and found the streets as their final home.

Terry appeared to gain sobriety after the final game. Except for a brief slip to The Cromwell to spin some yarns, he avoided inebriation for his final, brief days at the residence, and he left soon thereafter.

Marty hoped the fast-talking Terry found success again in sales. Terry left the residence as though he was headed on a business trip—a Samsonite hard-shell suitcase in his hand and a cigar in his mouth. He shook hands with Marty and Harry, then exited. In the parking lot, he paused. That was the end of Terry.

Harry eventually took the bus home from the Saint Anthony one last time. He had gone to the bottom and exited on top. As he rode his last bus—on time—the memories of the Saint Anthony filled him with sorrow and with joy. It was not the typical introspective last day of a career, filled with joy, a touch of remorse, fear, and excitement. Harry's career was different. He felt sorrow and joy for what he knew. The year of the softball team never left his memory. It carried him, on that final bus ride, with the memory that he made a difference.

Jim and the Queen were warriors. They were partners, they were advocates, and they never stopped fighting for the forgotten.

Jim was behind the Queen for every grand entrance, his emaciated figure eerie and his face Christ-like. His eyes did the talking. Jim had been down the rocky pathway, and his heart stretched a hand to those who followed. He didn't invent the Saint Anthony, and he didn't make the policy, but when hope was lost on the road, Jim's hand was the most important guide of all.

His obituary said it all: "Come to where the dew of mercy glistens, and rock on, brother."

The Queen's scarves flowed wildly to her last days, entering shelters, boardrooms, and city halls in a blaze of fury. She was the Queen of Housing and had little interest in becoming a CEO. In her mind, she was already there. The CEO agreed.

After 35 years in social service, the Queen retired. At the time, she presumed an idyllic lifestyle at a North Woods cabin would be a final reward.

In her own words: "I was going to live happily ever after in my cabin in the woods; my only needs were dogs, cable TV, a good sound system, and a library card. That plan lasted two months. I had not created a plan; instead, I had created a personal mythology that simply didn't work. I could not relate to retirement. What did it mean? What did it matter?"

The Queen quickly returned to work, taking a position as Justice Minister for a progressive Catholic Church in a Twin Cities suburb. She was a well-suited warrior for a congregation seeking to enact change, and with the means to do so. Her more appropriate title should have been Minister of Justice, as the Queen was a superhero.

Eventually, the Queen would relinquish her powers to illness. But even the ravages of pancreatic cancer could not topple her spirit. Befitting the Queen, she hosted her own memorial service, where she stoked a glorious fire of vulnerability, change, and beauty. She spoke at the largely hilarious and emotional service:

"William Butler Yeats wrote a poem about the change he saw in his countrymen after the agonizing Irish Revolution. The poem, entitled *Easter 1916,* captures the essence of emotional, intellectual, visceral, and transformational change. He wrote, 'All changed, changed utterly: a terrible beauty is born.' I related to this refrain. My own evolution/revolution has not been easy. It has been filled with awe and ambivalence, crucifixion and resurrection, [and] casual comedy[,] but a terrible beauty was born."

The Queen was a terrible beauty. She knew that life was a pathway for everyone, and that while it might be rocky, we are all beautiful for walking it.

The Bible played all sorts of roles at the Saint Anthony. Courtesy of another charitable mobster, every room at the residence had one. Some read it daily, and some read it when necessary. The Queen was not a Bible person, but one verse guided her days.

Jesus entered the temple courts and drove out all who were buying and selling there. He overturned the tables of the money changers and the benches of those selling doves. "It is written," He said to them, " 'My house will be called a house of prayer,' but you are making it 'a den of robbers.' " The blind and the lame came to Him at the temple, and He healed them.

To the very end, He looked out for the Queen. She wasn't Jesus, but she did his dirty work.

MARTY INTERLUDES

It was 11:30 a.m., 5 below zero, and Martin Peterson, a 54-year-old divorced father of three, was barefoot and still in his pajamas when he began the new year in heroic fashion by saving a young boy's life. It was 1993. Marty already had helped a woman escape a fire at 1345 Ames Avenue when he climbed onto the porch roof there and broke a window of a burning bedroom where a 2-year-old boy was trapped.

Saint Paul Pioneer Press, January 2, 1993*

The case manager woke up the day after New Year's Day and read the *Pioneer Press.* His two roommates were still sleeping, thankfully. The house was strewn with empty cans, a pizza box, and a stack of mailing trays from the post office. It was the remnants of an envelope-stuffing "party" for a political campaign. The case manager was not the candidate, but he wanted to make a difference. It was an unusual form of entertainment for the house full of single men.

Marty's picture was on the front page. The case manager had not spoken with Marty for over a year. Marty looked thoughtful and frail. He looked the same as he did when the case manager was still a case manager.

Marty's physical exploits didn't surprise the case manager. He was thin and weak well beyond his years, but a summer on the diamond and a few years of lifting books at the Union Gospel Mission Thrift Store could prove to anyone that Marty could climb the roof of a burning building and save a child.

The heroic action didn't surprise the case manager. This time, drinking didn't get in the way of family.

Alcoholism carried Marty to the edge of many things. He saved one family that cold day in Saint Paul, but he was never able to save his own. As a parent, he was rarely present, physically or mentally. When Marty's children were young, they saw two parents mired in the drink. Their only real connection to their father in those days was a special dinner he would prepare every two months: Marty's Magic Spaghetti.

Years later, Marty's son wrote, "The only thing more consistent than my father drinking a case of beer every day was his amazing consistency for making his Magic Spaghetti. My father was on his third or fourth beer by the end of the meal. We would say thank-you before the magic disappeared. Feeling whole and full for a moment."

As the children grew, they were often called upon to shuttle their drunk father away amid dangerous and embarrassing states of inebriation. The son once scooped Marty up from the corner of the busiest intersection in Minnesota. The whole world saw his dad face down in the grass. None of them stopped. The son was used to it.

As years passed, Marty and his children grew farther apart. The kids were productive. They had their own children. They were caring. They made peace.

Marty's children witnessed a raging fire. They tried to save him, but the flames were too hot. They were the heroes, and Marty knew it.

"It was a scary feeling to hear the kid screaming and you can't get in there, you knew he was going to die in there . . . it was a terrible feeling," Peterson said, rubbing his soot-covered hands and coughing from the smoke he inhaled.

Saint Paul Pioneer Press, January 2, 1993*

ELEVENTH INNING—EPILOGUE

MY FRIEND

A summer on the diamond did something to Marty. After the softball season, he made an unceremonious move to formalize his sobriety. It wasn't an event, just a realization of sorts. After 35 years, it was time to stop.

Without fanfare, but with veiled sadness, Marty departed the residence and entered the Christ Center at Saint Paul's Union Gospel Mission. Freddie walked him to the door of the Saint Anthony. Jim drove him.

The Union Gospel Mission was the Grand Bazaar of Homeless Men. Over 400 men were housed in an eclectic enclave of multiple service levels.

The barracks-style shelter on the main floor was a standard overnight men's homeless shelter. Since the mission did not accept government funds, they were allowed religion. For merely attending a religious service in the evening, and without a requirement to listen, one was awarded a bunk bed with a donated quilt, no stipulation on upper or lower, and a meal. The food was almost always legume-based. Without the ecumenical service, it was $3—cheap. The shelter was rowdy, smelly, and mostly hopeless.

Next to the shelter was the mission's multilevel transitional housing facility, a single-room-occupancy facility with about

100 rooms. Residents paid $150 per month, and they had their own room and a shared bathroom and kitchen. Many of the residents engaged in day labor services, some were on disability, and a few were permanently employed. The concept of "transitional" was loose at best, with many residents spending the rest of their days within its damp, concrete walls.

The Christ Center was adjacent to the mission and was a religious-based treatment program. The housing was a notch above the transitional housing facility next door, and the meals were separate and far less odor-inducing. The facility attracted numerous drop-off donations from professionals in lifelong recovery. Larry B. calmly and firmly steered the ship for about 50 largely destitute men, some who would arrive from the mission, some occasionally from the Saint Anthony, and a handful directly from the streets. He was a burly, mustached man who had seen his own share of destitution. He seemed tough like a Marine, and he looked like a Marine, but he didn't bark orders like one, his thick countenance never asking the ubiquitous, "What is your major malfunction, son?!"

He cared like a Marine, though, and he was driven like a Marine. Larry suited Marty nicely.

Over years of drinking, Marty had lost religion. But he never stopped praying, and he never lacked faith in the existence of a guiding power. The Golden Rule was his rule, and he knew that someone had to call the rules of the game.

Marty was tapped out long ago at the county for treatment funding, so the Christ Center was his only option. Perhaps he needed religion.

Marty lived at the Christ Center and engaged its program in the same way he had lived at the Saint Anthony, quietly and respectfully. He participated in everything that was required of him, gaining the immediate liking of Larry and the residents. Even the most difficult residents would give Marty the brother-nod on their way out.

Jim told Larry about Marty.

Marty finished his official time at the Christ Center, but he was allowed to stay and lend a helping hand and attitude. He was a good man to have around the house.

Marty eventually joined a new Catholic Charities program that offered an immediate job with slightly competitive, tax-free pay and a seemingly limitless array of services to move participants from reliance to self-sufficiency.

Marty worked on-site at the Union Gospel Mission, managing the thrift store, where he earned a living, maintained the required level of chit-chat, and, as a bonus, uncovered an occasional treasure in the donations that were dumped on the dock each day. The treasures were always books.

He met a 20-something case manager from Catholic Charities, who visited him several times a week, even though he only needed to visit once a week. The young man from Saint Paul would hear stories of the softball team, of Marty's life, and of life in general.

Their lives would eventually diverge, with the young man following a trajectory of public service and Marty taking the route of advanced age.

Marty's body would fail on that route, accelerated by years of drinking and over-the-top tobacco use. Long after the beer-can pyramids, Marty loved his Parliaments.

Years later, the case manager, no longer young and no longer a case manager, visited Marty in an assisted living home in Duluth, Minnesota. It was unclear what brought Marty to

Duluth. Perhaps he was seeking Terry. It was eminently clear why Marty required assisted care.

Marty's frailty was pronounced, he was smoking, and there was a smattering of empty beer cans on his nightstand. He smiled weakly, but wide, as the case manager walked through the door.

They talked for the afternoon, reminiscing about the Saint Anthony, the mission, and Saint Paul. Mostly, they talked about the team. They talked about Terry, Jim, Freddie, Wesley, Johnny Luck, and, one by the one, the entire team.

Marty stared out the window toward the picturesque hillside, a Parliament dangling from his yellow hand.

"It was really something, [playing with] those guys."

The case manager took his leave. A few years later, Marty would take his own leave.

There was a fire on a bitter cold December evening. His death certificate kindly indicated "end-stage chronic obstructive pulmonary disease with emphysema, prostate cancer, recurrent urinary tract infection, and pneumonia."

At the end of his days, Marty was the frail embodiment of the case manager's Golden Rule. Inside us all, we are men, and we are brothers; we are women, and we are sisters.

He also could play ball.

Marty Peterson wasn't Jesus, he wasn't Ted Williams, and he wasn't Herb Brooks. He was my friend.

Pray to Saint Anthony and you will find it.

HISTORY AND ACKNOWLEDGMENTS

It was a bitter cold February afternoon in 1989. After walking four blocks from the bus stop on University Avenue, I pulled, then pushed open the rusty doors at the entryway of the Catholic Charities Saint Anthony Residence in Saint Paul, Minnesota.

Initially, I thought the doorway heater ignited the pom-pom on my Minnesota Vikings knit hat, so I swatted at the top of my hat like Curly from *The Three Stooges.* Quickly realizing that my fear of the unknown skewed reality, I should have known the smell of cigarette smoke. But it was not my mother's True Menthol 100s. This smoke was infused with body odor, wet shoes, and the musty walls of an old building.

I was a victim of *soicumstance.*

I was a 20-something VISTA volunteer who had signed on for a year at $400 a month to start an evening drop-in center at Catholic Charities Job Services. I was fresh out of college, and I did not want to buy a suit. I wanted to make a difference; apparently, I could only do that while wearing K-Mart-special khakis. My heart told me that it was either my "soul or my signature" on the VISTA contract. It was the Peace Corps for America, and the Volunteers in Service to America saw me coming.

Not unimportantly, the program deferred the suit and my student loans.

It was my first week on the job when I was given the opportunity to spend a day at Catholic Charities service locations. Lazily perusing the sites was better than starting actual work where I would have to make actual decisions.

Wednesday was a visit to the Saint Anthony. I chose to straddle the day and night shifts, largely because I did not want to wake up early that morning, and possibly because I wanted to end my day at the Ace Box Bar down the street. The suit was not the only thing I was deferring.

My mother prayed to Saint Anthony just about every day for various lost items, including her mind on occasion, and especially for her three sons, definitely stooges. I knew about the saint, but I did not have a clue as to the residence.

Turning the corner from the entryway, with my pom-pom intact, I knocked on the open office door and greeted Harry Opus, the Saint Anthony Residence Day Manager. Harry was sitting with two older men. All three were smoking.

At that moment, my life changed.

Thirty years later, I see the faces. I hear the voices. I remember the foot odor. I taste the bologna sandwich on stale bread with warm mayonnaise. Not bad, actually, for those of us who enjoy an overabundance of Miracle Whip.

The day I started as a VISTA, I was living with my parents. Unusually, it was not the worst thing in the world. Like their elders, my mother and father pounded into our family that every human deserves the time of day from a Harris. In our house, it was everywhere. Be it a homeless guest at Thanksgiving or just a smile to a stranger, we were taught that no Harris was better than anyone else.

Standing in Harry's office, I thought of mom and dad.

Later that evening, I walked out of the building . . . but I never left.

During my time at the Saint Anthony, I learned the legend of 1986. A group of Saint Anthony residents formed a softball team and played their hearts out against real teams. Former baseball prodigy and 30-year alcoholic Marty Peterson led a cast of the downtrodden on a run for the ages. It was hard to believe.

But it was real. What happened in 1986 is true, although by its own fuzzy nature, this retelling required a few blanks to be filled in with plausible conversations. The people are real, the Saint Anthony is real, and what happened that year on the diamond in Saint Paul was real. It is a story about equity, justice, and perception. It is also a touch about America's pastime.

It was far from typical. Six years removed from the Miracle on Ice, a group of men defied the odds before a decidedly smaller audience.

In English classes, my professors at Marquette University would stipulate a rule that a story had a protagonist and an antagonist.

Life stories are not that neat. Life is not that neat.

A Season on the Drink went down that hallway, sat in Harry's office, talked with Marty, and played ball on the diamond at Raymond Field. Like I did, I hope you saw the hope in their eyes. Every day, it speaks to my heart.

I have done nothing alone in my life. My mother and father, Bill and Ardy, taught me that gratitude is love and humility is character. For this story, it started when I was given the opportunity to be a VISTA volunteer, and then a case manager, at Catholic Charities in Saint Paul. Mike Adrian and Tim Reardon believed in me, and I am thankful for the path that set my future. I was in awe of everyone around me, those who intertwined their own lives with the lives of the forgotten. They held them from the cliff, knowing that they would fall together.

Writing this story over the past decades has been a labor of love and remembrance. At the very moment I heard of the team, I embarked on telling a true story of hope. Like softball and this story, it was always about the team.

Editors and confidantes Ted Davis, Kevin Olson, Jim Hamilton, Dr. Liza Arendt, Debbie Russell, and Megan Ryan took many moments from their own incredible community work to keep me on course. Advocates and leaders John Taft, Heather Anfang, Brian McGill, and Jill Droubie offered important pathways. Mark Mishek, exceptional human and former Hazelden President/CEO, did what he does best—be an amazing, caring, thoughtful leader and friend. He was a beacon for the story, and for me. Catholic Charities leaders Father Larry Snyder, John Estrem, and Tim Marx kept the fire of service alive. Bill Hockenberger, former Saint Anthony Residence manager, pointed me in all the right directions. He was a gracious hand to the story and to anyone who called the Saint Anthony home. Prairie Editor Barry Casselman supported and regaled the effort with tutelage and friendship. Beloved Minnesotan and true friend of the book, Pat Coleman ensured that my facts were within the baselines and that history should be told as such. The professional guidance and rally cap of sportswriting friend and Detroit aficionado Brian Murphy focused the team. My Marquette roommate, Chicago author, advocate for the poor, and Phil Jackson–lover Dave "Whits" Whitaker thankfully reminded me that rewrites are part of the game.

The incredible Dave Winfield, one of the greatest ever, was a leader from the beginning, reminding us all that the diamond can change lives. I am honored and my gratitude is unending. Joe "Pogie" Gallagher was an advocate-extraordinaire—a friend to Saint Paul and to telling this story. Pogie makes it happen.

The Votel brothers—Tom and Kevin—led me through the forest in many ways; I am thankful and in awe. To the team at

AdventureKEEN, you could not be better partners. Thank you for believing in that summer on the diamond. You change lives.

National sportswriting superstar and mentor Paola Boivin provided extraordinary guidance and insight, and her Renaissance man–brother Dan Boivin was right there with her. I am deeply grateful to both.

Filmmaker, National Guard Soldier, and Worthington, Minnesota, native Joe Roos provided guidance, editing, and encouragement on the long home stretch. He is a great American, and I am thankful in so many ways.

World library treasure Peter Pearson was the man behind the curtain, spreading the word of libraries as pathways to love and opportunity. Every stack of books in every library in America has Peter's fingerprints on it. Along with rock-and-roll library star Beth Burns, and my library-loving mother breathing the fire of books down upon me, I tip a cap to the Friends of the Saint Paul Public Library. They make a difference. And yes, please donate to your local Friends.

Terry Schreiber, Ron Causton, and Jim Senske graciously shared the memory of baseball, neighborhood, and the promise of youth. Their contribution to the story was immeasurable, and the difference they have all made throughout their lives is invaluable. Sometimes, it only takes a moment to find a mentor and an inspiration, and I am grateful to have three more in my life.

For Adam Gillette, my great friend and volunteer editor MVP, I am indebted for many things. The hours and hours of detailed review on all those Sundays made me a better writer and person. Your commitment to the story and to spreading hope in the world is a measure of character. You are one of a kind, and the world needs you.

Eric Peterson, Marty's son, was with the story every step of the way. He is a hero in so many ways, and his message makes a difference. Thank you for sharing your family's life with the world.

For my friend Marty, this is your story. When I met you, I knew immediately that kindness was in your soul, and that you mattered. Your quiet voice is loud and clear to this day. Your path was rocky, but you have found peace.

For my parents and grandparents, who have long departed the world but are still with me, I owe my character. Bill and Ardy Harris, my parents, lent an ear to anyone with a word. My brothers Mike and Dan "Lord" Harris were there every step of the way.

Manoog and Sarah Yapalemian, my grandparents, saw hate firsthand and lived with only love in their hearts. They believed every person has a story to tell, and we should listen.

Nothing happens in my life without my wife, partner, and bench coach, Laura; our league-leading children Daniel, Ellie, Joey, and Andrew; plus, of course, mascot Ranger. My love and gratitude are unending. You make everything happen.

For the residents of the Saint Anthony, past, present, and future, and all those who need a hand of kindness and a glimmer of hope, the world is yours.

Wesley—left field for Smiley
Terry—pitcher for the Manager
Jerry N.—catcher for the Other Jerry
Jerry—third base for Jerry One
Johnny Luck—center field for New Guy
Jim—shortstop for the Boss
Harry—second base for the Other Boss
Ray—right field for the Mechanic
Marty—first base

A Season on the Drink allows us to see ourselves in the person next to us. That person could be anyone. As reported in the media, one of the figures in this story of respect and equality—one of the clergy who guided the residence to serve some of the neediest in our community—had his own demons. For victims, this cannot be understated. The Saint Anthony shows how we can take the path of loving unconditionally. Our hearts live with all victims of abuse, neglect, and the turning of hate's blind eye. See yourself in your neighbor.

A Season on the Drink
DISCUSSION GUIDE

1. Marty Peterson undergoes significant changes throughout the narrative. What do you think are the key turning points in his journey, and how do his relationships with the other residents shape his path toward redemption?

2. Terry is portrayed as both charismatic and deeply troubled. How does his presence influence the dynamics of the softball team and the broader community at the Saint Anthony Residence?

3. The Queen is a powerful figure within the Catholic Charities framework. In what ways does her leadership style affect both the staff and the residents? Do you see her as a force for good, or is her influence more complicated?

4. The Queen's backstory of recovery and her current role as a mentor are central to her character. How does her past inform her interactions with the residents, and what impact does she have on Marty and the others?

5. Discuss the impact of organized activities, like the formation of the softball team, on the residents' sense of purpose and belonging. How important are these communal efforts in fostering hope and resilience among individuals facing addiction?

6. Addiction and recovery are central themes in the book. How does the author portray the cycles of addiction, and what insights does the story offer about the challenges of breaking free from those cycles?

7. Community and belonging play a crucial role in the lives of the Saint Anthony residents. How does the formation of the softball team serve as a metaphor for the search for connection and identity?

8. How does the Saint Anthony Residence function as both a refuge and a reflection of societal neglect for those struggling with addiction? In what ways does the community within the residence support or hinder residents' recovery?

9. Dignity and respect are recurring motifs, especially in how the residents are treated by staff and outsiders. In what ways does the book challenge or reinforce societal perceptions of addiction and homelessness?

10. Redemption and hope are persistent undercurrents in the story. Do you think the book ultimately offers an optimistic view of recovery and transformation, or is it more tempered by realism and loss?

ABOUT THE AUTHOR

PAT HARRIS isn't just a lifelong Saint Paulite—he's a passionate community champion. His commitment to public service began in 1989 as a VISTA volunteer at Catholic Charities, where he first learned about the Saint Anthony Residence. In between raiding his parents' refrigerator and his grassroots community work, he heard tales of a Saint Anthony softball team that won it all. He knew then that the story needed to be told. This early career experience sparked a lifetime of civic engagement and advocacy.

Pat's 12-year tenure on the Saint Paul City Council was the opening act of a remarkable career dedicated to lifting up others around him. During his council service, Pat worked tirelessly to address poverty, library access, arts support, and homelessness—earning accolades like the Catholic Charities Lifetime Service Award along the way. In 2004, he founded Serving Our Troops, a nationally recognized program supporting Minnesota National Guard soldiers and their families, which earned not one but two Emmy Awards.

Pat is a leader in the public financial industry, serving governments across the country for over two decades. He proudly earned a BA from Marquette University and an MBA from the University of Minnesota Carlson School of Management. He and his partner Laura are parents to four dynamic children, plus one enthusiastic canine companion named Ranger.

Pat represents the best of civic leadership. He proves that true impact comes from showing up, speaking up, and taking purposeful action. Pat Harris isn't just writing Saint Paul's story—he's helping author its most inspiring chapters.